# GOODBYE LILY

# GOODBYE LILY

Carole Patti Clarke

Book Guild Publishing
Sussex, England

First published in Great Britain in 2010 by
The Book Guild Ltd
Pavilion View
19 New Road
Brighton, BN1 1UF

Typesetting in Baskerville by
Keyboard Services, Luton, Bedfordshire

Printed in Great Britain by
CPI Antony Rowe

A catalogue record for this book is available from
The British Library

ISBN 978 1 84624 432 2

# *Prologue*

Lily was my sister. But she still is, I thought. Death can't change that.

'What are you writing about, Lorne?' she would whisper as she lay on the tall, iron, electrically-controlled bed, stricken with cancer.

'I'm writing about Rose Cottage,' I would tell her, catching her glimpse from the corner of her eye as I sat on the low stool next to where she lay.

'Never go back,' she whispered.

'Where, Lily?'

'Rose Cottage, our childhood home. It's cold, ice cold.'

'A ghost?' I whispered.

She didn't answer and fell back into sleep. 'I'm also writing about you, Lily, how petite and pretty you are; your dusky complexion and dark chocolate eyes that sparkle when you smile.' I peeped up and looked towards her, her eyes now wide ... wide open as if staring into space.

'Will you take me dancing?' she whispered.

'The cha-cha-cha?' I asked jovially before she fell once more into sleep.

Lily would tell me stories, many stories, when I was a little girl. 'Many,' she would remind me whilst she stood neatly plaiting my hair, 'were told by our dear Uncle Dennis.'

1

One was about her journey, together with her Irish father and beautiful Indian mother, over the Indian Ocean into Atlantic waters that brought them to England long before I was born into a world of misfortune, denied of a mother's love.

# Chapter 1

I listened to the breeze whistling in the air as the coffin was lowered into the ground. I shuddered as the ropes were swiftly moved away and she was finally laid to rest. I didn't want to take the few steps, which I reluctantly did, to pay my last respects. My lips kissed the petal of the pink rose which was held tightly in the palm of my hand. 'I love you Lily,' I said to myself as I let it go. Within seconds it lay crookedly on top of the lid of her slim wooden coffin. I slowly walked away.

I could hear the sound of footsteps briskly walking behind me.

'Where are you going?' Uncle Dennis asked, placing his hand on my shoulder.

I turned around. 'Home,' I whispered.

'Aren't you coming for drinks? A hot toddy would do you good. You're freezing,' I was told as he gently touched my hand.

'I'm going home,' I whispered again. I could taste the salt from my tears as they rolled down my face and over my lips.

'Look at the sadness in your eyes. I'm coming home with you, my love. Give me those keys,' he said, stretching out his arm and opening the palm of my hand to take them from me. 'You're not in any fit state to drive,

3

and anyway it's not that often I get the chance to drive a Jag.'

I allowed him to take control. My legs felt weak with every step I took, the pain severe with the thought that she was gone forever. My heart was broken. I glanced towards the belfry as Uncle opened the passenger door whilst protecting me from the flow of ongoing traffic. The sad reminder of my childhood came back.

'Come on, my love, get in; it's bloody freezing out here.'

'That's where I used to be a bell-ringer,' I told him as I glanced up towards it once more.

Aware of his sense of urgency, I lowered my head and sat myself down in the seat. The door was quickly closed.

'These cars are too bloody big for me,' he said, leaning over to pull the lever and move the driver's seat before stretching his tiny legs out to allow his feet to touch on the accelerator. I ignored his frustration as he started to fidget around in the seat, mistakenly turning on the windscreen wipers at the side of the steering wheel.

'Right, we're off,' he told me, feeling for the indicator on the other side.

There was no conversation on the silent journey home. I allowed my head to gently fall against the headrest and deliberately closed my eyes to shut out the world. I listened to the flick of Uncle's lighter, and smelled the aroma of his cigar as he puffed away at it. I partly opened my eyes, squinting slightly as the morning sun shone through the windscreen. I turned towards Uncle. He smiled and I smiled back.

'That's better,' he said, patting me on my knee. I straightened myself up and looked straight ahead.

'That's not taken long, has it?' he said as we turned into the lane heading for Rutherford House. I swayed towards him as he took the last bend on the road far too fast. 'Home at last,' he said as the car slowed down. The button was pressed and we patiently waited for the creaky iron gates to open. There was no one to greet us. The old wooden front door remained closed as we pulled up onto the drive.

'Stiff gin and tonic; what do you say?'

'I'll pour you one,' I said to him as I collected the abundance of tissues that lay on my lap, before stepping out of the car.

'Still chilly, my love, even though that sun's pretty strong.'

I didn't reply as I lifted up the latch and stepped into the porch. I wanted to run upstairs to my bedroom and lock myself in, but instead I took a deep breath and allowed Uncle to follow me into the kitchen. 'Ice and lemon?' I asked before stuffing the tissues back inside my coat pocket.

'Yes please. Are you joining me for one?'

'I'll have a sherry,' I told him, leaning over the sink to wash my hands.

'Now you go and sit down. I'll be your barman for the day. Mind if I root around? Anyway, I have a rough idea where everything is. Lemon?' he asked.

'Over there in the fridge,' I replied, pointing towards it.

'Well, come on, do as you're told. Come and sit yourself down.'

5

Obeying his order, I made my way back towards the lounge. I stood and stared at Lily's photograph, which was proudly placed inside a silver frame on the corner of the long oak mantelpiece. 'Lily,' I whispered, 'why did you have to go?'

'Weighs a ton, this tray,' Uncle said, trying to keep it balanced before resting it on top of the large oval coffee table. 'Now, at least we don't have to keep getting up and down all afternoon,' he told me as I looked down at it. 'Well, only for fresh ice,' he added, popping the cork from the sherry bottle and pouring it into the large curved glass. 'Would have popped you a cherry on top, but can't seem to find any,' he said, passing it to me before pushing the large Victorian armchairs closer to the fire. 'Come on then,' he said, patting the back of the chair to beckon me over.

The gin bubbled in his glass as it was generously poured. I listened to the fizz from the tonic as Uncle undid the top of the bottle.

'Are you going to join me?' he said, sitting himself down.

The smouldering fire gave out little warmth as I sat down on the chair next to him. I bent forward and reached down towards the stone hearth, struggling to pick up one of the logs that lay there.

'Let me do that,' Uncle said, taking it from my hand and resting it against the dulling embers. 'That solemn look you have reminds me of when you were a little girl. You always looked so sad. She's gone, my love, that's a certain fact. You're going to have to face up to it sooner rather than later. I remember taking your sister, as a baby, through the streets of Calcutta. It only seems like yesterday.'

I felt the tears trickling down my face.

'Take a big sip of that sherry,' I was told, which I immediately did, finding it hard to swallow as it reached the back of my throat. 'Now sit back and relax,' Uncle said, quickly standing up to reach for the large scatter cushion from the couch before placing it behind my back. 'Snuggle into that,' he said, perching himself back into his chair and staring into the fire.

The ticking of the clock sitting on the mantelpiece seemed louder than usual as the room went silent. I took another sip of sherry. Uncle gulped a large amount of gin, coughing slightly as he swallowed.

'That was bloody strong,' he said.

'More tonic?' I asked.

'No, my love, I'm sure I'll get used to it. I wonder why your mother was so bloody rotten to you.'

I lit a cigarette and looked him straight in the face.

'Sad that her life ended so quickly, and to die a day before her forty-third birthday. Such a young age. Do you miss her?'

'No,' I replied, taking a long drag of my cigarette and blowing it out up into the air. 'You look surprised.'

'No, not really, my love, considering the circumstances at that time. She never liked living in England. Calcutta was her home. That was all she had ever known. It must have been a massive shock coming over here. I know that you all suffered great poverty. It must have been hell.'

'It was,' I replied.

'I know from your mother's letters she was becoming restless with her lifestyle.'

'Is that why she became a lady of the night?' I asked.

Uncle gulped whatever gin was left in his glass, gave a nervous cough, and stood up. 'Remember, she was a very beautiful woman. Top up?' he asked, picking up the bottle of sherry.

I reached out and passed him my glass. 'You haven't answered my question.' We both jumped slightly with the crackle of the wood as the flames burst through it.

'Look at that fire,' Uncle said, passing my glass back to me and returning to refill his.

'Well, are you going to answer my question?' I asked, my eyes following every move he made as I waited restlessly for an answer.

'I didn't have much contact with your mother for quite a number of years before her death,' I was told as he walked the few steps over, steadily holding his glass before sitting down again. 'Her attitude towards me was very aggressive the last time I called at Rose Cottage to see you all, so I was reluctant to make the journey up again. I know London isn't that far, but if you're not made to feel welcome it isn't worth it.' He took another gulp of his gin. 'You do understand, my love, don't you?' I nodded.

'That's better,' he said, resting his head back before stretching out his legs. 'Like one?' he asked, pulling a narrow tin out of his jacket pocket.

'Cigars are only for men,' I told him. 'I don't remember your visits. Well, maybe one or two.'

'You were only a little child, my love. Dare say you don't.'

I stared at him as he placed his cigar in between his lips. Thousands of questions that need answering were going around and around in my mind. He flicked the lighter twice and puffed away.

8

'I remember when Jenny, your mother, invited me to Rose Cottage for Christmas many, many years ago. I needed to determine just how many children your mother had, and I spent almost half a day selecting inexpensive gifts at Selfridges. It was a happy reunion and I fell in love with you all, especially you, even though you used to appear and disappear almost immediately. Lily worked at the bakery at that time. We bonded, but I could see the pain of her upbringing in her eyes. I became emotional on my return home to London, worrying about all the poverty in your mother's life and thought of all you little children. You all appeared to be so very strictly disciplined. I used to send your mother small sums of money to help out, not that I expected any gratitude, but I was soon forgotten when the money stopped.' He shook his head in dismay before bending down and reaching for another log.

'It sounds like a huge firework,' I remarked as he threw it onto the fire, listening to the spitting of wood as the flames caught hold. This time he sipped his gin before settling himself back again onto his chair. 'You know, Uncle, it was very difficult being brought up by an Indian mother.'

'Anglo-Indian, my love. Your grandmother was Anglo-Indian, and Jenny never knew who her father was. Some Portuguese soldier, I was told. Took a liking to your grandmother, had an affair, and then ran off when he found out she was pregnant. Then, of course, Jenny, your mother, was born. I suppose it must have been pretty bad in those days to be left in that position.'

'Did her mother ever try to find the soldier?' I asked.

'Believe he fled back to Goa. There was no chance. But I don't think it bothered your grandmother. She liked her men too much. That's gone down far too quickly,' he said, inspecting his empty glass before standing up once more. 'Surprisingly enough, she remained a devout Catholic.'

'Why did it surprise you?' I asked, watching him pick up the bottle of gin by its neck.

'Well, she was adventurous and free spirited. She liked to hang around the dance halls in the district. Make this my last,' he said as he struggled to focus on what he had poured. 'Well, at least for the time being.'

'What are you trying to tell me?' I asked, perching myself on the edge of the chair.

'Well, she certainly attracted the attention of many males.'

I looked curiously at him whilst he sat himself down. 'It all sounds too familiar to me,' I told him. 'What was my grandmother's name?'

'What, you were never told!'

'No,' I sharply replied.

'Grace was her name, and my father, your step-grandfather, was called Ernest.' I could feel the heat of the fire against my legs. 'In fact, that was where Grace met Ernest, in one of those dance halls she frequented, so I was told. Let me help you, my love,' he offered as he watched me press both feet firmly on the woven carpet in an attempt to move my chair further back.

A heavy cloud must have passed a shadow over the sun as the room darkened allowing the glow of the fire to show itself off. 'Thank you, Uncle,' I said as he moved my chair into a more comfortable position.

10

'It's a pleasure,' he told me, trying his best not to stagger. 'Anyway, at that time he was serving in the Army with the Devonshire Regiment stationed in Calcutta.'

'Who was?' I asked whilst he sat himself down.

'Ernest, of course. Anyway, an affair with my mother ensued. Well, Ernest's tour of duty had ended and he was posted back to his regimental headquarters in Plymouth, unaware that Grace had become pregnant with me.'

'How sad.'

'Well, not at that specific time, my love. You see, Grace managed to make contact with him and he returned to Calcutta.'

'Thank God,' I said before taking another sip of sherry.

'Yes, he joined the Calcutta Light Horse Brigade as a Regimental Sergeant Major. He was an expert in small arms, so they snapped him up.' He paused for a while, hastily opening the tin and pulling out another cigar. 'Well, Ernest married Grace in October 1935,' he said, popping his cigar between his lips. The steel bore no shine on a rather tainted lighter as he lifted it out from deep inside his jacket pocket. Uncle flipped open the lid, spinning his thumb several times against the tiny wheel inside. 'Short of petrol,' he mumbled, struggling to light the edge of his cigar against the dying flame. 'Am I boring you, my love?'

'Not at all,' I replied, moving my hand from over my mouth after taking a long, hard yawn.

'Why don't you come back to London with me for a few days?'

'Thank you, but no. I've got to try and get things back to normal. My life has been upside down for months with Lily being so ill, and I've got to get back to my writing.'

11

'How long will it take you to finish this book of yours?'
'Don't ask,' I replied.
'Will I get a mention in it?'
I looked at him and smiled.

'Anyway, after Grace and Ernest married, I was born one month later,' he continued. 'We lived in a large flat and had three servants to care for the day to day chores, and of course to look after Jenny, your mother, and myself.'

'Lucky you,' I told him.

'Well ... fortunate,' Uncle replied, 'although Grace, I have to say, was a very volatile person with a short fuse, especially where my father was concerned.' He paused again, taking two puffs on his cigar. 'Dare I have another?' he said to himself, lifting his glass up into the air to inspect what remained. 'Perhaps not. Don't want you to think your uncle's an alcoholic. Anyway, Grace's love and tenderness towards us was faultless. She was always prepared to take on the world to protect us from any problems we encountered. But she made it very clear that she had become bored with her marriage and once again began visiting dance halls and mingling with men.'

'God, it really does sound familiar,' I told him, sitting back in the chair.

'Yes, it's quite sad I suppose,' he muttered. 'You see, Ernest, on the other hand, was a quiet and gentle man who enjoyed the comforts of his home and listening to the radio.'

'Maybe Grace found him too boring,' I said. Uncle raised his eyebrows and frowned. I felt my comment invalid, and allowed him to carry on.

'You know, Ernest only tolerated Grace's behaviour

because of his devotion to her. Damn it, I will have another drink. You don't mind, do you?'

'Help yourself,' I told him. He coughed nervously and stood up, as if embarrassed. I felt quite dizzy bending down to reach for the packet of cigarettes that had slipped from the chair onto the carpet.

'We're down to these,' Uncle spoke.

There was no time for me to turn to where Uncle stood as, from the corner of my eye, I saw something flying towards me, making me duck my head in fear.

'Sorry, my love. Shouldn't have thrown them over to you like that.' Uncle quickly walked over, placed his drink on the tiny circular wine table next to his chair and, without hesitation, reached down to pick up the matches. 'Sorry I startled you,' he said, taking one out and striking it. I moved slightly forward, placing the cigarette in between my lips, allowing him to light it for me.

'All right, I accept your comments.'

'About what?' I asked as he sat himself down.

'About Ernest. He probably was boring, otherwise Grace wouldn't have gone back to her old ways.' He had a look of disapproval on his face. 'However,' he said, leaning forward to pick up the poker and tend to the fire, 'Ernest reached a point, one hot and steamy midnight, when Grace failed to return home. He took me to a park nearby and was going to end both our lives with his gun.'

This time it was me who raised an eyebrow.

'It's true, my love, it really is. I don't remember it, of course, I was little more than a baby at the time. I was to learn about it many years later. I lived with the bitter taste for quite some time after I'd found out. But now there's just sadness. Sadness at how Grace constantly betrayed him, and how desperate he must have felt.'

I stood up and reached for the poker, gently taking it from his hand. It was as if he was in a daydream, his eyes permanently fixed on the flames from the fire.

'Your drink's here,' I whispered, patting him lightly on his shoulder before passing it to him. The room went silent. I sat myself down. 'Oh why did you have to go and leave me Lily?' I said to myself, shuddering at the thought that we had just buried her. I pictured her smiling face from years gone by. I felt a lump inside my throat and allowed the tears to trickle down my face.

'Get that sherry down you,' Uncle told me, standing up to wait for me to drink it. It felt awkward as I swallowed. 'That's better. I'll refill your glass,' he said, taking it from me.

I brushed the palms of my hands along the sides of my cheeks to wipe away the tears.

'Come on, try and pull yourself together,' I was told as Uncle pulled out a crisp, white handkerchief from his pocket before passing me another sherry.

'Thank you,' I whispered. I didn't look at him as he sat gently down on his chair next to me. My eyes started to blur as I gazed at the pattern that was woven into the carpet.

'I became very close to Jenny during our upbringing. Sometimes step-brothers and sisters don't get on, but we always did. You don't mind if I continue, do you?' Uncle asked.

I looked towards him and nodded my head in approval.

'However, your mother often used me as an alibi for her meetings with boys. In exchange for my loyalty to her she used to procure her school friends for me. This practice continued for some time.'

'Looks like she never changed,' I said. Uncle looked up at me. 'Don't look so surprised, Uncle. You knew what was going on.'

'Not to the full extent, my love. Remember, I haven't seen you all for years.'

'Mother used to use me as her alibi. Looks like old habits never die.'

'An alibi for what?' Uncle asked.

'Men,' I replied sharply.

Uncle coughed as he took another huge gulp of his drink. 'Want to tell me about it?'

'Not particularly. It's Lily that I'm thinking of, not my awful childhood. Anyway, it's all in the book I'm writing. I'll give you a copy when it's finished.'

Uncle was slowly but surely showing the signs of too much alcohol, failing in an attempt to throw another log onto the fire. 'Bugger!' he mumbled as it hit the grate and rolled back onto the hearth. 'Remember, your mother was only fourteen when she became pregnant with Lily. Such a young age to have that responsibility,' Uncle told me, kneeling down and placing the log, this time more carefully, onto the fire.

'Are you trying to make excuses?'

'Not at all, my love, but it should be taken into consideration.'

'What, for the years of abuse I suffered? You must be joking.' I felt angry and quickly lit myself another cigarette.

'You can't spend the rest of your life feeling bitter because of your upbringing.'

'I don't. Well, I try not to. It's just all so bloody sad.'

'Anyway,' Uncle said, 'Grace was enraged when she learned that your mother had become pregnant, and she was determined to trace who was responsible for it, and, of course, it was your father. He was at that time serving with the Royal Air Force in Calcutta. Anyway, believe it or not, your father had requested an immediate posting back to England. Grace was going to have none of that and, with Ernest, they took issue with the Royal Air Force Authorities and his transfer was blocked, and the marriage arranged.'

'My feet are aching like mad,' I told Uncle, slipping off my shoes before curling up on the chair and resting my head on the arm.

'Are you tired?' Uncle asked.

'A little,' I replied, yawning once more.

'I feel like I'm telling you a bedtime story. It's as if you're a little girl again curled up like that. Well, after all the wedding arrangements for your mother and father were made, we moved into a large apartment, still in Calcutta, and the wedding reception for your parents took place there. It was a grand affair, and I remember being one of the pageboys,' he paused and chuckled to himself, 'together with three bridesmaids. I fancied the pants off one of them.'

What a horrible saying, I thought, placing my hand underneath my head to rest on it.

'Sadly enough, not long after your mother's wedding, Grace was diagnosed as having TB. Ernest arranged to rent a villa in Darjeeling, near the Himalayas, in an effort to improve her quality of life. Grace and I stayed there for three months. The villa was in a remote area and my only means of transport was by horseback. Are you asleep, my love?'

'No Uncle,' I said, opening my eyes and sitting myself up with the intention of keeping awake. 'I didn't know that you could ride horses.'

'Well, let's face it, they certainly weren't thoroughbreds. More like donkeys if you ask me.' I turned to him and smiled, taking another cigarette out of the box, allowing Uncle to strike a match and light it for me. 'You know, I was never made aware of my mother's condition. We returned to Calcutta where her health deteriorated even more.'

I could feel his emotions building up as he patted one finger after another on the arm of the chair. I sipped the remainder of my sherry, ready to excuse myself to go and freshen up.

'I recall being sent to live with family friends, until one December afternoon when Grace demanded my presence. She was in bed and burst out crying when I arrived.' At that point Uncle's eyes filled up with tears. I decided that it was the wrong time to excuse myself and reached out for his hand to give a little comfort. 'Anyway, she asked me to hug and kiss her.' Uncle's emotions got the better of him as he cried out loud. 'It still hurts, my love, even to this very day,' he told me, skipping a breath. 'Forgive me,' he said, 'you must feel bad enough with Lily gone. You don't need an old bugger like me reminiscing. They say that talking about these matters helps, but bloody hell, not in my case. Here's me telling you to face the fact that Lily's dead – I'm some joke, aren't I?'

'I don't mind listening, Uncle.'

'Well, you'll have peace after today. I'm leaving for London in the morning.'

'So soon!'

'Yes, I've got to get that house of mine sorted out. Being accused of preventing its sale. I must admit though, I have been awkward about it. Wouldn't you after being married for twenty-five years and she runs off with another man, then demands the home, my beautiful home, to be sold to obtain half the money from it? I'm devastated, my love. I miss her so much. To think of her sleeping with another man crucifies me. Anyway, we'll keep the log fires burning, shall we?' he said, purposefully picking one up and placing it on the smouldering fire.

'Uncle, things don't sound too good for you,'

'Well, you've just got to get on with it, my love, haven't you?' he said, giving out a short, nervous laugh. 'Do you mind?' he said, lifting up his empty glass and holding it in the air.

'Don't rush home in the morning. Stay another day at least.'

'Sure, my love?' he said as he slowly walked over towards the coffee table.

'Yes, I'm sure,' I replied, turning around in my chair and giving him a gentle smile to make him feel at ease.

'Do you mind if I continue my story about Grace?' Uncle asked, whilst lifting the bottle of gin and pouring himself a generous amount. 'I somehow need to get it off my chest.'

'Give me five minutes,' I replied, standing up and making my way towards the stairs. 'I just need to freshen up.'

'You look tired, my love,' Uncle said on my return. 'Shall I shut up?'

I curled up on my chair, lit a cigarette and encouraged him to carry on.

'OK, where was I?' he said.

'You were telling me about your meeting with Grace when she was ill,' I whispered, giving him a gentle reminder.

'Oh yes, my last meeting. Unfortunately, it wasn't to last very long. Mother whispered her last words to me saying that our Christmas presents were already wrapped, and asked God to take care of me. Ernest was standing at the opposite side of her bed. He stood and stared at me. He must have known that it would be the last time I would ever see her. He gently ushered me out of the bedroom, which was decked out with flowers. Our three servants would not look at me when I reached the lounge. Their heads were bowed as they were ordered not to show any emotions during my visit. However, I sensed that something was happening to my life. I returned to my temporary home and Grace, my dear mother, died later that day on December the sixth.'

I felt a lump in my throat. This time it wasn't for Lily, but my poor Uncle, who looked so frail as I watched him kneel down and place the last remaining logs neatly onto the fire, brushing his hands together to get rid of the dust before struggling back onto his chair.

'Ernest never got over Grace,' Uncle said, resting his head against the back of the chair. 'He became very morose and took to heavy drinking. Our bath was always filled with blocks of ice and bottles of gin. He just couldn't come to terms with his wife's premature death.'

'How old was Grace when she died?' I asked.

'Thirty-five,' he sharply replied, placing another cigar between his lips, then pressing the outside of his jacket pocket looking for matches.

'I've got them,' I told him, lifting up the box and pulling one out. I leant over towards him before striking it.

'Thank you, my love,' he said in between puffs. He sat back and rested his head once again against the back of the chair. 'Still want to listen?' he asked as I passed the ashtray over to him. I nodded my approval. 'To my shock,' he continued, 'my father left the Calcutta Light Horse Brigade. It was odd not to see him in uniform. He always looked so grand in it. He was tall and very broad. Handsome with it too, but a very lonely man. His only friend at that awful time was a bottle of gin. He seemed to get more and more frustrated with his life and decided that we should move to a villa in the country. We soon settled down and started to enjoy the country life. Ernest cut down somewhat on his drinking habits and eventually joined the Calcutta Racecourse as a senior steward. I would also help out with the general chores of mucking out.

'Our neighbours had a young daughter, Barbara, who was about fifteen at the time. She seduced me in the stables,' he chuckled. 'We became very close. This practice continued for many months and I felt secure that someone actually needed me. I remember eagerly getting ready for my usual rendezvous with Barbara. It was a clear, crisp morning and I couldn't wait to see her. All of a sudden I heard someone banging on the door. I told them to hold on, nearly falling over as I rushed to put my trousers on. It was a telegram for Ernest. I thanked the man as he handed it over then quickly slipped on my boots, closed the door behind me before jumping on my bicycle and pedalling as fast as I could to the racecourse. I'd never held a telegram before and felt quite anxious to hand it over to Ernest.

'Barbara was there when I arrived, brushing the stable yard. I told her I'd be back soon as I cycled past her. She made my heart flutter as she smiled. I eventually arrived at Ernest's office, leant my bicycle against the wall, gave two knocks on his door and was ordered in. I stood silently as he turned his back on me, listening to the envelope being ripped as he opened it. "Jenny, your sister, gave birth to a baby girl at St Helier's Convent, Calcutta, in the early hours of the morning." I walked over and shook his hand. He patted me on my back. "You're an Uncle now, Dennis," I was told as he sat back at his desk and continued with his work.

'I slipped silently out of the room and cycled the short distance back to the stable to give Barbara the good news. She ran straight into my arms as I told her that from that day I was an uncle. We kissed tenderly and aroused the passion we had for each other. Seduction inevitably happened.

'There had always been friction between your father and Ernest. Religion was partly to blame. You see, Ernest was also a very strong Roman Catholic and never wanted your mother to marry anyone who wasn't the same, especially an Irish Protestant, which your father was, so I knew that I had to be patient before a visit to your mother and father, and the new baby, would be permitted.

I was desperate to see your mother after being absent from her for quite some time.

'My love for Barbara was getting stronger. The days and weeks went by quickly and, in that time, she had taught me to ride horses, as well as many other things!' he chuckled again.

'I was surprised to see Ernest at home one particular morning as I appeared in the lounge dressed for work. Ernest spoke in Punjab to one of the servants. He disappeared and then arrived back with a fresh set of clothing for me. "Get changed," he ordered. 'I realised that at last he was finally going to take me to see your mother.

'We boarded the tiny train which would take us into the heart of Calcutta. Ernest held a small parcel wrapped in brown paper. I presumed it was a present. I stretched up, barely reaching the rope that formed a loop, to try and keep my balance as the train made its journey through the mountains. Everyone was squashed together. The humid atmosphere made me break out in a sweat. The sensation of it trickling down my back before absorbing itself into the material of my shirt, made me feel quite irritated.

'Anyway, with relief the train started to slow down, finally stopping at our destination,' he carried on. 'Everyone seemed to want to leave the carriage at the same time. I was pushed around in all directions. Ernest couldn't understand my frustration as he looked down at me disgruntled as I openly complained.'

Uncle paused, took a minute sip of his gin and then continued. 'I jumped off the step onto the creaky wooden platform. The humming of voices and the cries of little children made me feel quite relieved that I now lived in the country. I glanced back before making my exit. The grey smoke bellowed from the engine as it twirled itself up into the air towards the sky while everyone tried to board. I hastened my step. Ernest swiftly walked along the tiny streets. I knew not to complain and tried to keep up with him, following two steps behind.

'I was used to seeing poverty. The heart of Calcutta was well known for it, and we had lived in the city until quite recently, but it was still a shock, my love. We couldn't avoid walking through some of the many slums that were there. It sickened me to see young mothers sitting in the streets, their hungry babies too weak to cry. There was one in particular, sitting there with a child resting its head over her shoulder. Her hand was permanently held out, her long fingers bent slightly as if they had been put in a cast, in the hope of someone dropping some food inside them. Her large black eyes stared down towards the ground. I quickly felt inside my pocket and pulled out three rupees, bent down and placed them inside the palm of her hand. She moved her head slightly and stared me straight in the face. There was no expression from her. I'll never forget the sheer sadness in her eyes.

'I'd lost sight of Ernest by then and panicked. The smell of rotting garbage made me feel quite sick as I pushed my way through the crowds. It was obvious that the country life that I was living was doing me the world of good.'

'Did you manage to find Ernest?' I asked, feeling anxious.

'Yes, my love, eventually I spotted him, but only because

he was so tall. Ernest, of course, showed his displeasure again as I finally caught up to him. Anyway, the walk took us up towards the mountains. Ernest stopped suddenly, pulled the telegram out of his pocket, checked the address then pressed the rusty doorbell adjoining the gate. I jumped slightly as a herd of goats ran past us. Obviously, the sound of the bell ringing had disturbed them. I could hear their cries in the distance as they wandered aimlessly in search of food.

'Ernest pressed the bell once more, this time firmly pressing his thumb against it. A woman appeared draped in a cream cotton sari. "What is your business, sir?" she asked in broken English. Ernest passed her the telegram through one of the gaps of the dark green painted iron gate. He was thanked. On reading it she passed it back, then picked out a key that was joined with others on a large brass loop and placed it inside the keyhole. A tiny bird fluttered its wings and flew over the arch as if to welcome us as the quaint gates were opened. "I am Sister Rosemary, and welcome you both to God's home. Mother and baby are doing very well," she told Ernest. "Follow me."

'It was an almost silent journey as we made our way in single file along the narrow cobbled pathway, bordered at each side with large shrubs. Ernest coughed twice, nervous of course. The straps of my open sandals stuck firmly across my feet. It was the first time that I had worn them. It felt quite uncomfortable.' Uncle paused again, lifted his glass up towards his mouth and slowly sipped his gin. 'I'm sobering up somewhat telling you about all this,' he said.

'You should be the one writing a book,' I told him, lighting another cigarette.

'No, my love, I wouldn't have the patience. It's taken me three weeks to write my will out and I still haven't finished it. Huh, I wish I could be there to see her face.'

'Who?' I asked.

'My ex. I've left her 25p,' he chuckled. I looked at him, puzzled. 'Yes, a penny for every year I was married to her. It should by rights only be 23p if you take into consideration that the last two years of our marriage she was having an affair, but I thought I'd be a little bit generous,' he chuckled once more. 'Can you imagine her reaction when my solicitor informs her that she's in my will? She'll run down to his office anticipating that I've left her the whole of my estate. That's how much of a mug she takes me for. At least I'll have the last laugh if nothing else.'

He stretched out his tiny legs and sat back in his chair before continuing his tale. 'Anyway, Sister Rosemary led us through a leafy archway. I stood for a second, mesmerised at this beautiful building that stood and looked down on me. The brass bell stood proud in its own belfry on top of the slanted roof. My eyes squinted at its bright reflection against the sun. I watched two elderly nuns tending the plants as we walked along the vast lawn. Doves flew in and out of their cotes. A cockatoo sat lazily on the branch of a tree. It was like paradise. A huge palm cast its shadow over a square wooden table, a cloth made of cream lace placed in a triangle over the top of it. It was set with miniature cups and saucers matching a tall floral teapot. It gave out a homely touch to the silence of this very beautiful place. "Iced tea?" we were asked. Ernest immediately thanked her. I was desperately thirsty and felt quite impatient as I watched it flow from the spout. First, Ernest was handed his, followed by me. Needless to say, it was downed in a second.

' "Well, at least you made it in good time," Sister Rosemary told him, her head turned towards Ernest as we continued to walk. Ernest questioned her whilst we took the steep steps up towards the veranda. The dark green shutters adjoining every window were wide open, complementing the white-washed walls of this huge building. "They're leaving for England in the morning." Ernest turned and looked at me and I at him, and nothing more was said.

'We were escorted through into a large stone-flagged hall. I was surprised at how cold I felt, and shivered slightly as we were led up the lengthy winding staircase. Everything seemed so clinical. Our footsteps echoed on the bare wooden steps as we climbed each one. I found myself needing the support of the iron bannister. Ernest must have been a lot fitter than I was as he held his back straight and took every step with ease.' Uncle paused, took a deep yawn and I followed suit.

'Coffee?' I asked.

'Suppose I'd better,' he replied, yawning once more, making me do the same.

'I'll put the kettle on,' I told him, stretching as I stood up to make my way into the kitchen. 'Strong or weak?' I called, holding the jar of coffee in one hand and a teaspoon in the other as the rumbling kettle began to boil. I waited motionless for his reply. He had obviously not heard me and, anyway, it was quite bad manners for me to shout from one room into the other, I thought. I placed the coffee and spoon down on the shelf to walk the short distance from the kitchen to the middle room where Uncle was. It didn't surprise me to see him sitting there fast asleep. I crept over towards him and gently opened his fingers to take the glass that he was clutching from his hand. There was no disturbance as I lifted his head slightly to place a cushion underneath, allowing him to rest more comfortably. I removed the ashtray and returned with a clean one. The tiny silver tin which held what remained of his cigars, along with the box of matches, I neatly placed on top of the spiral wooden wine table by his side.

Dusk was slowly coming in, allowing the fading sun to peep now and again in between the clouds, casting shadows into the room where Uncle lay sleeping. A blanket was in order. I wearily climbed the stairs, searched through the linen cupboard, chose one that would be suitable and returned to cover it over Uncle's frail physique. I stood and gazed at him, reflecting back at Lily's photograph, which stood in its frame next to the ticking clock. The mantelpiece looked bare and sad as she smiled from her picture. I gave out a sigh, allowed a few teardrops to fall and slowly made my way upstairs to shower.

I wished it was last week, last month, last year, any time but not today, as I stepped into the shower allowing the sprinkling water to run from the top of my head down to my toes. Uncle's words were going around and around in my mind. 'She's gone, my love, that's a certain fact. You're going to have to face up to it sooner rather than later.'

I felt I was suffocating as the glass door surrounding the shower unit was suddenly covered in steam. There was no view out, and I imagined that Lily was standing there holding a towel and brush waiting for me to dry my hair as if I was a child again. I felt frightened, and instantly pulled the door across to open it. I reached out for my white towelling dressing gown that was hanging from a hook behind the bathroom door and slipped it around my body. Although feeling more refreshed, I couldn't help but feel downhearted whilst making my way along the landing towards the stairs. I could hear Uncle gently snoring on my return and crept quietly over to check him. He was certainly out for the count. I felt weary as I wandered through into the kitchen and decided to ignore the two unused coffee cups, instead pouring myself a stiff drink to try and unwind for a while before retiring early to bed.

Dusk had finally set in as I wandered through the room where Uncle was sleeping, towards the open door that led me into the blue room. The click of the switch sounded more prominent than usual as I turned on the Victorian table lamp that sat on the right hand side of the desk, allowing it to illuminate the significant amount of paperwork that was scattered on top. I searched for a little bit of space before placing my glass down. Reality hit me once again as I pulled out the hefty leather chair and sat down. The endless weeks before Lily died had prevented me from sitting here to write my book. I didn't feel happy with the knowledge that I now had the freedom to do so. The fact that I had been beckoned to be by her side, to hold her tiny hands, to tell her how beautiful she was, to give her every ounce of love I possibly could, but now my time was my own. I stared at the gold fountain pen, dry of ink, the cigarette ends lying in an ashtray with traces of lipstick imprinted from weeks gone by; the remains of stale coffee left in the bottom of the white china cup accompanied by a layer of blue mould; the bank statements still sealed inside discoloured envelopes dried out by the heat of the sun.

I stared straight ahead through the large Georgian window. The darkness of the night left nothing in view, just the sad reflection of myself as I sat and silently cried. I didn't wipe the tears away as they rolled down my face, falling in drops onto the sheets of writing paper that lay in a disorderly manner in front of me. I felt too numb.

I jumped as Uncle snored quite loudly, skipping a breath in between. I wanted to cry forever but my emotions were drained. Wiping my face with my hands, I picked up the tiny brown bottle which was lying on its side next to a heavily stained coaster. To my relief there were still some left as I shook it, listening to the tablets rattling against one another. I struggled to open the tight-fitting top before tipping the bottle slightly and allowing them to fall into the palm of my hand. At least I'll be able to sleep, I thought.

Stretching out my arm, I reached over for the batch of letters in their bright pink envelopes that my friend Susie had religiously sent to me. Pulling one out from underneath the elastic band which firmly held them together, I halfheartedly smiled as I took the letter from its envelope, unfolded it and read with great interest what she had written. I gave a sigh, regretting that I had never taken the time to reply. How lazy of me to take advantage of the thought that she would always be there for me. Her words reminded me of the mischief that we got up to as children.

*Do you remember when I nicked those apples from Foster's orchard,* she wrote, *and you watched out for me? Didn't we run like hell that afternoon? You couldn't eat one because they were too hard, so I scoffed the lot. I had diarrhoea for the next couple of days. That should have taught me not to steal any more, although I did repeatedly steal fags from Dad's box. Anyway, you, you sissy, wouldn't take a drag from one of them in case it made you cough. I shed some tears for you too. Those dreadful times you were locked away in that horrible bedroom. You were so naïve and always thought that things would get better. Don't think that I don't know what went on at Rose Cottage because I damn well do. Haunts me to this day. Anyway, get your backside on an aeroplane and get over here for a while.*

I smiled to myself. Maybe I will one day, I thought, as I carried on reading. It was obvious that everything was working out well for her and I noticed, as I continued to read, how erratic her handwriting had become.

*It's roasting hot today. These cocktails are going down a bloody treat,* she scribbled.

I smiled once more and gave up any attempt to read on. I lifted my glass. 'Cheers, Susie,' I said before swallowing a rather large amount of vodka. I felt an urgency to write to her and, without hesitation, put pen to paper.

*My Dear Susie,*

*How rude of me to ignore your wonderful letters without sending any reply, and how selfish of me to make the effort to write to you because I'm at my lowest ebb. It's hard to think that we practically grew up together and now you live on the opposite side of the world. Reflecting on your last letter, it seems that you have found happiness at last. It doesn't surprise me. You were always determined never to let anything or anyone get the better of you. You always had a positive outlook on life. You taught me a few tricks – wish you had taught me that one. I know how fond of Lily you were all those years ago, and it is with such sadness that I write to you with the awful news that she was buried today – cancer. My body feels ravaged with pain. She was always there for me, wasn't she, even until the very end of her life? You know more than anyone how she helped me through the severity of my childhood. We both, I suppose, didn't realise how long and harsh those years would be growing up at Rose Cottage. I always had hope because Lily always gave it to me. Hope of a happy future, of growing into a young woman and ridding myself of the shabby life that I was forced to lead. Strangely enough, Susie, she didn't teach herself what she taught me. Her life was a constant battle and her beauty made her cursed. The men that encroached into her life were highly undesirable and throughout her short life there was very little happiness. When there was she cherished it. I will never understand why such a beautiful, well-spoken lady fell for the dregs of society. Sadly enough, Lily became addicted to the bottle and died without a companion by her side.*

*It's been a long day, as you can imagine. I'm sitting here with a triple vodka and will finish the evening with a tablet to ensure that I sleep. It's naughty, I know, but I simply can't stand the thought of a restless night. My Uncle is staying overnight. He's already retired, even though he hasn't made it out of the armchair, taking into account that he's had one too many. I must say, I've been glad of his interesting company and will somehow miss him on his return to London tomorrow. I'm holding on to the saying that time is a great healer, but the pain is deep and I'm frightened. I feel jealous that God chose to take her from me, and angry and frustrated to be denied sharing my joys and fears and also sharing hers with a lady that I loved and adored so much. Susie, I kissed her goodbye this morning. She was dressed in a cream and gold sari. Her hands clasped a bouquet of white lilies. I walked away, turning around once more to take a last look at her before making my exit. I stood outside just a few feet from the door knowing that the lid of her coffin was finally being closed. Everything was still as everyone stood in silence. The pall-bearers finally appeared, their shoulders firmly in position as Lily was carried towards the hearse. I don't think I have to say any more, do I?*

*Sorry, I desperately needed you to share my thoughts and feelings. Thank you if you have. I'll sign off now. I know that you will understand why. I promise to write to you again. I will, as soon as this sombre mood leaves me and the colour comes back into my days. Thank you for the memories,*

*Lorne*

I gave a sigh, put down my pen, picked up the sleeping tablet and swallowed it down with the remainder of the vodka that was left in my glass. With the sound of Uncle snoring and the ticking of the clock, I felt quite sleepy. It was time to retire for the night. The lights were dimmed and Uncle was kissed gently on his forehead before I made my way to the stairs. My body felt like lead as I held on to the bannister, slowly taking one step at a time. I gave out a long hard yawn as I reached the top, persuading myself to make one last effort to brush my teeth before climbing on top of the bed. I was too tired to pull the quilt back as I lay there. I felt a burning sensation in my eyes as I stared straight up at the ceiling. I turned on my side, buried my head in the pillow and sobbed. I didn't remember falling asleep and was startled to be disturbed by the sound of birds singing. I opened my eyes and found that the darkness of the night had gone and dawn had broken.

# Chapter 2

I could hear clattering in the kitchen and gently lifted myself off the bed, wandered into the bathroom, turned on the tap and splashed my face with the cold running water. I felt weak as I squeezed the toothpaste from the tube along the toothbrush. I made little effort brushing my teeth before rinsing my mouth and spitting out the liquid into the sink.

What the hell is going on? I thought, listening to the constant clatter from the kitchen. I refastened the belt of my dressing gown around my waist and made my way downstairs. The door to the kitchen creaked as I pressed down the handle and opened it.

'Needs oiling,' Uncle told me, holding two saucepans at the same time. 'You look wretched, my love. Will you sit down?' he said, placing the pans down on the hob and walking towards me. A kiss was given on my cheek while he swiftly pulled out a wooden chair from the kitchen table for me. 'You should be wearing your slippers,' I was told as I sat down resting my feet on the tiled kitchen floor. I ignored what was said and admired the table Uncle had set for breakfast. 'Scrambled, boiled or fried?' he asked, bending down and lifting the carton of eggs out of the fridge.

'I'm not hungry,' I replied.

'Scrambled it will be,' he said, opening the carton and walking back towards the cooker.

I felt a little aggravated as he started to whistle while cracking open the eggs and dropping them into the pan. The grinding of the pepper mill went through me as he moved it from side to side. The bread shot up from the toaster.

'Bugger!' Uncle said as he lifted it out and placed it onto the breadboard. 'That was bloody hot.'

I jumped a little as the cup and saucer were clumsily put down on the table next to where I was sitting. The effects of the sleeping tablet I had taken the previous evening hadn't fully worn off, which left me feeling very sensitive to the noise Uncle was creating around me. I reached for a cigarette, trying to ignore the scraping of the knife along the slices of toast as Uncle spread the butter. I felt sick looking down into the glass of thick tomato juice that Uncle had rushed over to give me.

'Dreading the journey back to London,' he said as he placed the toast onto two plates. 'Wish I'd driven up now. I always end up with some unsavoury character sitting next to me. Still,' he said as he tipped the pan to one side and scooped out the eggs with a wooden spoon, 'I'm looking forward to my return. I'm missing the buzz I get from city life. It's so bloody quiet out here. Sure you won't change your mind?' he asked, walking over with the plates and placing them on the table before dragging his chair out and sitting down.

'About what?' I asked.

'Coming back to stay with me for a while. I don't want you sitting here in solitude with your grief. You've got to get on with life now,' I was told as he leaned over and passed the plate with my scrambled egg. 'Careful, my love, it's bloody hot,' Uncle said, picking up his knife and fork and tasting a bit.

Not wanting to distress him with all the trouble he had gone to, I followed suit. I couldn't attempt to fully please him and apologised for not having much of an appetite. 'Sugar?' I asked, pouring the tea from the pot into his cup. I waited until he had finished swallowing for his reply.

'I'm being tested for diabetes at the moment so I'll say no.'

'Uncle, that's terrible!'

'I'll cope, my love, as long as this keeps ticking,' he said, pressing his hand against his chest. 'That's all that matters.'

There was an air of silence. Uncle concentrated on what he was eating, pausing now and again to sip his tea. I rested my elbows on the table, holding the teacup in between my hands.

'What are you thinking about,' Uncle asked, 'while you're sitting there daydreaming?'

'Lily's funeral,' I replied.

'Drink that tea before it gets cold,' I was told as he carried on eating. 'I'll be leaving at lunchtime,' he said, bending his elbow to check the time on his watch. 'Suggest we go for a long walk.' Uncle turned his head and looked through the large kitchen window. 'It's such a beautiful morning.'

He could see from the expression on my face that I wasn't too happy with the idea as he turned back to my direction before reaching over for the pot of marmalade.

'So what are you going to do?' he asked in a stern manner. 'Sit and rot in this house grieving?' I could see that he was slightly annoyed with me by the way that he spread the marmalade across his toast with his knife. 'Sorry, my love,' he said as I glanced over to him, 'I just can't help but worry about you.'

Placing my teacup back onto the saucer and leaving it on the table, I stood up and took a long stretch. 'I'll go and take a shower,' I told him. Uncle smiled. 'Need a woolly jumper?' I asked. 'There's still an early morning frost.'

'Wouldn't mind, my love,' he replied. A shred of marmalade fell down as he bit into his toast. Uncle quickly caught it and placed it inside his mouth before finishing the remainder of his tea. 'I enjoyed that,' he said, standing up to clear the plates. He stopped my attempts to help and ushered me upstairs to shower and dress.

My return was swift, feeling a lot better on freshening up. 'Catch,' I said, throwing the jumper just a short distance towards him.

'Will it fit?' he asked, slipping it over his head. 'Just the job,' I was told as he pulled it down over his chest.

'It's a perfect fit, Uncle,' I told him.

'You don't mind, do you?' he said, looking down towards his feet. 'I pinched them from the porch.'

I refrained from making any comment as Uncle stood there in a rather large pair of green wellington boots. The noise from the rubber as they flapped against his knees made me smile as he walked over towards the wine table to collect his cigars. The brim of the wellingtons was much too wide for Uncle's tiny legs.

'I feel like a country gent,' he said, as he reached for

his jacket. He was obviously happy to wear them. 'All I need now is a flat cap,' he called.

I quickly collected my boots from inside the porch and slipped them over my trousers.

'Don't you need a coat?' he remarked as I stepped back into the kitchen.

'I'm wearing another sweater underneath this one,' I told him, pulling the neck of my polo jumper out slightly to feel some cool air. 'I'm hot enough as it is.'

'Right, let's get going then,' Uncle said, bending his elbow inviting me to link my arm with his.

I closed the door behind us. Uncle took a deep breath. It was obvious that he was thankful to be out in the fresh morning air. We walked briskly along the drive, stopped, and I pressed the buzzer for the large iron gates to open before stepping onto the narrow country lane.

'Look,' he said as he turned his head towards the sky, 'there's not a cloud in sight. What are you going to do with your life when I've gone back to London, besides of course finishing your book?' he asked as we stood still, allowing a car to pass.

'Find peace with myself,' I replied.

'That's a hard thing to do, my love. I've tried it many times. It somehow works best when I've had a few drinks,' he added. 'Especially after a few glasses of scotch. But it doesn't last, my lovely, at least not in my case. Still, it's a wise thing if you can do that. You've lived such a turbulent life, I can't say I blame you. Anyway, where did I get up to regarding the visit to your mother in the Convent? I somehow forgot. Suppose through all those gin and tonics I drank.'

'Sister Rosemary had invited you inside,' I told him. 'And Ernest and you were making your way up the winding staircase.' He looked a little puzzled as we continued to walk. There was silence as Uncle tried to reflect back.

'Of course,' he said after a few seconds. 'Well, I was pretty exhausted when we reached the top,' reminding me again of how Ernest took every step with ease. 'There was again no conversation as we were led along the narrow, oblong corridor. Tiny black painted doors standing firmly closed faced us on either side. The sun's rays allowed very little sunlight as it beamed through the skylight, staying firmly in one position. The bare wooden floorboards picked up every sound of our footsteps. I found the atmosphere very depressing.'

Uncle pulled a broken twig from its branch twirling it from side to side in his hand as we walked along the country lane.

'Even though I miss city life, you're damn lucky to live out here,' he said, taking in another deep breath and enjoying the freshness of the morning air. 'Well, back to Ernest and me,' he said. 'Sister Rosemary stopped all of a sudden. It was obvious that we had reached the door that would lead us into your mother's room. Ernest ordered me to remain outside the door when Sister Rosemary opened it. I tried to take a quick peep inside but the door was quickly closed. I sighed and leant against the walls of the corridor. I must admit, though, I did try and listen to what was being said because I could hear the murmur of voices, but it was all too much of a blur, although I did hear Lily's cries. It was obvious that she had been disturbed. I should imagine that Ernest wanted to hold her in his arms. Must admit it, my love, I couldn't hold on to my emotions and covered my face with the palms of my hands and quietly sobbed.'

'I can just imagine you standing there in that long, dark corridor. Oh, Uncle.'

'Well, you see, my love, I was so anxious to see Jenny and Lily, your sister, that my emotions did rather get the better of me.'

I gave out a sigh of sympathy in support of him, knowing how frustrated he must have felt before Ernest would allow him to enter the room.

'Oh look, a squirrel,' he said, his voice breaking.

'Uncle,' I said, 'are you crying?'

'Silly old bugger, aren't I?'

'Shall we go home?'

'No, let's just walk. It doesn't matter where we end up,' he said. 'It's going to be a long time before I can do this again, especially with my favourite niece.'

I gently wiped the few tears that he had shed away with my fingertips, kissed him on his cheek and guided him slowly to continue our walk.

'Anyway, to put your mind at rest, my love, the tiny black door finally opened and I was instructed by Ernest to enter. There was no rush. I composed myself, lifting my head high and straightening my shoulders before walking in like a gentleman. I coughed slightly as this time it was me who was nervous.

'Your mother was sitting on the edge of her bed. She was dressed in a floral sari and looked beautiful. She immediately opened her arms out to me. I walked the short distance towards her, knelt myself down and allowed her to hold me. "Oh I have missed you," I whispered to her. She smiled, showing off her brilliant white teeth. Her dark skin felt like silk as I kissed her on both sides of her cheeks before standing up next to Ernest. I waited to be invited to have a look at the new baby.'

'Why did you have to wait?' I asked, feeling an ache in my arm as I unlinked it with Uncle's.

'It would have been highly bad mannered of me to take matters into my own hands and do so. Sister Rosemary must have seen the anxious look on my face and invited me over to the tiny drawer that had been pulled out of its set and placed on top of its own wooden surface. I took the few steps with haste, stood on my tiptoes and looked down into the drawer where your sister was lying. I asked permission to touch her tiny hand that had slipped out from the cotton sheet that was wrapped around her. I was overwhelmed with emotion on making my first contact with Lily. I don't have to tell you how beautiful she was,' Uncle said.

I suggested to Uncle that we take a walk along the canal and pointed over to the tiny boatyard that came into view. 'We can have a pot of tea if you like; there's a little café inside.'

He was pleased with the suggestion and started to search through his pockets. 'Will we have enough with a fiver?' he asked.

'Oh yes. Anyway, I should be the one who's paying. After all, you are my guest.'

'Well, we're not going to argue over a pot of tea, my love. What with the hospitality you've given me, it's out of the question,' he replied, as we stepped into the yard.

41

A rusty anchor lay on its side. Shoots of grass had sprung up in between the concrete flags as we walked towards the weathered building. Uncle stepped forward, reached out for the latch and lifted it up. 'The bloody door won't open,' he said, pressing the weight of his body against it. He tried once more, using all the force he had. This time he was successful. 'I nearly broke my back trying to open this door,' he called over to a plump, grey-haired woman as we stepped inside. She stopped sweeping the bare wooden floor and leant against the handle of her brush.

'Don't complain to me,' she told Uncle. 'I'm just here to try and make a bob or two.'

'It's a poky little place if you ask me,' Uncle said, pulling out a spindly-legged chair for me to sit down. I reminded him that it wasn't London. He agreed and sat down next to me. 'Can we smoke?' he asked.

'I'll bring you an ashtray,' the plump woman replied.

Uncle felt for his tin of cigars and pulled it out from his pocket. 'Thank you,' he said as the woman appeared with a cloth in her hand and began wiping the surface of the circular wooden table that we sat next to. Her short, stubby fingers held on to the tin ashtray. Uncle reached out and took it from her hand.

'What was in the parcel that Ernest had wrapped up, I presume for my mother?'

'Well, my love, Ernest must have waited for my presence before he handed it over, to your mother, of course.' He paused, as he lit his cigar. ' "This gift is a token from Dennis and me for all the love and deep affection we have for you," Ernest said as he bent down and placed it in your mother's hands.'

Uncle stopped speaking as the stainless steel teapot, followed by a bowl of sugar lumps and a jug of milk were placed on the table. We waited until she had returned with two cups and saucers and a teaspoon for each of us. The woman was thanked again and our conversation continued.

'Anyway, your mother had difficulty untying the piece of string that was wrapped around the gift. Sister Rosemary soon went to assist her and carefully untied the knot. The crisp, brown paper fell apart showing off a hand-painted box which held a blaze of coloured patterns. Jenny looked up towards Ernest before lifting off the lid. An abundance of miniature coloured tissue paper, almost like confetti, lay on the top.'

'Milk?' I asked, interrupting his conversation as I poured the tea.

'Just a touch,' he replied. 'Anyway, I got quite excited as your mother placed her hand inside, allowing her fingers to rummage around underneath the paper. "It's a necklace," Jenny whispered.' Uncle looked at me. 'You look disappointed,' he said, 'but there's a little tale behind this. You see, Grace's father, your mother's grandfather, made himself a living by diving for pearls in the Indian Ocean.'

I gave a disconcerted look.

'It's true, my love, it really is. He didn't earn a great sum; it depended on how many he could catch. Some days were good and some were bad. What a bloody awful way to make a living considering the risks that had to be taken.' Uncle frowned slightly at the thought. 'There were many pearl divers who eventually suffered from the effects of decompression.'

I looked puzzled and Uncle explained. 'Well, when that happens they either end up permanently deaf or with serious mental disorders, their lives, of course, in ruins.'

'Shall we continue our walk?' I asked. 'The atmosphere in here is quite stuffy.'

Uncle agreed and stood up almost immediately to pull my chair out. The woman was paid and Uncle suggested she keep the change. 'You see, my love, these pearl divers had to hold in their breath for long periods of time as they dived for their search,' he told me as we both started to make our exit. 'It was inevitable that there would be accidents.'

'How awful,' I remarked as Uncle lifted up the rusty latch to open the door.

We welcomed the freshness in the air as we stepped outside. I held onto Uncle's jacket as we made our way down the sloping embankment before meeting the narrow pathway which was to take us on our walk along the banks of the canal. A flock of chattering geese flew swiftly over us.

'Wondered what the hell that was,' said Uncle, almost losing his balance, as we watched them disappear from view.

The crunch of gravel underneath our feet was the only sound to be heard as we silently walked once again with our own private thoughts. The last of the early morning mist rising from the dark, still water of the canal gave it a slightly eerie feeling. I stared at a clump of bulrushes, their thick stems standing high, fed by the water. A cluster of buttercups caught my eye. I quickly bent down and picked one out from between the shoots of grass where they grew. I turned to Uncle and tickled his nose with the yellow petals. Uncle sneezed, excused himself and then smiled.

'The child is still locked inside you, my love. It's something that I've noticed while spending this brief time in your company.'

My mind flooded back to the awful memories of Rose Cottage and the cries for help that no one heard. I felt my heart ache. Uncle clicked his finger and thumb together quite sharply a few inches from my face. 'Where did you go?' he asked as I blinked my eyes.

'Somewhere I've never left,' I whispered.

'Take that look of sadness away,' he snapped. 'I realise that you had to endure the punishment of a loveless childhood, and how unpleasant it must have been for you for many years.'

'How can you?' I asked raising my voice. 'You weren't there, Uncle, to hear my cries and see the constant beatings and the life of solitude that was forced on me.'

'Are you going to condemn yourself for the rest of your life?' he shouted as he stood me still, taking a firm grip with his hands around my arms. Teardrops filled my eyes and rolled down my face. Uncle rested my head on his chest, allowing me to let my frustration out. 'It's locked deep inside you, my love. Let it go.' He was silent as I cried in his arms.

'I'm sorry,' I whispered, raising my head before wiping my face with my hands.

'Look, we have a friend,' he said, pointing his finger to a plump duck as we began to walk slowly along the bank.

I smiled as the duck, with its short legs and webbed feet, wobbled in a clumsy, swaying motion towards us. The harsh sound of quacking made us feel uneasy as he came closer.

'Look at him fly,' said Uncle as the duck flapped his wings in the air before splashing down onto the water, leaving a series of ripples behind him as he paddled away. Uncle refrained from getting too excited and coughed slightly with embarrassment.

Relieved that our passage was now clear, we took the walk more briskly.

'I've been thinking,' Uncle said.

'About what?' I asked.

He stopped for a second, bent his elbow and checked the time on his watch.

'Going to the local market, maybe to buy a trout or whatever.'

'Have you time?' I asked.

'With your permission, I have.' I looked slightly bewildered. 'There's something I must do before my return to London. Can I stay on for a day or two?'

I immediately flung my arms around him.

'Does that mean yes?'

'Of course,' I replied, squeezing him as tightly as I could.

'I'll cook you dinner; you can chill the wine; there'll be some logs on the fire and after we have eaten, we'll sit down and have a fireside chat. How does that sound?'

'Wonderful, Uncle, just wonderful.'

\* \* \*

46

I felt surprisingly relaxed, relieved that I had Uncle's company for a little longer. I asked myself why Uncle felt that he must stay. Still, it was none of my business, and the fear of the door being closed behind me on his early departure had lifted.

'I'll have to cut down on the booze when I return home, well at least try to. And these don't help either,' Uncle said as he lifted the tin of cigars from his pocket and shook them. 'Mind if we sit down for a while?' he asked as we approached a rather rustic cast iron bench.

Uncle didn't wait for my reply and hastily sat himself down.

'We'll take a short cut home,' I told him as I sat down myself onto the hard surface next to him. I felt anxious as Uncle took in deep breaths, pausing in between. I sat silent until he recovered.

'I'm OK now,' he said, breathing normally. I gave a sigh of relief. 'I'm not that young and fit any more,' Uncle said, patting me on my knee. 'Still, there's life in the old bugger yet.' We both responded with a smile, stood up and started to make our way home.

'There is something that haunts me, Uncle.' He bent his elbow once more and I linked my arm in his. Uncle looked at me with slight apprehension. 'The doubts were constantly put in my mind from being a young child.'

'About what?'

'That I was illegitimate.'

Uncle lifted the palm of his hand up towards his mouth and gave a large cough. 'Total rubbish,' he snapped. 'Your parents were married before Lily was born – remember? Anyway, I must finish telling you about the present that

47

Ernest and I gave to your mother. You see, your great grandfather became restless. Being a pearl diver had been his life. Uneducated, he knew nothing else. Money was short and, frustrated with his lifestyle, he decided to become a dishonest man. He took a huge risk by not handing in all his catch. Because he got away with it the first time, it encouraged him to continue. He would make constant trips to Bombay and hawk the pearls on the black market. He rarely returned home, spending most of the money in bars and on loose women. Used to the money, his dives into the ocean would take longer than usual in order to collect as many pearls as he possibly could. The inevitable was to happen. One particular morning he took his last dive and never emerged from the water. His body was never found.'

'How tragic, Uncle.'

'It was, my love. Anyway, your grandmother's family was informed and Grace and her mother found themselves destitute and had to leave their home for more humble surroundings. With ill health looming, and living under the stress of great poverty, Grace's mother became a beggar on the streets of Calcutta. Unkempt and riddled with arthritis, she became a burden to herself. Her death, maybe her relief, was swift. Some say it was an act of suicide. She was seen passing through the busy market place before stepping out and wandering aimlessly in between a crowd of moving oxen, leaving her body crushed to pieces. Grace fled from the lodgings they had shared, unable to cope with the sudden loss of her mother, collecting a handful of tiny boxes which were their only possessions and began roaming the streets aimlessly. Her attention was taken by groups of men chanting to her as she wandered through the red light district. Realising that she was practically penniless, it became her second home for quite some time.'

'So she was a prostitute,' I remarked. I pressed my arm firmly against Uncle's, pushing it gently against his to guide him across the road, relieved that home was in view.

'Anyway, the tiny boxes were never opened for many years,' Uncle continued. 'They were not important to Grace as she assumed that there was nothing of value inside them. It was only when Grace fell in love with Ernest and they settled in a home together that she asked Ernest to help her stack the boxes on a wooden ledge in the drawing room, which was too high for her to reach. Ernest complained that he had more important matters to deal with that day and, in his haste, let one slip through his hands. As it hit the floor the box immediately split open. I remember Ernest telling me how Grace jumped on top of the chair in fright as the contents were scattered on the floor.' Uncle gave a slight giggle. 'Ernest bent down and picked up one of the shells that had fallen from the box. He knew immediately as he felt the rough, glassy surface that it was the shell of an oyster, and cracked it open at once. "Look here!" he told Mother, beckoning her down from her chair. And there it was for them both to see. Inside the open oyster lay a beautiful pearl. Ernest reached up to collect the remaining boxes that lay on the ledge, asking Grace to go and bring a knife from the kitchen. Piercing the lids open on her return, he gave a sigh and turned to look at her. "You've been carrying a small fortune around with you," he told her. 'There were probably other thoughts going on in Grace's mind as the remainder of the oysters were opened, leaving an abundance of gleaming pearls. Ernest, although a quiet man, had a strong character.'

Uncle paused as we reached home, allowing me to press the digits of the gate in order for them to open. 'His love being so strong for Grace, he insisted that the pearls be made into a necklace for her,' I was told as we walked slowly down the driveway. 'There was to be no argument although Ernest knew that Grace would have been happier to sell them to buy the fancy clothes that she craved. Ernest would sit, night after night, with little lighting, carefully piercing a hole in each pearl. Grace would show her boredom. As an army wife she had been used to his absences, which she took advantage of.'

'Meaning what?' I asked as I opened the door into the kitchen.

Uncle slipped his jacket down from his shoulders and hung it over the back of a chair. I filled the kettle with cold water and lit a cigarette. We both sighed at the same time as we sat down at the kitchen table. I slipped off my boots, leaving them exactly where I had put them on, took a large drag of my cigarette and leant back on my chair. 'You were saying,' I said, 'about Grace taking advantage of Ernest's absences.'

'Oh yes,' Uncle replied. 'The dance halls always lured her back and it became, again, a regular habit. There would be the odd times that Ernest would return in the hope of finding Grace at home. He would sit next to the ticking clock, counting every second until her return.'

'How the hell did she get away with it? – Coffee?' I asked, standing sternly up from my chair.

'Ernest knew to turn a blind eye. There would have been nothing to gain if he didn't. The idea of living life without her was unthinkable.'

'It's so weird, Uncle. Weird that it's so identical to the way my parents were.'

'You must remember that your mother grew up in that environment.'

I poured the boiling water into two teacups and stirred the coffee with a little aggression. 'Yes, well, so did I,' I said raising my voice slightly, 'but it didn't turn me into a whore.'

'Pop a touch of scotch in for me, my love,' said Uncle, which I freely did.

His hands eagerly reached out as I passed his cup over to him. 'Sorry, Uncle, my frustrations are not directed at you. I didn't even know her.'

'She was a good woman in spite of her indiscretions,' I was firmly told. 'It's vital that you rid yourself of the pain that you constantly carry around. Thought of getting any help?'

'My God, I'm not that bad.'

'You'd be surprised, my love, you really would. I've seen the pain inside you after just a couple of days in your company.'

'That's for Lily,' I quickly told him.

'You can't beat a cup of coffee, especially with a touch of scotch in,' Uncle said, drinking what remained in his cup. 'What's the solemn look for?' I was asked. 'Want to drive me to the market? Remember I promised to cook you a meal tonight.' Uncle stood up and grabbed hold of the car keys from the kitchen shelf and placed them on the table in front of me. 'I'm only going to be a nuisance for a short while,' he said.

I smiled, stood up and took hold of the keys. Uncle slipped his jacket back on and followed me out towards the car. The door was opened for me and I placed the keys in the ignition, allowing Uncle some time to make himself comfortable next to me. I then slowly made my way along the drive and onto the lane.

'Mind if I smoke?' he asked. I pressed the button to release the electric window. Uncle struck a match and lit a cigarette. 'Anyway,' he said, taking a drag of it. 'I must finish telling you about these pearls before we reach the market. You'll be getting quite bored with it all if I don't.'

I didn't turn to acknowledge what he had just said and continued to drive.

'Concentration was needed until the last pearl was sewn on and tightly placed in position onto the threads of cotton that Ernest had twisted together to form a thin length of string. It was a fiddly job to finally join the necklace with a tiny hook and eye made from gold, but he was a patient man and, with the help of a magnifying glass, the necklace was at last secure. He scrutinised it closely and sighed with relief that the job was well done as he held in his hands a beautiful string of pearls.'

'You've made goose pimples go down my back,' I told Uncle, cautiously turning around a large bend before joining the road that would take us into the busy town.

'Dare say I have, my love. I can feel some myself.'

I stopped at a red traffic light, turned to Uncle and

smiled. 'I'm looking forward to having dinner with you tonight,' I told him before the lights changed and our short journey continued.

'Later that same evening Grace returned home to a cold atmosphere,' Uncle told me. 'The pearl necklace had been safely put away and she was questioned about her whereabouts. It was out of character for Ernest to do so. The urgency he must have felt to hand over the necklace that he had finished making for her while she was obviously mingling with other men must at that point have been too much to bear. Grace refused to give any answers, slamming the door of her bedroom behind her. Ernest, confined to sleep on the armchair for the night, quietly wept.'

'How terribly sad, Uncle,' I remarked as I indicated to turn into the car park. We roamed around trying to find a suitable place to park. Uncle sat back silently. I reassured him as he frowned that there was enough space, while manoeuvring my car in between two vehicles. 'Will you finish telling me your story?' I asked, pulling the handbrake on and switching off the engine before turning to face him. 'Only it's deep in my mind and I'm anxious to hear the ending.'

'There isn't any ending, my love. Ernest took it to his grave, his heart still broken so many years after Grace's death.'

'But the pearls?' I asked.

'Ernest never gave them to Grace, but locked them away in a hand-painted box deep inside a large wooden trunk that held only his personal possessions.'

'That's odd,' I said. 'Why go through all the care and attention to make the necklace and yet not give it to her?'

Uncle shrugged his shoulders. 'Ernest didn't go into detail with me about that night Grace returned home late. It was obvious that she must have been quite blunt to make Ernest sit and weep.'

'What a mystery,' I whispered.

'Yes, I don't know what must have been going through Ernest's mind when we boarded the train that day to visit your mother and the new baby. Reflecting back,' Uncle said, 'he was rather silent, his shoulders stiff and upright at all times. I remember him clinging on to the brown paper parcel, placing it close to his heart. It was almost uncomfortable to be near him. Unknown to me at that time, in the parcel was the string of pearls. Whatever reason he had must have been extremely deep, knowing that he had denied Grace what was rightfully hers. So you see, my love, the necklace was special.'

'So, Mother was the one who finally received it.'

Uncle didn't reply. There was an air of silence as we sat there with our own thoughts. 'Come back to London,' Uncle asked, taking hold of my hand. 'I'll never give up asking until you do.'


Uncle got quite excited as we stepped out of the car, looking through every shop window as we walked through the precinct arm in arm. He clearly found the town charming and was relieved when he found a cashpoint. We passed the corner café, where Lily and I would occasionally meet. I imagined her sitting on the same chair at the same table, waving at me to welcome me in. I tried hard not to look through the plain glass window, but I had to. My body was ripped apart with pain. I wanted to throw up there and then.

'Take me home,' I asked Uncle as the tears rolled uncontrollably down my face.

Uncle squeezed my hand tightly and led me, with a little force, across the street towards the market. 'Bloody pigeons,' he remarked, stepping in between them as they searched through discarded waste. 'I wish I could bring that smile back,' Uncle said as he pulled out his handkerchief from the pocket of his jacket. 'No doubt there'll be plenty more,' I was told as he wiped my tears away.

The market square was full of activity. I jumped with the sudden bellow from a trader as he tried to sell his goods. I felt suffocated amongst the crowds of people and urged Uncle to hurry. He took notice and we were soon standing in the queue, patiently waiting for the fishmonger's attention. I pulled my face as a whole trout was thrown on the scales. Uncle agreed on the price.

'Would you like the head cut off?' we were asked. Uncle nodded straight away. I jumped once more with the fast action of the large knife as he picked it up by its thick wooden handle. I blinked as it was immediately thrust against the neck of the trout, slicing its head off. With a touch from the fishmonger's hand, the head slid from the board. I gave a shiver as it slurped on landing into a round, white plastic bin propped by three wheels against the flagstone floor.

The fishmonger winked at me while straightening his cloth cap over his short, cropped blonde hair. His blue eyes had a sparkle in them. His fair, clean complexion was attractive. He smiled, forming a tiny faint line at each side of his mouth. I smiled back with embarrassment. He picked up the trout with his long fingers. His nails, cut short, were immaculately clean. Uncle searched in his wallet while the trout was wrapped in a sheet of brown paper. Our eyes met once again. I turned to Uncle, embarrassed. The money was passed and the trout handed over.

'Will you come back and see me?' the fishmonger asked, speaking in a quiet tone as Uncle occupied himself by inspecting his change.

I had only just realised how handsome he was. 'Yes,' I whispered, 'yes, I will.'

His attention was alerted by a rather irritated, overweight woman, complaining about how long she had been waiting. His smile was warm as he moved away from me to assist her.

'Handsome devil, isn't he?' Uncle remarked, looking over in his direction before we turned to walk away.

'Well, yes, I suppose he is,' I replied. 'How old do you think he is?' I asked Uncle when he stopped further along.

'This looks interesting,' he said out loud, picking up a thick brown leather-bound book. 'Mmm, Churchill. Might be a good read. Early forties I'd say, my love. Rather a good Prime Minister in his time,' he called to the old man sitting on a stool behind the book stall. Too tempted, I glanced back. It was as if he knew. Whilst in the flow of a conversation he suddenly stopped for a second. Our eyes met again from a distance and I quickly turned away.

'Bugger!' Uncle said, struggling to place the book he had just bought into a thin plastic carrier bag. A light breeze blew in the air as the cloud slowly thickened above us. 'Let's head for home,' Uncle said, 'looks like there's going to be a storm.'

I walked straight ahead in front of Uncle, trying not to give in to the temptation to turn around and take one last glance at the handsome man I had just encountered. We left the market square and moved hastily as the heavy drops of rain fell from the sky. 'You were right,' I called to Uncle as we quickened our step.

'Bloody English weather,' he snapped, slipping the bag which carried his book underneath his jacket.

A loud blast of thunder bellowed through the sky and a flash of lightning encouraged us to run as fast as possible. 'Hurry,' Uncle called as the car came into view. 'Switch on the engine,' I was told as the door opened.

Our soggy clothes squelched against the leather seats as we slammed the doors behind us. The keys slipped through my wet fingers as I attempted to start the ignition. 'Damn!' I called, bending my arm and shoulder down in search of them. Another blast of thunder ripped through the air followed by a bright glare of lightning.

'Thank God we're sheltered,' Uncle said as the keys were finally placed in position and the engine switched on. The windscreen wipers worked frantically and the view was dim. The heavy rain hit against the headlights as I carefully drove through the car park to make my exit.

'Jesus Christ!' said Uncle as a bright flash of lightning lit the sky. The storm had taken charge making the journey home slow and conversationless, as I concentrated on steering us through the downpour.

The last bend was turned and I breathed a sigh of relief. I fiddled for the feel of the tiny plastic oblong buzzer which was hanging down amongst a mass of keys adjoined to the ones placed in the ignition. Pressing the soft red button in the middle firmly down with the edge of my thumb, the large iron gates slowly opened. Water flowed out of control from the blocked gutters surrounding the rooftop of the house, bouncing aggressively onto the tarmac as we arrived on the driveway.

'Looks like you have problems,' Uncle said, moving his head close to the window and looking up.

I jumped once more with the crack of lightning and another deep roar of thunder echoed through the sky. 'I'm making a run for it,' I told Uncle as I opened the door of the car and headed as fast as I could indoors. Uncle arrived a couple of minutes later, coughing and spluttering.

'Pour yourself a scotch,' I called down from upstairs while stripping off in the bathroom before stepping into a rather baggy pair of tracksuit bottoms. I swiftly moved into the bedroom, leaving the coat hanger shaking inside the wardrobe as I grabbed a fleecy top, pulled out a pair of socks from the large pine drawers, grabbed a towel I had lazily left hanging over the rod of the four poster bed, and rubbed it vigorously against my hair as I made my way downstairs.

'Uncle,' I said, watching him shiver as he sat on the edge of the kitchen chair holding a glass of scotch. He conveniently sneezed in front of me. The excess water on his hair dripped slowly down his neck. 'There's a warm towelling dressing gown in the spare bathroom. Why don't you go and slip it on?' I told him passing him my towel. Tilting his glass towards his mouth he took a large swig,

58

draped the towel over the back of his neck and excused himself.

I slowly wandered across the kitchen and rested my hands on both sides of the sink. I leaned slightly forward and stared through the kitchen window. Condensation was slowly forming around the squares in the glass as I looked out. I was glad of Uncle's absence for that short time as I stared out at the torrent of rain that lashed vigorously down onto the drive. I remembered the last remaining weeks of Lily's life. How brave, I thought, as she clung on to every minute that she possibly could. My mind replayed the events, allowing her words to echo around in my mind. I could feel her touch as if she was still there, reaching out for my hand. I allowed my imagination to take hold of hers as I stood there at that lonely kitchen window. There are many true men out there for you, my dear sister, she would faintly say, believing in her heart that I would one day find happiness with a man by my side. Enjoy the company they want so dearly to give you. Don't be scared. Love is free. Take hold of it, and when you do, never let it go. She seemed so restless with her words on that particular afternoon. There was no blinking. Her still brown eyes stared directly into mine. Her eyelids slowly closed as I sat and stared at her beautiful face. I remembered it so vividly it was as if I had just that second left her bedside and slipped into another room. My mind clashed with the thunder that bolted through the sky once more. The slow sequence of events was so clear. I remembered how I slowly started to release my hand from her weak grip that she held around my fingers. My touch about to leave hers – she mumbled. I moved closer to her. 'I'm still here, Lily,' I whispered, feeling the closeness of her hand once more. Saliva dribbled from her mouth down towards her chin. I reached over with my other hand and wiped it away. 'I'm not going to leave you,' I told her as she partially opened her eyes. I squeezed her hand as gently as I could to reassure her. 'Let them take you in their arms,' she whispered. 'Let them make passionate love to you. Don't waste this wonderful time you have here. Allow yourself to be loved.' 'I will, Lily,' I told her, resting my forehead on her chest.

I gave an enormous sigh, purposely trying to cut Lily, and the picture I had of her, from my mind.

'I've been sitting here for the last couple of minutes, my love.' I jumped at the sound of Uncle's voice. 'Where did you go to?' he asked. 'In that world of your own?'

'To the hospice, Uncle, I've been back to the hospice.' I felt my voice breaking in between and quickly turned back and howled with grief.

'You've got to try and pull yourself together,' I was told. 'It's not going to be easy, I know that.'

'No, Uncle, no,' I screamed, turning fiercely towards him. 'I can't pull myself together as you sit there with your whisky as your healer. I've spent two days trying to pull what you call myself together.' I missed catching a breath and panicked. 'I'm in pieces, can't you see?' I cried out.

'I'll start preparing dinner,' he said.

My vision of him was blurred as I stood up. 'I don't want dinner,' I screamed. 'I don't want to sit and smile and make stupid conversation for your contentment. Don't you realise my heart is broken and no one, not even you, can fix it?' I cowered down against the floor.

'You're like an injured animal; let me help you,' Uncle soothed.

'Don't touch me,' I screamed as his hand rested on my shoulder.

'Shall I go?' he quietly asked.

'Yes, go, just go, Uncle,' I cried, covering my face with the palms of my hands.

'I'll light the fire before I do. At least tonight you'll be warm.'

Emotionally drained, I couldn't stand up straight and staggered like a drunk in search of Uncle. I leaned against the open door and watched him strike a long match against the stone hearth to light the tightly rolled newspaper tucked in between the logs inside the iron grate. He knew that I was there but ignored my presence and continued to feed the slow-burning fire with logs.

'The victory is God's,' I whispered with a quake in my voice.

'God isn't your enemy, my love. Come here.'

I felt riddled with guilt as I approached him. 'I'm so sorry, Uncle,' I said, crouching down next to him, flinging my arms around his neck and squeezing tightly. 'I hurt your feelings and I didn't mean to. Please forgive me.'

'You didn't hurt mine, my love,' he replied patting my shoulder. 'You only hurt your own. And anyway, I saw the twinkle in that man's eyes today.' I moved my head slightly up to his. 'And dare I say I also saw one in yours.'

'The fishmonger!'

'Ha, ha,' Uncle said.

'It didn't take you long to figure that out. I'll go back and see him one day.'

Uncle's reaction surprised me. 'Yes, you will,' I was told, 'and the sooner the better.' Uncle got hold of my face and lifted my chin gently up towards his. 'I'd go and splash that pretty face of yours with cold water. It's swollen. How about a stiff gin and tonic?' he called as I excused myself and climbed the stairs to freshen up.

'Good idea,' I called back, trying to sound strong despite the weakness I felt.

My reflection was ghastly as I leaned over the bathroom sink and looked into the mirror. I gripped the tap and turned it slightly, allowing the water to run freely around the oval washbasin. I filled my cupped hands and felt my face tingle with the splash of cold water as it touched my face.

'This book I bought looks bloody interesting,' Uncle called.

'I'm sure it is,' I called back, reaching for the hand towel and patting my face dry.

'Drinks are ready.'

'I'll be down in a second.'

'Feel better?'

'A little,' I replied, taking hold of the tall slim glass that Uncle passed to me.

'Cheers,' Uncle said, clashing the rim of his glass next to mine. 'Well, come on.'

'Yes, cheers.' The clink of our glasses rang out against the spitting of logs burning on the open fire and I tried, almost in vain, to abandon the grief I still felt.

Uncle patted the corner of his new book twice as he

sat down in the armchair and rested it on his knees. 'At least you'll get some peace tonight,' he said as he opened the pages at random. He looked towards me and gave me a warm smile. It was spontaneously welcomed with a smile back in return.

'You're restless, my love,' he told me as I found myself moving around in the armchair trying to find a comfortable position. The gin in my glass nearly spilled over as Uncle reached across and pulled the arm of the chair closer to him. 'I'm exhausted,' he said, placing one hand over his mouth and yawning. 'Mind if I have a nap for ten minutes?' I eagerly gave my consent.

An air of contentment filled the room. My pain, thankfully, had eased. I leaned my head back against the tall-backed chair and watched the fire in the grate in silence.

'Bugger!' Uncle muttered, while in a deep sleep. It amused me and I wondered where his dreams had taken him.

The burning logs dropped lower, leaving the dust to fall through the narrow slits of the grate. I looked over and, with a slight stretch of my neck, stared up into the round face of the old mechanical clock that sat proudly on the mantle above. It was a deliberate stare as the point of the hand ticked the minutes away and I hated that haunting sound, hated it for taking me further from the past into a future without the gentle guidance of Lily.

'Where's my drink?' Uncle said to himself, sitting up with a jolt. 'Ah, it's there,' he said, noticing that he had left it stuffed between the arm and seat of the chair that he was sitting in. I felt his embarrassment as he turned and looked at me, quickly turning away before looking back towards me once more.

'I wondered where the hell I was just then,' he said, straightening his hair with one hand and picking up his book that had slipped by his side with the other. 'The bloody trout!' he shouted, standing up unbalanced before dropping his book onto the carpet. 'I've left it in the bloody car.' I stood up and took hold of his glass as he passed it over to me. 'I'm going to get pissed wet through again,' I heard him say, the rain sweeping towards him as he lifted the latch and opened the main door that led him onto the driveway.

A strong gust of wind swept through the open door, scattering loose sheets of paper that had been lying on top of a miniature writing bureau inside the hallway, onto the floor. I bent down and picked them up one by one before holding the door ajar. 'Hurry,' I called, holding my breath as the rapid wind swept in once more.

'I'm back,' he called, shivering on his entrance as he held the wrapped trout at arm's length. 'There's another storm brewing,' Uncle said as he made his way into the kitchen and dropped the trout sharply on top of the steel sink. 'I'm going to get changed,' he said. 'I feel a real sissy in this.'

'You're probably right,' I thought, turning and looking at him. The only things visible were his two tiny feet with protruding ankle bones on either side. He fastened the belt of the robe a little tighter around his waist in an irritated manner and quickly disappeared.

The howling wind whistled a lonely lament as it clashed against the window panes, finding weakness in the old wooden frames as they clattered with age against the storm. The rapid succession of crackling wood alerted my attention back into the drawing room. The sudden dramatic force of fiery sparks landed in succession, dying into dark embers on the woolly fireside rug. The tall bright flames from the burning logs battled inside the darkness of the chimney breast against the force of the intruding wind.

'Uncle,' I called. 'Uncle,' I called again, raising my voice.

'What's the panic?' he asked, slipping his arms inside the sleeves of his jacket, lightly stepping from one foot to the other as he hastily made his way down the stairs. He stretched out his arm and gently brushed me to one side. 'Blast!' he called out touching the head of the poker that the heat from the fire had penetrated. He bravely made another attempt to pick it up, this time with caution. Uncle made the scene more dramatic than it was. Bending his knee, he placed one foot on the hearth and plunged the iron rod into the grate, thrusting the point suddenly against the logs. 'Get back!' he shouted at the burning wood as it rolled towards him, moving the rod in and out as if in some sort of fight, the poker his sword.

'Hungry?' he asked, proudly stepping back feeling in complete control. I passed him his drink and thanked him as he placed the poker back in its stand and heartily took a large gulp. He quietly complained by the look on his face as he swallowed.

'I'll pour you a fresh one,' I said, reaching out and taking his glass from him.

Uncle checked the lapels of his blazer and straightened his sleeves before following me into the kitchen.

'Uncle?' I said on his approach to the sink.

'Yes, my love.'

'How do you know if you are really attracted to someone?'
'When you look them in the eye and your heart flutters.'
'That's old fashioned.'
'Maybe, but it still happens. It happened to you today.'
'It didn't.'
'You can't pull the wool over my eyes, my love. Come over here and turn on the cold tap for me,' he asked, unwrapping the paper before lifting up the trout to inspect it once more. 'Pass me the salt. It's a slippy bloody thing,' he said as he opened it, taking a firm grip before washing it under the cold running water. 'What's the face for?' he asked as I pulled it in a girlish fashion as he slapped the fish onto the board.

Relieved that I could step back from Uncle's presence, the gin was poured to his liking.

'I'll set the table,' I told him, leaving his glass on the shelf.

The double glass doors stuck slightly to their hinges before finally opening. The dining room held an air of silence. I looked at every empty chair, the detailed embroidery on their high backs fading with age, standing neatly in position. The lustre had left the large rectangular table and the signs of tarnish were there for all to see. 'Come on, get some life into yourself,' I whispered to myself. That's what Lily would say, I thought, wouldn't you Lily? I felt that she was there, pushing me quietly along, urging me to find warmth and happiness in my life. I promised Lily that I would before she died, but now I just stood there, feeling sombre in the dullness of the room. I stretched out my arm, pressing my fingers onto the switch to light up the chandelier.

'Very French,' Uncle said, appearing in the doorway and looking up to where it hung.

'Don't you think it hangs a little too low?' I asked, folding my arms and staring profoundly at the ceiling.

'It's designed to hang low,' Uncle said, admiring the beauty of the structured black dome. 'It's rimmed with gold,' he said, inspecting it closer.

'Imitation, Uncle.'

'Oh well, you'd never tell. What's the rush for anyway? Dinner won't be ready for at least an hour,' he called as I quickly left the room. 'Where are you?' Uncle asked.

'I'm in the blue room,' I shouted through the open doors. 'Why don't you sit near the fire and enjoy your drink?'

'Does that mean I'm not wanted?'

'Only for a while, Uncle.'

I lifted the tiny thin latch opening the lid of a small ornamental box which sat on the oblong dresser. Staring for a second at the tiny key that once shone of brass, its discoloration no surprise considering it had lain solitary on top of the wooden base for a number of years. I was surprised at its weight on lifting it out, trying to ignore my feelings of apprehension. I knelt down and pushed it hastily inside the lock of the cabinet below.

'What are you up to?' Uncle asked, peering his head around the door as I turned the ring of the key to its side.

'I'm going to bring some life back into this place,' I replied turning the key once more.

'What, from a cupboard?'

I ignored his remark, first staring below and then above on the shelf at what had been stored.

'I feel like I'm intruding. Am I?' he asked.

'No, not at all,' I said, bending down to my knees. I quickly glanced in his direction. 'Sorry, Uncle, it's just…' I stopped for a second and stared inside again. 'It's just that, well, it's not been opened for at least three years.'

'Good God, what's so special inside?' he asked.

'The love of man,' I replied with a sigh.

'Pardon,' he said coming a little closer.

I took a long deep breath. 'Here, take these for me.'

Uncle gave a nervous laugh as I reached inside and picked up two tall bronze candle holders. 'They're heavier than I thought,' I said with urgency in my voice as I lifted them out, so he would hurry and take them from me. 'You've gone terribly pale, Uncle,' I remarked as he gave a little shiver before stretching out his arms slowly and taking them from me. 'With that look on your face, anyone would think that I was going to pass you the remains of a dead body.'

'Well, actually, it did cross my mind.'

'Uncle!' I said, relaying my shock at the very thought. 'Look, Uncle,' I said beckoning him over to me. 'Everything is still as it was. There's the candle.' The tiny piece of burned wick fell onto the top of the shelf as I picked it up. The dried melted wax that had dropped with the heat of the flame crumbled on my touch.

'Not much of it left,' Uncle remarked as I passed it over for him to hold.

'I remember wrapping these as if it was yesterday,' I said, placing my hand inside the cupboard once more.

'What's all this about?' he asked with frustration in his voice.

The gentle rustle of tissue paper took Uncle's attention as I lifted it out, unwrapping the two napkins. 'I remember folding these,' I told him, my attention drawn to the crease lines that were still impressed on the white linen cloths as I opened them out, laying one on top of the other across my knee. I held my breath and inhaled deeply.

'Another sigh.'

'Yes, Uncle, another sigh. I remember the excitement preparing dinner for that night, nervous that the raspberry and honey sauce I had made with the help of a recipe would complement the duck that was to be cooked and sliced that evening. I remember running out buying bunches of flowers that day, filling the house with colour in every room and rushing back out, peering through shop windows that were dressed with beautiful clothes, relieved on finding something new to wear. I was complimented on how I looked in that long fitted dress made of black lace, my shoulders bare, feeling the warm, loving atmosphere that had been created. The light aroma of perfume lingered behind me with every step that I took towards him before he embraced me in his arms.'

'Tell me,' Uncle asked, touching his fingers on my hand, 'what happened that evening that hurt you so much?'

I shook my head to let Uncle know that I couldn't countenance the idea of verbally going through it. 'You'll find out all about it in the book that I'm writing,' I whispered.

Uncle patted my hand and released his touch. 'May I?' Uncle asked, looking at me for approval before reaching inside the cabinet and lifting out two crystal glasses. 'There's a lipstick mark on this one,' he said, holding it up against the light.

He was right. The imprint of lipstick was still there.

'Well then, let's get it cleaned up,' I suggested, unintentionally shedding a tear.

'Where's it all going?' I was asked. 'Shall I leave you to it?'

'Do you mind? It's just that with you doing all the cooking, I'd like to put a womanly touch to the dining room and, anyway, it's about time that all these were used.'

'Have you anything to put inside this?'

I shook my head while pulling out the tissue that was tightly squeezed inside a tall, slim glass vase.

'Then I'll find you something out of that huge garden of yours.'

'Uncle, please don't go out.'

'It will only take me a second.'

'Well, at least wait until the storm dies down.'

'If you insist, my love. Maybe I'll read some of the book I've just bought,' he said, moving his wrist up closer to him to check the time. 'I've got at least three quarters of an hour to kill. I can see the expression on your face. Immensely boring, I should imagine you're thinking,' he said as he stood up. 'You can't change the course of history, my love, and Churchill is certainly a part of it.' He moved his jacket up and then down onto his shoulders, pulling the collar closer to his neck, making his statement quite clear.

'I do love you, Uncle,' I said as I placed my hand on the dresser in order to pull myself up.

'What, an old fool like me?'

'Yes,' I answered, standing up. 'Not that you're a fool,

certainly not, Uncle, and you're not that old.' He held his head high and with pride, excused himself from the room.

The pain wasn't as severe as I had thought. The last streak being polished from the glass with the crisp cotton tea-towel, and the tall, thin candles lit with the strike of a match, the table was set. I stood back and looked with unexpected admiration at how the room had been given back its unconditional warmth. I gave a sigh – of sadness or relief, I didn't know. It was just a sigh.

'Finished?' Uncle called.

'Yes, finished,' I called back. It was obvious he had noticed the flames flickering from the candles through the bevelled glass doors that led through into the drawing room. I pressed down on both handles and opened the doors wide. The single applause from Uncle echoed as I finally took my place in the armchair next to him.

'You'll be ready for this,' I was told as he leaned forward and passed me a chilled gin and tonic from the top of the wine table that now seemed to have a permanent place next to him. 'Uncle,' I said.

'Yes, my love,' his attention taken from the page.

'How long did you stay at the Convent?'

He raised his eyes. 'I'm somewhat confused,' he replied.

'When you went to visit mother and Lily, who had just been born,' I reminded him.

'Bloody war,' he said, 'it's taking over my mind.'

'Could it be anything to do with the book you're reading?' I asked.

71

'Mmm, maybe,' he replied, tapping his fingers on the cover as he closed it.

Uncle noticed my attention focusing on the photograph of Lily.

'I can't remember the length of time we stayed that day with your mother. Lily was restless, which is usual for a newborn, I suppose. We were ushered out of the room many times. Ernest would pace up and down along the narrow corridor. The cries from your sister would linger. When silent, we knew that she had suckled at your mother's breast. I sensed how irritated Ernest was on those long stretches we were left standing in that corridor. "The baby should be christened a Catholic, and today," he told me. "What do you say, Dennis?" I, of course, shrugged my shoulders. Ernest always liked a straight, prompt answer. No doubt he was irritated even more when he wasn't given one. "I'm thinking of sending you off to boarding school, a private European one, of course. It's in the Himalayas. At least it's run by Catholic priests – St Vincent's," he told me. I remember shuddering at the very thought. "What's that look for?" Ernest snapped. Looking up at him, my eyes couldn't help but show the signs of sadness at the thought of being abandoned once more in my life.'

There was a few seconds of silence between Uncle and myself, leaving us with the sound of the howling wind that crashed fiercely around the outside walls of the house.

'The weather's still pretty dreadful,' Uncle said. 'Let's hope it's calmed down by morning. Anyway, if I recall, we were allowed back into your mother's room with instructions from Sister Rosemary that our stay couldn't be longer than a couple more minutes. Rest for a new mother is essential, we were told, as she moved away from the door to let us through. Lily was fast asleep, back in the drawer that had been made into a temporary cot for her. "May I?" I asked, taking the pearl necklace from your mother's hand as she sat once again on the edge of the bed. "Do you like her?" your mother whispered as she glanced over to Lily. I didn't get time to reply. "We'll be back to see you before you depart for England," Ernest said quite sternly. "I only hope to God that that man looks after you," he told her. I panicked slightly but finally managed to undo the catch of the necklace. Your mother jumped at the touch of my cold hands as I fastened the pearls at last around her neck. Ernest turned away and tapped his fingers on the tiny ledge while staring out of the window. "We'll say goodbye tomorrow," Ernest said, walking over and opening the door, beckoning for me to follow. I kissed Jenny and swiftly left the room.

'By then my feet were blistering. The straps across my sandals had dug into them. You can imagine how uncomfortable I felt with each step that I took. "What's that limp for, Dennis?" Ernest asked as I followed behind him along the corridor towards the staircase. I straightened my walk as best I could and wasn't questioned again.

'Ernest threw a handful of rupees into a circular clay bowl that had been placed on top of the flag floor at the entrance. "We'll be back tomorrow. Quite early if that suits you," he told Sister Rosemary. She nodded her approval and escorted us back along the lawn. We respectfully said our goodbyes and started to make our way back to the heart of Calcutta. I was informed that we should find a suitable guest house nearby, and a substantial meal to end the day. I felt bitterly disappointed at Ernest's aggression and, with the looming thought that I could be sent off to boarding school, my appetite diminished.

'The walk was silent apart from the squawking seagulls making me aware that we were close to the city. I felt quite suffocated as we walked back through the narrow streets. The pavements were lined with people squatting. You could smell the squalor. It was quite unbearable. "I have decided that we should go home," Ernest called, turning to me as I followed behind. I nodded quickly in agreement and hastened my step with his. Ernest shouted at me to run as the train was slowly starting to make its journey. We jumped onto the platform and ran as fast as we could. Ernest, of course, was first and offered me his hand as he hoisted me up into the carriage. I thought of Barbara, the stable girl, on that cramped journey home and couldn't wait to return to her and hold her in my arms.'

'Were you in love with her?' I asked before taking a cigarette from its packet.

'Madly,' Uncle replied as he finished off the remainder of the gin in his glass. 'We were greeted on our return home by Ernest's loyal servant. Immediately, our slippers were handed over to us. I remember crouching down in the hallway with an expression of pain upon my face. The servant had the same expression as he watched me carefully remove my sandals. Ernest ordered a variety of light snacks before requesting dinner to be ready by nine that evening. I was desperate to see Barbara and asked if I could be excused from having such a late meal. Ernest looked disgruntled once more but nodded his approval and then requested that two bowls of lukewarm water be put into our rooms, recommending that we both go and freshen up. On my return I found Ernest in the dining room.

' "Iced tea?" I was asked.

' "If you don't mind, no," I replied, picking up the jug of water from the table as Ernest poured himself a rather stiff gin.

' "Are you joining me?" he asked, pulling out a chair for me to sit down. Dare I question him, I thought, as the servants presented each of us with a bowl of lentil soup laced with chillies. After all, the boarding school was not what I wanted. Ernest broke a chapatti in half and passed one over to me. I decided not to broach the subject with him and we both sat and ate in silence. No doubt Ernest had Grace on his mind as he left the soup unfinished, wiped his mouth with his serviette and walked over to the cabinet to pour himself another drink. I excused myself and left the room immediately. I know that you might think that was rather rude of me, but Ernest couldn't stand anyone near him when he wanted to drown his sorrows. He would just sit in self pity and drink.'

'Over Grace?' I asked.

'Of course, my love. I slipped out to see Barbara that evening. I'd forgotten about the blisters on my feet as I pedalled my bicycle. "Barbara," I called as I cycled closer. "Dennis," she called back. I quickly jumped off my bicycle and she once again ran into my arms.'

'How romantic.'

'Well, yes, it was. She took me into the barn and tenderly made love to me. As we lay together feeling content, I whispered to her that I may have to go away. "Where to?" she asked. I told her that Ernest had mentioned the Himalayas and that there was a boarding school out there, but assured her I was praying I wouldn't have to go as I couldn't bear the thought of not being able to see her. We wrapped our arms around each other and kissed tenderly before my return home.'

Uncle gave a sigh and stood up. 'I'll serve the dinner now,' he told me, placing his book carefully on the seat of the chair before asking me if I would serve the wine.

'Uncle,' I said as we made our way towards the kitchen, 'do you still love her?' He didn't answer as tears rolled down his face. I knew then that he did. 'I'll take the wine through,' I called amongst the clashing of saucepan lids and a very flustered Uncle.

# Chapter 3

Dinner was eventually served and my applause on excellent presentation left him quietly pleased. The wine was poured and with a clink of our glasses we wished each other well.

'This is delicious,' he said. 'Try some.'

I agreed, the trout tasted excellent.

'There's something missing,' he told me. Uncle excused himself and a sudden bang of music made me jump. 'Sorry,' he called, turning the volume down before returning to dine.

'Tell me,' I asked, continuing my meal, 'why did you never marry Barbara if you loved each other so much?' The soft sound of piano music playing in the background made me feel quite emotional as Uncle looked at me with sadness.

'We did love each other.'

'Was she beautiful?'

'Extremely.' Uncle paused and took a sip of his wine as he stared into the flicker of the candlelight. 'Have you any idea, my love, what it feels like, the pain, sometimes extreme even to this day, to have loved and lost?'

'Yes,' I immediately replied.

'Sorry, I know that Lily has just been buried.'

'It's not about Lily. Why did you lose her, Uncle, if your love was so strong?'

'It certainly wasn't my intention. You see, when dawn broke that following morning I quickly washed and dressed before running downstairs to meet Ernest in the breakfast room. It was a tiny, dark room with shelves filled with books from floor to ceiling. It was the room where Ernest would spend as much time as he possibly could, reading until the early hours of the morning, always with a jug of percolated coffee by his side. "These bloody riots are still continuing. It's getting worse," Ernest told me, lifting his head up from the newspaper while I helped myself to a bowl of prunes. "I'd advise you not to venture far. Not on your own," he warned. I asked him if it was that bad. "It looks as if it's going to get that way. Couldn't you sense the mood of the people as we walked through the streets?" he answered. "But aren't we safe out here in the country?" I put to him. "For the moment, but it's not looking good. We'll make our last trip into Calcutta today."

'Ernest worried me that morning. It wasn't like him to express how anxious he was. What's that puzzled look on your face?' Uncle asked.

'Sorry, but I don't understand. Why should there be riots in India?'

'Well, at that specific time, my love, India was seeking independence from the United Kingdom. India was regarded as the brightest jewel in the English Crown, but the Indians desperately wanted to be a free nation. I must admit, I wasn't aware of the tension until Ernest pointed it out to me. It was more noticeable on our second journey back. I didn't feel at all safe, even though Ernest was armed. The asparagus is overcooked,' he said, slicing it

78

with his knife. 'Sorry, my love. It's been rather a one-way conversation, me going on about the past. I suppose you find me an immense bore.'

'Of course not, Uncle. In fact you're quite interesting.' I smiled as he immediately drew me back into more conversation about that part of his life spent in India.

' "Don't look at anyone, Dennis," Ernest told me as the train came to a slow stop. Our departure from the station was swift. Ernest flagged down a cart pulled by two bullocks and we set off on our shaky journey to bid farewell to your mother. "There's growing hatred between Muslims and Hindus," Ernest said as the journey took us through the crowded streets, "and this place is full of them." Ernest treated both sides with contempt. I myself only felt sadness at the sheer poverty these people faced every day of their lives.

'Our journey took us through the mountains. I felt quite sick by then as the wheels of the cart struggled over the loose stones that were scattered along the road to take us to our destination. Ernest obviously thought that with the tensions rising, travelling by foot was too dangerous.'

'It's strange to think that Lily was there at the time,' I told Uncle. 'The girl that I grew up with came from so far away, with just a drawer to sleep in at the very beginning of her life. Oh, Uncle!' I held my hands over my face and wept.

'I was at that time ignorant about the true facts of what India was going through. Ernest held the truth from me only to protect me from any anxieties I might have had.'

I knew that Uncle was purposely carrying on with his

conversation as my tears flowed, and I allowed him to do so. My grief controlled, I wiped my eyes. Uncle refilled my glass, ensuring that I took a rather large sip. I thanked him for the food and apologised for the remainder that was left on my plate.

'It is rather filling,' he told me, placing his knife and fork onto his plate.

'Do you mind?' I asked, lifting a cigarette out of the box.

'I'll join you. Have you got any plans for tomorrow?' Uncle asked, striking a match and leaning over.

'I was supposed to be meeting Prudence.'

'Who?'

'Prudence,' I replied, thanking him. 'We usually meet on the last Thursday of every month just for coffee. She's a nicely spoken lady, rather eccentric. Suffered from manic depression for years. She was in and out of institutions. At one time she thought she'd gone mad, especially when her husband and children walked out on her. I should imagine that was her turning point. She couldn't bear living without them and hated herself.'

'What a depressing cup of coffee you must have with her,' Uncle said.

'Actually, no. Tired with her illness, she volunteered for intense therapy. It was one of the hardest battles she had ever faced and now, three years later, she has a bubbly personality, loves going places, works out in the gym to keep her tall, slender body in shape, practically lives in the beautician's, applies make-up to a once pale, drawn face, changes the colour of her short cropped hair whenever she chooses and gets on with it.'

'Did her family return to her?'

'No, Uncle. Prudence worried me the last time I saw her. It was about three weeks ago. I felt anxious as I approached her. Her hair had been dyed jet black and she sat there with a look of gloom. "It's Crumblewinks," she said as she looked up at me. "I cooked steak last night with onions and gravy, his favourite. He'd been in a sulky mood over the last couple of days, so I ignored the fact that he hadn't touched his dinner." '

'I'm sorry to interrupt,' Uncle said as he burst into laughter. 'I'm sorry, my love, carry on,' he said trying to control himself, only to burst out laughing once more.

'Anyway, I'm not going to say much more, only that she tucked him into bed that night, switched on his bedside lamp and left him to sleep.'

'Don't tell me he had his own bedroom?'

'Yes, Uncle. Even down to his own dressing table, with his grooming brushes neatly laid out and framed photographs of himself standing on the top.' Uncle burst into another fit of laughter.

'It's not funny, Uncle. Prudence woke up next morning to find him dead.'

'In bed?' Uncle asked, still laughing.

'Yes,' I replied. 'Crumblewinks was all she had and she treated him like her child. That's why she'd had her hair dyed black, in mourning for him.' Uncle nearly fell off his chair, his laughter now uncontrollable.

'It's very sad,' I told him. 'She's now turning religious because of it.'

'I've not laughed like that for years,' Uncle said as he eventually calmed down. 'Do you mind if I have a shot of whisky? This storm isn't dying down,' he added as a strong gust of wind forced the rain to lash heavily against the window. 'Shall we sit by the fire?'

'Uncle, it's so hard to realise that I can't pick up the 'phone any more and speak to Lily,' I told him, following him through.

'Let me carry that,' he said, taking the glass of wine from my hand and allowing me to sit before handing it over to me, giving me a gentle sympathetic pat on my shoulder. He poured his shot of whisky, blew his nose into his white cotton handkerchief, threw a couple of logs on the fire and sat down next to me.

'Don't mind the intrusion,' he said, 'but are you seeing anyone at the moment?'

I smiled. 'No, Uncle, I'm not. I've not had a date for the last three years.'

'Good grief, that's shocking. You mean to tell me that you haven't even been taken out for dinner?'

'No. When Lily was diagnosed as terminally ill my life revolved around seeing her as much as possible.'

'Surely there have been opportunities?'

'A few,' I replied.

'For God's sake, don't end up an old maid.'

'I won't.'

'You're bloody right, you won't. I still say you should return to London with me.'

There was a couple of minutes' silence. The music had stopped playing, leaving the faint sound of the ticking clock that stood on the mantelpiece above, the tiny crackles of burning wood below and the whistles from the howling wind. Uncle sat back in his chair lighting one of his favourite cigars.

'It's nice to be able to sit and talk to you,' he told me. He bent his head back, puffed his cigar and blew the smoke up into the air in appreciation of being able to continue his story. 'Now, where was I up to? Oh, yes, I remember now. We were making our way up to the convent. That's right,' he said, taking a large swig of whisky. 'Ernest tapped the driver of the cart we were travelling in on his shoulder. It came to a halt creating particles of dust that floated into the air. Ernest coughed profoundly, stood up and got out, leaving the carriage to sway. I held onto the sides and jumped off after him. They communicated with each other in Punjabi.'

'Can you speak Punjabi?' I asked.

'I can get by but not that much, and what I can I daren't repeat,' Uncle said with a chuckle.

I smiled, took a sip of wine and sat back to listen once more.

'It was quite obvious that our means of transport would be waiting for our return as the old man tied up the straps of the reins and nodded in agreement. It was easier the second time around. Ernest pressed the rusty bell. Sister Rosemary appeared, opened the gates and welcomed us once more. "We have said our prayers this morning for their safe journey." Sister Rosemary held onto the wooden cross that hung low against her chest. "England is very far away and we pray that they find peace and happiness there."

' "So do we," Ernest said, "but there are many pitfalls out there."

' "Don't I know it, sir, but God will guide them, I'm sure of that," she added.

'I felt a little sick in the stomach, my love, as we made our way along the lawn up towards the convent.'

'It must have been awful for you, Uncle, to say goodbye.'

'It was, it was. You see, I didn't know if or when I would ever see your mother again and, of course, my niece, Lily. Sister Rosemary told Ernest that they were packed and ready and waiting. I thought I would have been prepared for our goodbyes but my stomach turned at the very thought. More wine?' Uncle asked, noticing my almost empty glass. 'You see, my love,' he said, taking the glass from my hand, 'Ernest started to get very cold in his ways. Not just to me but with everyone.' Uncle walked around the back of my chair towards the dining room. 'Although I hadn't had much contact with my sister after her marriage, I felt totally distressed at the thought of her departure from India.'

I listened to the wine bubbling from the neck of the bottle as he poured it into my glass. I stayed with my head resting against the back of the chair and stared into the roaring fire.

'Thank God,' Uncle said on his return, passing me the glass of wine, 'that I had the love of Barbara and our servants to go home to. Would the lady of the house mind if I had another shot?'

I assured him that it was there for his pleasure.

With thanks he poured his whisky and sat comfortably back into his chair. 'You're not a bitter person, are you?' he asked, reaching slightly over to touch my hand.

I turned to him in surprise. 'Of course not.'

'I know Rose Cottage still haunts you, but the key that locked you in doesn't exist any more. You're the only one who holds the key now, no one else. Excuse my intrusion again, if you don't mind me saying, why do you deny yourself a life, then?'

I moved my head back and looked up at him.

'Have I hit a sore point?'

'No, Uncle. I'm quite content with the way I live, thank you.'

'I know that you are writing a book,' Uncle said, 'but what happens at the end of the day after you have put that pen down?'

Frustrated with his remarks, I lit a cigarette and took a rather large drag.

'Your bowls are full of fruit with nobody to eat it; your vases are full of flowers without anyone to pick out their beautiful scent; the vacant rooms of your home have no sound,' he said, taking a sip of whisky. 'But worst of all...' I looked at him with horror as to what his last remark might be, 'you lie and go to sleep at night on a bed that is loveless.'

'You sound like a bloody vicar,' I told him.

'Do I really?' he asked, looking surprised. We both broke out in a fit of laughter. 'Well, I'm certainly going to leave you with sombre thoughts if nothing else,' said Uncle as we slowly began to compose ourselves.

I tried to ignore what had just been said. Our laughter disguised the seriousness of Uncle's words.

'Why don't you slip off your blazer, Uncle? It's pretty warm in here now,' I told him.

'Maybe. It is slightly tight under the arms. God knows

when I'll wear it again,' he said, resting his glass and standing up. 'You see, I save it for special occasions,' he added as he slipped his arms through the sleeves, folding it neatly and resting it over the back of his chair. 'There's a lady, if I might call her that, at the Conservative Club. It's only a short walk from my home so I frequent it quite often. She works behind the bar. She's a bit on the tarty side; you know, low cleavage and all that sort of stuff, but I fancy her like hell.'

'Uncle!'

'Well, I'm only human. I might wear it the next time I go in.' Uncle sat down and lifted his glass, this time just taking a sip. 'Not that there's a chance for me. Still I can dream,' he added.

'You do amuse me, Uncle,' I told him, smiling broadly towards him.

'Dare say that I amuse myself sometimes, trying to knock twenty years off my age to get a woman's attention, silly old bugger that I am.'

Uncle stretched out his legs and I curled myself up into the chair. We both sat staring into the glowing fire, allowing each other time to filter through our thoughts.

'I feel much more relaxed now, don't you?' he asked. 'After all, it's been an exhausting day, but lovely. And you, my love, ending up with a handsome admirer and in the market of all places.'

'Uncle, that's all that it was. Just because he smiled at me and I smiled back means nothing.'

'Didn't you speak to each other?'

'Briefly. He asked me if I would go back and see him.'

'And?'

'Well, I said yes, but it's out of the question. I couldn't possibly.'

'Wouldn't you like to see him again?' Uncle asked.

'Yes, but it isn't going to happen, and anyway dating is the last thing on my mind. Sorry, Uncle, but we keep throwing each other off track. The clock keeps ticking and before I know it you'll have returned to London. Would you mind continuing your story? I'd love to listen. I promise I won't interrupt.' Uncle smiled, reassuring me by the touch of his hand that it was of no consequence if I did.

'I had to consider your mother's feelings and show no emotion at the sadness that I felt. We were escorted into a rather cold, musty hall, and found her sitting on a tiny bench. "Dennis," she called to me, reaching out her hand while holding Lily in the other. I ran over the stone-flagged floor towards her and kissed her hand several times. "May I?" I asked, looking at Lily. Jenny smiled as I hesitated before having the courage to gently pick her up and take her from your mother's arms. She was wrapped tightly from head to toe in a lightweight woollen blanket. I touched her pretty face. Her dark complexion felt like silk against the tips of my fingers. Ernest slipped his hands inside his pockets and stood with his back to us, staring directly out of the window as if deliberately detaching himself from your mother. God knows what was going through his mind. Sister Rosemary, who had disappeared for a while, rushed back in holding a camel-haired overcoat. "This should keep you warm. Stand up," she said to Jenny. "Turn around," she said abruptly, shaking it a couple of times. "Slip your arms through the sleeves," Sister Rosemary told your mother as she hoisted the back of the coat over her shoulders. "That will do fine. The climate will soon change on your journey. Pardon, sir," she said, moving over to Ernest. "I don't seem to recall your surname." Ernest turned around, "Dorrell," he replied. "I believe the climate changes many times in England. Am I right, Mr Dorrell?"

'Before an answer was given, Ernest became distracted. A shadow cast itself into the bright rays of the beaming sun. The echo of footsteps caught our attention. "Thank goodness," your father said, as he appeared looking flushed and extremely anxious. I must admit he did look very smart in full Royal Air Force uniform. He placed his luggage on the floor and immediately walked over to Ernest and shook his hand quite firmly. "There was a mix up with the dispatch papers," he said as he looked over to Jenny.

' "I could sit and listen to you talk all day," Sister Rosemary said to your father, "with that lovely Irish accent of yours." She giggled slightly and I was amused that she had finally let some of her human side show. "There's transport waiting to take you on the first leg of your journey," Ernest said. "Dennis and I will accompany you before you board the ferry." He told them that the ship they would be sailing on for England had been docked in the harbour overnight; that it had been checked and he couldn't see any possible delays. He then called to me to take all the luggage, insisting that it must be fastened on the front seat next to the driver. He assured me that the driver had plenty of spare rope and I was to make sure it was securely fastened.

'I felt sick in my heart as I looked down at Lily before your mother took her from me, knowing that I would never hold her as a baby in my arms again, and to think that I went to her funeral only a couple of days ago. What a bastard life is.'

Uncle's tears rolled down his cheeks uncontrollably. I felt helpless as I knelt down next to him and rested my head on his lap, realising that his memories of Lily went a lot further back than mine as a child growing up with her. I stayed silent and still, allowing him to pour out his feelings of grief. I didn't share it with him, keeping the misery of losing her myself locked inside. This was a moment for Uncle to release his emotions without having the burden of coping with mine.

'Sorry, my love,' he said, gasping a little for breath.

'Don't be sorry, Uncle,' I replied, aware of the distress in his voice. I didn't dare look up at him. I couldn't bear to see his tears. There was nothing that could be said, but I felt the pain, the deep agonising pain that he was going through. I lay still and waited. Eventually his sobbing eased. 'These winds haven't died down yet,' he said, with a slight falter in his voice, as they beat forcefully against the structure of the house.

I jumped as Uncle blew his nose fiercely into his handkerchief.

'Sorry,' he said, patting me on my head.

My knees felt numb as I lifted my head from Uncle's lap and stood up. 'How about another shot?' I asked.

'Dare say I wouldn't mind.'

He gave me a little smile and I gave him a big one in return before making my way into the kitchen.

As I passed Uncle his drink I said, 'I'm worried about you, Uncle. I feel a great sense of loneliness inside you.'

Uncle took a sip of whisky and leaned once more against the back of the chair. 'My dearest, dearest niece,' he said, stretching out his arm and taking hold of my hand. 'I could never be lonely, my love. My life is full, so full of very precious memories that I carry around in my heart every day of my life.'

Uncle took a firm hold and gripped my hand tightly, releasing the pressure almost immediately. I knew not to question him on his wellbeing any longer. He gave a big yawn, his resources weakened, and I suggested that I would not be offended if he wanted to retire.

'It's quite rare that I have the opportunity of company, especially so late in the evening,' he told me. 'Without wanting to intrude, would you mind if we chatted a little longer?' His face looked strained with dark shadows under his weary eyes. Unfortunately, he had found no escape from the traumatic event of Lily's death. 'I know that my visit was unexpected,' he said, 'and even though the sadness lingers, the generous hospitality that you have given me ... well, let's just say, at a time like this, I'm so thankful for it.'

'Your words embarrass me, Uncle. I hope that I'm allowed to return the compliment on the mental strength you have given me, your selfless companionship throughout my laughter and tears, and on the subtle way you have led my thoughts to stray from the raw emotions I have for Lily by capturing my imagination with your intriguing conversation about that part of your life in India.'

'The pearls,' Uncle said, with a slight raise in his voice,

proud of the compliment he had been given. I smiled at his pleasure while he took a large gulp of whisky before continuing. 'It was Ernest who gave notice before your mother's journey that they should be removed. "They'll be ripped off her neck in seconds," he said, "with all the peasants out there." Your father stepped over and carefully slipped them from her neck. "Dennis," Ernest called to me in an abrupt manner as I stood and watched. "Get a move on immediately." I must admit I made quite a bundle. Lifting the heavy luggage took quite some doing. I took a deep breath and hoped what strength I had would allow me to carry them without embarrassment. Looking back, I must have looked so clumsy. Nearing the gate, which was to be my last exit, I turned around and glanced once more up towards the convent, never realising the picture that I saw would stay in my mind for ever.

'The luggage was dropped by my feet before shaking the old man several times as he lay fast asleep sprawled across the seat of his carriage. Ignorant of my request, I hurled the luggage up where it landed with quite a bump next to him. He stood up sharply and complained bitterly. There was a language barrier so it meant nothing to me. The only thing he seemed to understand was money and he soon quietened down when a couple of rupees were shown.

'I picked up the twisted rope. The quality was poor and rather short in length. Guided by my actions, he soon realised that a helping hand would be needed and that the luggage had to be fastened as securely as possible. Are you sure you want me to continue? After all, it seems as though that is all we have mostly talked about while

I've been here. It's so bloody deep-rooted in my mind that having the opportunity to release it to someone like you, who has genuine feelings, is giving me great comfort. You do understand, my love, don't you?'

'Uncle, I'm full of gratitude for your giving me an insight. It's hard for you to realise, I know, but my childhood didn't consist of being able to sit and listen, or even ordinary chatter. It was a bleak, dark world, Uncle, forced from having any opinions. The ridicule I was subjected to if I did made me feel worthless. I soon learned, growing up at Rose Cottage, that I had no choice but to take defeat and suffer the humiliation of feeling worthless for those many years. At least I'm not ignorant any more about some of the facts regarding my mother.'

'Christ, I feel so bloody patronising,' Uncle said, draining the last drop of whisky from his glass.

Aware of his feelings, I stood up. 'A gin and tonic would go down nicely; same again?' I asked, taking the glass from his hand.

'Have you ever found happiness?' he asked.

'A million times, Uncle. Most might have been fleeting moments, but I've found it.'

'Don't you ever get lonely living in this house? It is rather large.'

'Yes,' I replied, passing him his drink.

'Cheers, my love.'

'I've poured myself quite a stiff one,' I told him, sitting back down. 'Maybe too stiff,' I said, shivering a little as I took a sip.

'Oh, knock it back.'

I smiled.

'Sorry, I shouldn't have said that to a lady.'

'Uncle, stop being so courteous. I've knocked quite a few back in my life. And don't look so surprised.'

'Well, I'm sure you have, my love; dare say I've done the same.'

It was difficult for me to conceal my amusement at Uncle referring to his habit in the past. Exhausted of emotions, he took another sip of whisky, slipped his jacket down from the back of his chair, felt inside his pocket and pulled out a short, fat cigar. He seemed much more relaxed. I could smell the aroma as he puffed quickly, allowing the small quantities of smoke to fill the air. I felt quite mellow. No doubt the large gin and tonic I was drinking had some part to play.

'That evening we had released the emotions that had built up during the course of the day. Although we had tried, I suppose it was far too early to expect an evening of light entertainment. The barrier of grief stood firm, but there was no more crying to do, at least for now.

There was a lull before we turned to face each other, both obviously having something to say.

'Sorry, Uncle,' I said, insisting that mine was of no importance.

'No, go ahead,' he replied.

I was adamant, and had to insist firmly that he take the lead.

'I was going to suggest, well, if you wouldn't mind, that I finish off the facts about your mother's departure,' he said, reminding me of how he had to tempt the old man before he would co-operate with tying the luggage firmly in place.

'Of course I don't mind, Uncle,' I answered, taking another sip of the gin. A little spilled down my chin. Uncle caught hold of the serviette that rested over the arm of my chair and wiped it immediately.

'Sure you wouldn't like an extra splash of tonic?' he asked.

'No thank you. I want to make sure that I sleep well tonight, and this will just do the job.'

Uncle made a gesture with his hand and saluted the idea. The tension had lifted and we both smiled, I with some amusement.

'It was of utmost importance that the luggage was fastened securely, for if it became loose, Ernest would have become incensed with anger. The rope was knotted and pulled with the help of the old man as tightly as possible. I caught his breath several times as he exerted himself. The strong, unpleasant odour made me feel quite sick.'

I frowned at Uncle at the very thought.

'I shook the load vigorously,' Uncle continued. 'There was no movement. Satisfied, I stood back for a second and rubbed the sting from my hands before patting the old man gently on his shoulder. He grinned through the few remaining teeth that were left decaying inside his mouth. The oxen that would pull us along on our journey had no disguise as I stood there looking down towards them. Their thin layer of skin clung tightly around their swollen ribs. Alerting them with a tug from his rope, their heads hanging low towards the ground, the driver sat himself down to await our instructions.

'I could hear the sound of voices drawing closer through the dry, heady atmosphere. I jumped down from the carriage and waited attentively. The tall shrubs surrounding the convent hid them from view until their sudden appearance caught my attention. Ernest, the more dominant figure, walked a few steps ahead in a rather stern manner, I thought, as I looked towards him. If only Grace, my precious mother, had been alive. She would have tried to make their departure a joyous one.

'Sister Rosemary held Lily with affection as she walked side by side with your mother, your father walking a short distance behind, partly pulling out the documents from the inside pocket of his jacket, double checking that they were safely within his possession. After all, Lily and your mother were classed as Indian citizens and he would have gone through endless bureacratic wrangles to enable them to leave India.

'I hid my sadness deep inside as I smiled openly towards your mother. She stood bearing the overcoat with unease. Sister Rosemary handed Lily over to your father to say a final prayer before our departure. Without permission, I approached Jenny and slipped her coat down from her shoulders and held it over my arm. Her relief must have been immense as it left the sari she wore clinging tightly against her back. No doubt, if not for my actions, she would have had to persevere feeling quite uncomfortable in order to show her gratitude for the kindness the Sisters of Charity had shown for her wellbeing on the long journey ahead.

'Now stop looking so sad,' Uncle said to me. 'Good God, I can't believe I'm holding up this glass with its contents dry.'

'I'll pour you another,' I said.

'No, no, I intended this to be my last for the evening, and so it shall.'

I accepted what he said and relaxed back into the comfortable atmosphere. There was silence, but only for a few seconds. Although he tried to resist, the temptation was too much.

'Well, if you insist, may I?' He didn't linger from his request and shot up from the chair to refill his glass.

'Shall I straighten your cushion?' I asked before he sat down. 'I'm sure you'll be more comfortable,' I added, noticing that it was squashed into the back of the chair.

'You'll do nothing of the sort,' he told me as he spilled a little of his whisky from his glass as he leaned forward to straighten it himself. 'Sister Rosemary said her prayer. Everyone's heads were slightly bowed, except mine,' he chuckled. 'I glanced towards your father. His hair was short and neat and he showed the distinguished peak of his cap as he kept his head bowed. The stiffness of starch on the light blue collar of his shirt seemed to make his Adam's apple protrude even more. His jacket, padded on the shoulders, fastened with three dazzling brass buttons, disclosed a rather large knotted tie. He was slender and tall and his waist, I imagined, rather slim. The crease along the length of his trousers was immaculate, his tightly laced boots so shiny they reflected the rays of the sun with glory.

'There was no pause from Sister Rosemary as Lily began to cry. Your father rocked her up and down in his arms. Your mother instinctively looked up, the prayer now ended, and Lily was immediately placed into her arms.

'Patting the luggage, congratulating myself on a job well done, I showed my displeasure to the old man who had, while waiting, rolled a rather limp cigarette. It had a distinct smell as he puffed away. He smiled in ignorance, his features coarse, and then gave a sudden, sharp cough before throwing it to the ground. Poor old bastard, I thought, before turning my attention back towards your mother and father as they stepped up onto the carriage, your mother taking her time with the help of your father.

'Lily's cries lingered. "The movement of the carriage will quieten her down," Sister Rosemary reassured your mother. "Tell her, won't you, as the years go by," she said, looking directly towards Lily, "that this is her birthplace? One day she may return. I will be old and weary by then, but I'll know instinctively who she is, and my arms will be open to greet her."

'Ernest, who had no time for sentiment, gave his thanks and hurried me along to join him for our journey. "Young man," Sister Rosemary said to me as I put one foot onto the carriage. She opened my hand and placed a tiny wooden cross on my palm, taking hold of my fingers and closing them tightly around it. "God will look after you, my son," she said. I felt her warmth and as she released her touch I stared into her glazed eyes with question. The look that was there gave me the answer. Her experience of life was beyond imagination. She knew that it held no guarantees, not even for a young man like me. She believed, through her devout faith, that the cross that she had placed in my hand would help to give me protection from the perils I might come across throughout the course of my life.'

' "Dennis," Ernest ordered. I quickly took my place. The wheels of the carriage creaked as they slowly turned. There was no haste in the old man. For him, this was just another journey. Ernest kept a strict eye on him and had conveniently taken up the seat at the rear of the carriage in order to do so. There was no steady motion. The stones that had rumbled down from the mountainside became quite an obstacle. I glanced back. Sister Rosemary, clasping both hands below her waist, stood still and watched. Without any thought I jumped down from the carriage, ran the short distance towards her and took the liberty of kissing her on both her cheeks. Your mother giggled as I jumped back onto the carriage.

'Ernest called out to the old man in a stern voice, ignoring my behaviour. He called out once again. With a wail and a harsh movement of the rope, the oxen began to move at a steadier pace. I turned around once more. The mountain was steeper than I had thought and she had disappeared from view.

'Sister Rosemary had been right. The movement of the carriage did soothe Lily; in fact it left us all feeling quite tranquil. The faint rustling of the mountainside breeze whispered in our ears as our journey took us further down. The old man gripped tightly, pulling in each side of the rope to ensure that the oxen moved at a steady pace, although Ernest, as vigilant as he was, surprised me by admiring part of the scenery. I glanced over at your mother, Lily lying peacefully in her arms. If only this could be a joyous occasion, I thought, reminding myself that with each turn of the carriage wheel we were closer to them leaving India behind for a future many, many miles away.

'Our senses picked up on the polluted atmosphere as the carriage started to descend towards the city. At last on firm ground, the rope was loosened, allowing the oxen to increase their pace. The foul stench was quite unbearable as we passed by mounds of rotting garbage before entering the busy town. A bus with no upper deck slowly passed us. Its windows, free from glass, made no difference to the stifling conditions inside. Crammed to its limits, men, women and children hung their heads out over the structure to breathe in the existing air.'

I took a deep breath.

'Is that in sympathy?' Uncle asked. I smiled before moving up and curling closer into my chair. 'Your mother was taking great interest in her surroundings,' he continued, 'as we turned into one street and then another. She was leaving her culture behind and taking her baby daughter to something she could only imagine.' Uncle sighed, puffed at his cigar and sat silent.

A sudden flickering caught my attention. I turned and looked through the open doors towards the dining room. The wick from the candles had burned low leaving just a flicker of candlelight casting shadows on the ceiling above. I listened to the raging wind continuing to howl. The old elm tree that stood magnificently against the house had suffered a blow. Its cracked branch beat constantly against the window. Feeling anxious, I looked at Uncle and thanked God that I wasn't alone.

'I'll clear the plates,' I whispered over to him.

'Please don't,' he said as I made an attempt to move. 'It's been a painful journey surfing through the past but somehow you have given me the incentive to talk about it. May I continue?' I nodded in agreement. He responded immediately.

'My stomach turned as we made our connection onto the road that led us along the banks of the river. The huge rocks and the shallow water were a sign that I would soon be bidding farewell to your mother, father and Lily. The wide open river eventually appeared in the distance. Finally, we were side by side. The dark, murky waters stretched beyond the eye. This was their passageway to the open sea that would take them to England, a place about which your mother and I had little knowledge. Ernest grew tense and leaned over slightly to check ahead. He was more observant than I and pointed out the huge paddle steamer before warning the driver to slow down. "I'll expect a telegram on your safe arrival," Ernest told your father as we came closer. Ernest's manner was cold. There was no bond between them, Ernest made quite sure of that.

'A call was made to the driver to pull up. I jumped off and ran around to help Jenny down onto the step, keeping a tight hold of her arm before she stood firmly on the ground. Lily made no sound as she lay inside her blanket on your mother's arm. She was, of course, oblivious that India was her birthplace and that her future lay many miles across the sea. I only hoped that one day she would learn about India, not just the poverty but its culture, and recognise that she was born into one of the most beautiful places in the world. My sentiment was cut short. Ernest called for my attention and I was ordered to help hand down the luggage to your father. The old man coughed and spat out onto the ground as I hoisted myself up, struggling fiercely to untie the number of knots that had secured the luggage throughout our journey. A strong hooting from the vessel diverted my attention. Grey smoke bellowed from the funnels, circling up towards the sky. Reality was here. "You take the small one," your father called, dropping two of the cases down. "Hold on to it tightly, Dennis," your father said as we made our way through the crowds. "It contains your sister's belongings and the small necessities that the baby will need throughout our journey," now raising his voice higher above the crowd as we continued to push our way through.

'I glanced back. Ernest had taken your mother and Lily under his wing and stood no nonsense if anyone got in their way. I stopped with your father at the end of a swiftly moving queue. "Hurry," I called to Ernest as we stepped closer towards the deck. I kept a watchful eye, anxious for them to join us. Ernest stopped among the crowd and reached out for Lily. A few seconds passed as he settled her in his arms before hastening his step towards us. The hoot from the vessel was more profound. Your father took hold and gripped onto your mother's case. "Dennis," he called, leaving me behind while trying to manoeuvre the luggage along the creaky wooden steps. His voice was lost among the gush of water underneath the huge wheels that began to turn. I felt the warmth of Jenny's hand touching mine, but lost it immediately as she swiftly moved along. Ernest bent down a little so that I could say my goodbyes to Lily. I kissed her gently on her forehead before she was taken on board and handed over to your mother. Ernest returned in seconds, standing by my side as the vessel slowly started to move. Your mother stood against the steel railings and waved but was directly moved back by your father. Steam hissed through the funnels and the wheels propelled with great force. I felt physically sick and stretched out my arm lifting it as high as I could, swaying it furiously from side to side to bid farewell.

'The ripples in the water soon died down. We stood and watched until the vessel that carried them disappeared from view. I don't remember the walk back to the carriage. This time I sat across from Ernest. It was hard to believe, as the carriage set off at a smooth pace, that they had finally gone. There was an awful tingly feeling in the back of my throat. I heaved a few times before leaning over the carriage. I felt the wrench in my stomach before being violently sick. Ernest stared towards me, slipped his handkerchief out of his trouser pocket and passed it over. "It's affected you badly," he said. I didn't reply. I couldn't. I remembered the fun Jenny and I had as children, and our laughter echoed in my ears.

'Ernest and I sat silently throughout the remainder of our journey. A tear was shed by him as he looked aimlessly around at the surroundings. I was quite shocked and gave him the dignity of looking away.

'The old man was paid and I thanked him for our safe journey. We rushed once more, I jumping onto the platform, Ernest taking rather large steps to board the train to take us back to the country. It was a rugged ride back, holding onto the strap in order to keep my balance as we were jolted from side to side. I realised that I no longer had the cross that Sister Rosemary gave me. I didn't remember dropping it, but I must have released it from my hand in panic while untying the luggage and left it lying on the front of the carriage. Although deeply saddened by its loss, I only hoped that the old man had found it and, if so, that it would hold some meaning for him at some point in his life. When his weathered hands became too frail and the wheels of his carriage came to a final halt leaving the only life he'd ever known, purposeless, I could only hope the cross would guide him to the warmth of a loving atmosphere where the door is never closed inside the hearts of the Sisters of Charity who would give him care and protection for the remainder of his life.

'Throwing me slightly forward with a sudden jerk, the train slowed down. I held on tightly until it stopped, with relief that the burden of our journey was practically over. It was mid-afternoon, the heat wickedly strong. Small crowds merged together, eager to board, as we stepped down onto the platform. Our faithful servant called out for our attention over the ripple of voices. "Spotted in good time," Ernest said, eagerly walking over towards him. He was thanked for his punctuality and, with a humble look, we were offered our bicycles, which he had transported by hand for our speedy return home. "Jump up," I told him, patting the seat with a gesture for him to join me. My balance was deliberately unsteady as I turned the pedals around as fast as I could. The servant clung tightly around my waist. "You're taking a load of bubblegum," I called to him as he shouted in Punjabi in terror, only to scream in excitement with the twist and turn of the wheels. Ernest was way in front and ignored the calls of fear and laughter that echoed along the windy lane. "Mr Dennis, Mr Dennis!" he called. "Please, no more." "So you can speak bloody English when you want to," I shouted before giving one more twist on the wheel. He screamed, to my amusement, once more. One more twist and another scream. It was now time to slow down on my cycling skills. The servant, exhausted, leaned his head against my back, panting out deep breaths. Stopping the bicycle with a shriek from the wheels while pressing the handbrake tight and fast, the servant jumped off and ran as fast as he could towards the house, mumbling in his own language under his breath. I must admit, I did wallow in delight at his misfortune of placing his trust in me.' Uncle chuckled. I smiled broadly with amusement before he continued.

'I immediately slipped my shoes off in the hallway on entering the house. Ernest beckoned me to join him, holding open the door that would lead me into the dining room. His jacket was cast over the chair in an untidy manner. A hefty measure of gin had already been poured. I grinned over towards the servant as he hurried in with ice for Ernest. "Playtime's over," Ernest told me. "Pull over a chair, Dennis," as a glass of lemon water was poured for me. "I know that you're an astute young man," I was told as I took my place, "and, yes, there is an untold difference between your sister's husband and me. I do know, to his credit, that he loves her dearly, and that softens the blow of losing her; after all, only a young man himself, he took the courage to be with her here in Calcutta to greet in the New Year. You had retired early to your room that day with a fever, if I remember." Ernest took a huge gulp from his glass and swallowed the whole lot in one.'

Uncle was silent for a while as his memories played in

his mind. 'I remember your father coming to see Jenny the following day. He stood in the drawing room, with his cap held in his hand, waiting for Jenny. She had caught my attention earlier. Her bedroom door ajar, I could hear the moans of frustration as I peered in. "What do I wear, Dennis?" she asked, glancing towards me through the dim coated mirror while standing looking at herself in her bright orange sari. I shrugged my shoulders. "Dennis, for once," she shrieked in frustration turning to me, "be more forthcoming," as she threw one sari after another onto the bed. "The one you're wearing looks quite nice to me," I told her. "Oh, Dennis," she said, with an irritable tone in her voice as if I was talking nonsense. Actually, I was,' Uncle chuckled, 'it didn't suit her at all. I just hoped that my opinion would stop all the fuss.

'You could hear Grace's voice bellowing around the kitchen among the clatter of earthenware as the servants were repeatedly spoken to in anger. "It's not a good day here," I told your father as he looked quite anxious. Aunts and Uncles were arriving that day for afternoon tea and Grace always threw a tantrum if the catering wasn't exactly right.

'I asked your father if he would care to sit down. My request was politely refused. "Oh, by the way, a happy New Year to you," your father said. "Yes, of course," I replied, wishing him the same on the shake of a hand. "Dennis," Grace called, lifting up the latch on the old wooden door that led into the kitchen. "Good morning," she called over to your father as I excused myself from his company on my approach towards her. "You look much better today," she said, placing her hand on my forehead to check if I still had a temperature. "Your sister's being taken to the bazaar," she whispered. "I want you to be her chaperone, and don't pull your face, Dennis," she said as she leaned back and took a handful of rupees from the ledge in the kitchen before placing them in my hand. She quickly closed the door behind her and abruptly raised her voice again, this time speaking only in Punjabi to receive the full attention of the servants. "There's quite a bit of swearing going on in there," I told your father, trying to be humorous. I felt quite inferior on my judgement of conversation and thought hard of what to talk about to keep your father's interest. I was no longer concerned about myself. I heard Jenny's whispers again. "Sorry," I said to your father, feeling uncomfortable on having to leave the room. "How do I look?" she asked in a quiet voice. "You look fine," I told her. "Are you sure?" "Yes, now please hurry," I said. "Oh, by the way, I have to escort you to the bazaar," I told her in a hushed tone. "Make sure you stay well back," she said. "It will cost," I told her. "I know," Jenny whispered as I stood to one side to let her through.

'Your mother walked into the drawing room, quite confidently considering all the fuss she had previously made. Actually she did look rather nice, her long black hair pinned back from her face and wearing a rather daring red colour on her lips. The beige silk sari she had finally chosen blended with her complexion. I looked down at the decorative sandals securely hooked between her toes and listened to the bobble of beads tinkling against each other with each step that she took.

'Once we had left the house I did what was expected and kept my distance. I hated that job. There were more

106

exciting things for me to do, although it was fun passing the pretty girls who gathered in small groups around the busy market. I winked at a few which I suppose, at that time, was quite a daring thing to do. Some smiled, turning their heads away embarrassed. Others were more interested in the silks and hand-made embroidery than to take much notice of me. After all, I was a bit scrawny.

'Your mother was quite excited going from one stall to another, while your father took the initiative and bought her a bright blue silk scarf, threaded with gold edging. I caught sight of their first kiss. Jenny looked towards me. I quickly turned and immersed myself in the crowd.'

'You're so considerate, Uncle.'

'I had to be, my love. Your mother would have to pay me a handsome sum to give suitable, dishonest answers to the questions that Grace would subject me to on our return home. I did also take advantage of my time and rooted hastily through a mound of second-hand books among the twist of arms as people reached out in the hope of finding a book that would suit their needs. I couldn't believe my luck as I spotted a book I wanted and immediately picked it out from the pile of overturned books, although there was no sign of any interest from the crowd; I clung on to it and threw over the few rupees that I had. A nod was given and it was mine.

'I felt almost suffocated, squeezing in and out of the crowds in search of your mother. I almost started to panic but then caught sight of your father and whistled frantically for his attention. I cursed under my breath as they lost themselves among the crowd. Still, there was no way that they would have gone home. Grace would have been enraged at the thought of them being alone together. I dare say I would have been in a spot of bother.

'With that thought in mind I took a more steady pace, stopping to amuse myself at a display of wire faces covered in papier mâché which stared weirdly towards me from whichever direction I stood. I tried to impersonate their structured faces, twisting my face at all angles to try and resemble theirs. I caught a glimpse of a shadow and sensed someone standing a few feet in front of me. My face still twisted, I looked up. It was soon straightened. The trader gave a wicked glare, as if ready to jump over the stall and grab me by the throat. "You naughty rascal," he told me. "Go away, go away," clapping his hands together at the same time. I felt quite embarrassed and sheepishly mingled back into the crowd.

'The feeling of boredom set in and I missed the chit-chat of a companion. Litter was being discarded, leaving cartons of unfinished refreshments thrown down in any old manner. I got quite irritated at having to watch my step, avoiding the squelch underneath my feet from the spillages that had settled on the ground, while trying to catch sight of Jenny and your father. Groups of men stood in packs, exchanging their goods – mostly smuggled. The black market was fierce, with lots of money to be made. You knew to keep your head down and show ignorance when walking past.

'Identifying your mother among the crowd was almost impossible. I called out once or twice, mistaking her for someone else. Your father wasn't tall enough to stand out. The uniform he wore was the only key to success I had on finding them.

' "Like a taste, Dennis?" her voice called from behind me. I turned quickly. Jenny stood there offering me a share of the milkshake she was drinking. "What have you bought, Dennis?" she asked, trying to search for the title of the book I held in my hand. "Dennis is a clever one," she told your father. "He's always reading, aren't you, Dennis?" "Come on, Dennis, tell me what you've bought. It's a history book, isn't it?" "Sshh, I can't tell you now, it would only embarrass you if I did," I whispered. "Dennis," your mother said, giving me a devilish look. "It's not what you think, it really isn't," I told her. I felt quite awkward and looked towards your father. He smiled as if I was misleading him, too.

'Your mother had to be coaxed away with some persuasion, taking interest in almost everything that was left on display as we drifted along, slowly making our exit towards the long stretch of road for home. "You're going to have to sit with your Great Aunt Popsy on our return, aren't you, Dennis?" I was told. "Not if I can help it," I told your mother. "She'll have her arms wide open waiting to embrace you," she teased.

'Your mother still wanted to amuse herself as we finally left the bazaar behind. She giggled at the thought, knowing how much I would loathe being in my aunt's company. "He's her favourite," she told your father. "She dribbles now and again when she speaks and Dennis has to constantly sit by her side, don't you, Dennis?" she added, giggling once more. I took the huff as younger brothers do and hastened my pace, leaving enough distance behind to avoid any more teasing. "Dennis," Jenny called. I ignored her and quickened my pace even more.'

'Was it that bad having to sit with your aunt?' I asked Uncle.

'Well, yes it was. Her habits were more than just dribbling, I can assure you of that.'

I didn't dwell on finding out what, but could tell from Uncle's expression that it couldn't have been very pleasant.

'I would stay in my room on her visits and dread the call that my company would be desired in the drawing room. Ernest would call my name, sometimes twice. Not bearing him to have to call a third, I would reluctantly go down. Grace and Ernest would always give me a look of encouragement. Ernest would raise an eyebrow towards me. That was my prompt to show my compassion and suffer her welcome embrace.' Uncle pulled his face as if he was still actively in her company. 'You see, my love, she was quite wealthy and would hand out small amounts of money to us all at certain times of the year. She was always giving her opinion on facts she knew little of but was never challenged. Her face was lined with age and she had lost the sparkle of youth, and she detested your mother's beauty.'

I wondered what book Uncle had bought that day at the bazaar for him to be so secretive about its title. Tempted to ask, I pondered before deciding to refrain. After all, there was a possibility that it may have been quite personal.

'By now, home was only a short distance away,' Uncle told me, pausing to take a sip of whisky. 'I listened as Jenny and her beau playfully amused themselves. Although never trusting Jenny, who had an eye for the boys, I wondered if this time she had finally found love.' Uncle

110

gave a sigh and paused to reflect on memories gone by. 'Your mother called once again. "Dennis, Dennis, I've something very important to ask you." There was an anxious tone in her voice. I could hear the flap of her sandals as she ran close behind me. I stopped and turned. There was a near bump as I held out my hands cautiously to stop her running into me. "Will you be my alibi?" she asked, catching her breath before holding on to my arms and bending down to straighten her sandal that had slipped from between her toes. I remained silent. "Oh, stop sulking, Dennis," she said. "I'm not," I replied, trying to disguise how much I resented being teased in company. "Will you," she asked, "or are you going to wait for me to beg? I'll return the favour. Dennis, will you?" I must admit I nearly brought her to her knees.'

Uncle bent down, balancing a cigar on the edge of his mouth while holding onto his glass of whisky, and prodded the old iron poker inside the grate, allowing the flames from the fire to bellow up towards the chimney.

'So that she could sneak off with your father. "Tell Ernest that I've fallen over and I had to rest my ankle for a while in case it's broken." "Don't be stupid," I told her. "Well, can you think of anything better?' your mother asked. I reminded her that Ernest always knew when the bazaar closed down, how accurate he was on his timing and that he would expect our immediate return. However, she pleaded with me. I told her she wouldn't thank me if I said yes.

'Your father by then had caught up to us, and no more was said. Jenny looked at me with sadness as we turned into our street. Looking back in my later life, I didn't realise at that time how important it was for them to be alone together to seal their love. I regretted that I was too much of a coward to face the severe punishment from Ernest if I'd returned home without her.

'I pushed against the door quite hard, apologising for its stiffness to your father, who offered a hand. The chimes that hung down from the tall ceiling tinkled as we stepped into the tiny hallway. The chatter stopped on our entrance into the drawing room. Ernest stood tall, holding a glass of his favourite port. There was no excitement when he introduced your father to the rest of the family. I ran upstairs to hide the book that I had bought underneath the mattress I slept on and made a point, on my return, of ignoring Aunt Popsy's soppy welcome by noticing the glass that she held was empty. "Gin Fizz?" I asked, taking it from her. There was no time for an answer as I swiftly removed the glass from her hand and poured a generous amount before handing it back. She took the glass without notice and perched herself on the edge of her chair to question your father. Suddenly, she moved her head back on hearing his voice. Unable to cope with understanding the rhythm of his accent seemed to irritate her. It would have been much more acceptable if he'd been an English gent. The rest of the family spoke little English and took little notice of the conversation Aunt Popsy forcefully had with your father. I felt sorry for him. The atmosphere was tense so I suggested to one of my aunties, who was slightly younger than the rest, that she take the remainder of the family into the garden. "It's beautiful out there; even the doves are cooing," I told her while opening the shutters, allowing the rays of the sun to filter through. It was voted a good idea. Aunt Popsy's lips touched the rim of her glass. Taking a small sip she requested the need of some fresh air, too. She slowly, with the help of her walking sticks, stood up from the chair. I didn't rush to her aid, neither did I look towards Ernest for his silent instructions, and she slowly made her way out towards the garden.

' "Lemon water?' Jenny asked, looking towards your father. The pitch in her voice disturbed me. The offer was accepted and, sensing her unhappiness, I moved over to help her lift the hefty jug from the table. She looked towards me with sadness on her face, knowing that Great Aunt Popsy had taken a dislike to your father and that at Popsy's request the rest of the family would follow suit. I felt the tension in your mother as she held the glass towards me. There was an uncomfortable silence except for the trickle of pouring water. Ernest coughed before finally offering your father a seat. He was thanked and Ernest pointed to where he should sit and questioned him about his return to Chickagon. "I presume you'll be making your way back soon?" Ernest asked. Your mother stepped between them, passing the lemon water to your father and watching with amusement his expression on the bitter taste.

'The distinct smell of pancakes crept in from the kitchen. I decided to peep my head around the door in the hope that I would be spoiled with the offer of testing one out. Grace cursed me for interrupting an important conversation with her younger cousin, who lived on the wild side, amusing Grace with naughty conversation. Her cousin giggled. "Go, go, go," she said, moving her long plaited hair to one side while stroking it in a playful way with embarrassment. I quickly retreated to face the sticky atmosphere that lingered inside the drawing room. Your father stood, cap in hand, leaving his drink almost untouched. It wasn't a deliberate excuse to leave, but I would have found one if I had been faced with the same situation. "May I call back whenever the next opportunity arises?" he asked. Your mother looked at Ernest, hoping for a decent reply. He was cornered and reluctantly agreed.

'Ernest raised his voice, calling for Grace's presence. She wiped her hands on the cloth pinny fastened around her waist and bid your father farewell in a jolly sort of way. Ernest stretched out his arm from a distance and shook hands. Jenny was allowed one minute in the privacy of the hallway to say goodbye. Not daring to stay a second longer, the door flew open and she ran past Ernest and myself in floods of tears and ran up to her room. "You'd better go and have a word," Ernest told me as he listened to Grace's laughter on her return to the kitchen. I was useless at things like that and tried to think of words to console her while climbing the stairs to her bedroom. I knocked gently on the door before entering. "For goodness sake, pull yourself together. It's not as if you won't be seeing him again," I told her. "How do you know?" she sobbed. "And stop snapping." I told her I wasn't and it was just that I couldn't cope with women crying. She eventually sat up, looking towards the mirror which hung low by a piece of string on the opposite side of the room. "Will I see him again?" she asked, in doubt, as she walked towards the dresser and peered through the mirror at her bloodshot eyes. "Probably," I replied. "Yes or no, Dennis?" she demanded. I scrunched my shoulders. A large powder puff was thrown towards me as I left the room, returning a few moments later with the book I had bought. She lay back flat on the bed in quite a huff, choosing to ignore me by staring up towards the ceiling.

' "I'm amused as to why you're so annoyed, and especially with me," I told her, sitting myself down on the edge of the bed. She placed her hands behind her head, tutted, and then in a sharp, stern manner crossed one foot over the other. I sensed the look in my direction as I opened the book at random. The crisp sound of opening pages attracted her attention. I didn't respond but pretended to look with great interest as each page was turned. She sat up and looked down towards the book in my hand. "What tiny print," she remarked, coming closer. "You know how you've always wanted to speak, as Aunt Popsy would say, the Queen's English?" I said, looking towards her, "well here's your chance. I'll teach you and this will help a great deal," I remarked, passing her the book. "But what is it?" she asked. I told her it was a dictionary, and an English one at that. She looked confused, deliberating over its contents before saying, "You bought this for me?" "Consider it a rather early birthday present. I'll spend a considerable amount of time with you every evening, teaching you," I told her. "God, you sound just like Ernest," she mocked. I told her not to blaspheme. "Will I speak like you, Dennis?" she asked, poking fun at me by holding her nose up in the air. I responded by telling her that we'd be missed downstairs and I ought to go and help Mother with the entertaining. I reminded her that Ernest wouldn't tolerate our absence as I threw the powder puff back in her direction on my way out.

'The remainder of the afternoon went slowly by. I was tired and somehow felt quite tense. Mother didn't look at all well and encouraged me to make polite conversation so that she could escape back into the kitchen for short periods at a time in order that she wouldn't be missed. Jenny showed off her fancy nails she had painted from Grace's cargo of different colours, which she would discard at a whim in the direction of your mother, who would spend hours experimenting on each nail until the colour she liked suited her. It was regarded as being too westernised by my great aunt, but Jenny took advantage of her feelings and proudly paraded herself, showing the rest of the family how pretty she thought they were.

'Dusk was drawing in and my aunts clambered for their shawls to ward off the slight drop in temperature. Ernest had had it quite easy, staying fixed to his chair in the corner of the drawing room discussing politics with my uncle, who was almost grey in the face with age. With luck, Aunt Popsy complained that she felt rather exhausted, and that meant to the rest of the family that it was time to leave. There was a battlefield of chatter on their departure and Jenny giggled as Popsy crushed me tightly to her chest to bid farewell before she joined my aunts and uncles outside.

'The carriage that had brought them moved slowly off and with a quick, short wave, I watched as they disappeared into the distance. The house seemed pretty silent. Your mother helped the servants carry the china. The cups she carried rattled against the saucers as she moved along, giggling once more in my direction. I stuck my tongue out at her, showing my displeasure before she stepped into the kitchen. Grace rewarded herself with an evening out. "You don't mind do you, Ernest?" she asked. He gave his permission but then took solace in finishing off the remaining port that stood in the bottle beside him. I was worried. His expression was still when the door finally closed and Grace had gone. He called for quietness in the kitchen. No doubt Jenny was teasing the servants. "She'll be leading them a merry dance," he explained.

' "There's talk about Ghandi at school," I told him, sitting down next to him, "but nobody understands what's going on." "May we take this matter up at some other time, Dennis?" he asked. I excused myself from his company and walked the short distance towards the large, oblong window. "Is there anything you would like?" I asked, closing the shutters firmly together. "No, Dennis, no," he replied. There was an almost sombre mood with the usual pattern of Ernest sitting there dwelling on Grace's absence. The bottle eased his anxiety, and he would ensure that enough was drunk in order that he would sleep; not in his room may I say, but in his chair beside the dimly lit lamp in the drawing room with the clock ticking by his side. I wished him goodnight. He looked at me in an almost painful sort of way. My manner reflected some sympathy without a word being said before I climbed the stairs in the hope that it would be a decent night.

'I had no realisation of the time as I was suddenly woken from my sleep. Mother had obviously returned home. Her weak cough continued throughout the night and disturbed me immensely. But several hours later our home was back to normal, with a rumpus once more in the kitchen. Your mother and Grace always had something to fight about. I was amazed at how trivial it was and collected a bowl of freshly made food, ignoring their frustrations, and sat and ate in front of them, lingering over my fantasies that my English tutor, who was much older than me, would seduce me in between our lessons. Ernest insisted that the noise must stop at once as he entered the kitchen rolling the newspaper under his arm then taking a sip of tea from the cup that Grace had passed over. She didn't take much notice of him and busied herself, pen in hand, on a list, inspecting each cupboard. She complained that more visitors were expected as she jotted down with haste the groceries that were required for the day. "I couldn't possibly tolerate having to entertain, not again. Well, at least not for a while," she grumbled. Ernest took another sip of tea. Jenny stormed off, no doubt in frustration that her argument with Grace had come to a halt, and slammed the door behind her. The silent atmosphere that was left was to Ernest's liking. Taking one more sip of tea he left the room without a word. "He's such a bore," Grace said as he closed the door behind him. There was no acknowledgement from me. My fantasies were getting deeper. Too deep to ruin them with the mixed emotions they all seemed to share that morning.

'God, here's me rambling on, leading you from one situation to another. It's this bloody scotch I'm drinking,' I was told. He stood up with a slight stagger, feeling for the arm of the chair for support before taking the few steps to pour another. 'I must continue to tell you about Ernest on that early evening and the discussion he had with me when I was called to join him in the dining room,' he told me as he concentrated on tightening the screw top back on to the bottle, satisfied that a reasonable amount of scotch had been poured.

'I'll never forget that bicycle ride from the station, and to think of the torment I put the servant through. Still, it was bloody good fun,' he chuckled, seating himself slowly back down into the armchair.

'Was the dictionary ever used?' I asked, reminding him that he bought it at the bazaar in order to teach mother. He looked frustrated, fiddling with the tiny tin lid that held his cigars. I offered my help and was thanked.

'Silly old bugger, I am,' he said when it was finally opened.

I smiled, watching him struggle to pick one of the remaining two that were left, and waited patiently as Uncle took his time securing one in his hand before unravelling the band enabling him to force the cigar out of its wrapper. I immediately struck a match. The ordeal was over and he sat back puffing away to his heart's content, sitting back in silence with his thoughts. I also followed suit as I gazed towards the glow of the fire, only to be distracted by the sound of the broken branch still sweeping against the window pane. The candles had lost their glow, burned out by the long evening Uncle and I had shared. I gave a sigh. Although willing to retire for the evening, I expected a restless night. Uncle gave a loud snore, making me jump as well as himself. Startled, he blinked his eyes several times.

'I could have set the damn house alight, silly old fool, I am,' checking that he still held his cigar in between his fingers before sitting up much straighter in his chair leaving no temptation to doze. He gathered himself together, asking to be reminded about what I had just asked him. 'Was it about the dictionary? Blimey, it was,' he said, blurting it out before I had a chance to answer, letting me know that he still had his wits about him.

'I walked into your mother's room quite swankily, knocking of course before I entered, holding the dictionary in one hand and a roll of unused paper and pencils in the other, but the offer of a lesson was rejected. "I'm not as clever as you, Dennis," she said, trying one earring on after another while looking vainly into the mirror. "And anyway, I'm practising plaiting my hair this evening." She leaned up closer to the mirror, colouring her lips in vibrant red. Maybe I had given the impression of being rather superior and, again, was refused on my offer of coming back the following evening. I suggested that we start with the alphabet. "I already know that," she replied, pouting her lips in admiration of her reflection in the mirror. "We'll have to come to some sort of compromise," I told your mother, "if I'm going to give you my damn best on this, I expect the same in return." I felt pretty heated up and walked out of the room clutching the dictionary in my hand. It wasn't too long before I heard a gentle knock on my door. "Yes," I replied.

'"I won't choose my vanity over your precious time again," your mother said. "You mean you won't be looking in the mirror admiring yourself while I'm trying to teach you?" I called out. "No, Dennis, I won't," she replied.

120

"And is it your intention to work hard alongside me?" I asked her. "Yes," she replied, "it is."

'A promise was given and I immediately responded by walking over and opening my door. "If that's the case our lessons will start right now in this room and will continue until some progress is made." She looked at me quite humbly and, giving her the benefit of the doubt, I welcomed her in.'

Uncle's momentum was quick as he delved way back, seeing it clearly in his mind as if it was only yesterday. I felt a pang of sadness, knowing that he had little else left in his life but precious memories of the past.

' "I'm no cleverer than you," I told her. "Wiser maybe, but men usually are," I said with sarcasm in my voice. The tension was lifted and the job of teaching her was to begin. Night after night we sat in harmony, although it was a relentless task, tripping over simple words was always an occurrence. With hindsight I should have left things the way they were to avoid disappointment. Progress was slow and me? Well, I was extremely tired. "You're lazy," I shouted one evening. "Use your tongue; it's your instrument." She looked puzzled. But I stuck to it and tried to get her to impersonate me as I sat like a fool rolling my tongue around inside my mouth and clasping it in between my teeth to pronounce certain letters that were vitally important. Although, with the fun put to one side, I could see that her interest was diminishing as each lesson went by, not helped by the silent atmosphere downstairs every evening, with Grace's constant absences, fulfilling her desire to mix in the dance halls rather than sit with Ernest for company.

' "Aunt Popsy is expecting us to stay with her for a couple of days and until we receive instructions from Ernest, which could be at any time, you had better try harder. She'll be aghast if your grammar's correct," I told her. There were stolen moments when I thought I'd won, and would applaud when I knew that her pronunciation was correct. I must say I became quite informative, as well as impatient. "It's hopeless," I said at one point.

'During the late evenings I spent alone in my bedroom scrambling through the pages, my back would ache as I hunched over, peering at the tiny letters by candlelight for the right meaning to practical words. The dictionary became well used. The neat, straight pages tossed from one side to another left it somehow a little bedraggled. It appeared to be unfortunate when I was winning with your mother, that I would be called from downstairs to join Ernest for supper. The interruptions by him became a regular habit. It was to be dreaded. We would swerve our chairs quietly before sitting around the table next to him. Every crunch from the dry food we ate would be heard in the stillness of his company. Nevertheless, it was a task we had to endure, but it left no time on those evenings to practise on your mother's vocabulary.

'Grace had returned home quite early one evening. It was a surprise to see her. Unknown to be home before midnight, she was nursing a swollen ankle and cursed the uneven road for her misfortune. Ernest ran to her aid immediately. I discreetly left, leaving all the fuss to find sanctuary in my room.

'The screams of joy bellowed through the house the next morning. I, wondering what was so exciting, clambered

122

out of bed, secured the string around my pyjama pants and, in a drowsy manner, ran down the stairs to see. A letter had arrived. The shabby envelope addressed to your mother had taken its toll on the long journey before safely reaching her hands. It was obviously from your father and I poo-pooed the idea of wanting to listen to its contents before returning to my room and crawling back into bed. It wasn't long before I was disturbed. "He's coming to see me," Jenny said, barging into my room. "Dennis, he's coming in three weeks' time." "Ernest won't be pleased," I told her, turning over and pulling the blanket over my head to try and go back to sleep. She slapped the letter on top of my head before running out full of excitement.

'The thundering sound of smashed crockery sent a shiver down my spine. "You thieving pig," Grace shouted from downstairs. I could tell from the tone of his voice that the servant was begging her forgiveness. He had obviously been caught stealing again. "I had better go down," I told your mother as I hastily passed the open door to her room. She giggled at the repeated sound of Grace's voice. "Pig, pig, pig," she shouted. I ran down the stairs with the intention of calming the madness that was going on yet again over some petty theft. The poor boy had tears rolling down his face as I pushed the door open. Grace, hobbling on one foot, vacated the kitchen, mumbling under her breath. He tried to explain, by reaching up towards the cupboard, that he had been caught dipping into a box of raisins, showing me the spillage on the floor, when, out of fright, he'd dropped them. I patted him on his shoulder to calm him down before he crawled on his hands and knees to pick up the scattered raisins lying on the stone-flagged floor. He was stopped as he attempted to put them back into the box and, with my encouragement, he ate them out of cupped hands while I leaned against the door to prevent Grace's return. The poor bastard thoroughly enjoyed them, even though he was so distraught,' Uncle said, giving a huge sigh.

'I went out riding on my bicycle that afternoon. Although looking forward to my annual break from school to spend at my leisure as I cycled through the streets and up into the countryside, there was a nagging doubt that things were soon going to change. Why, I didn't know. Maybe the uneasy atmosphere at home had unsettled me.

'I felt the muscles in my legs begin to ache as I cycled up the steep hill. The flapping of my open shirt brought comfort with the warm breeze blowing in the air. Beads of sweat ran down my chest as I cycled harder to reach the top. Exhausted, I quickly took refuge, dropping my bicycle against the thick blades of grass before hiding under the shade of an old palm tree. Emily came into my mind as I lay there. It had been a long time, too long, since I last saw her. Emily's father was a colonel in the British Army and I, coming from a mixed marriage, wasn't quite becoming for their daughter. I thought of the innocent fun we had together, and urged myself to have the courage to call and see her before returning home. I had always held an attraction for Emily, my love. I suppose it was her sweet, gentle nature and her pretty face which didn't go amiss. Anyway, put my frolicking to one side. It was to be our platonic friendship that held its true value. I became quite excited wanting to tell Emily of my love for Barbara and pictured her face glowing with happiness with my news.

'My journey back was speedy with very few obstacles on the downward track. Relieved from exhaustion, I took one hell of a breath as I cycled along the windy driveway before catching sight of the secluded colonial home where Emily lived. The old man tending the garden stopped pruning and stared as I propped my bicycle up against an old tree trunk before hesitantly walking along the coloured stone pathway. I felt extremely nervous as I pressed my finger against the bell and waited for the huge white door to open. I was thankful that my bravery to call had paid off as she was alone with just the housekeeper and was delighted to see me.

'The stone bench she invited me to sit on under the shade of a huge canopy was rather cold. "It's quite safe," she said, concerned as I peered up towards the rusty iron bars that supported it. Maybe she thought I was being finicky so I quickly devoted my attention to her. She was intrigued with my gossip, which never strayed from the peculiarities of home, before she left for a while, returning with two large milkshakes. I had explained about the lessons I was giving your mother, and she thought the theft of the raisins from the kitchen was quite amusing.

'The question of your mother arose again, encouraging me to tell her of the guilt I felt. "You see, Emily, Ernest wanted me to be a carbon copy of himself and started correcting my grammar at a very early age. A tutor was brought in on a daily basis and with his tuition I soon learned to pronounce most words correctly, in an English manner of course."

'Emily smiled delightfully and I summoned the courage to touch her hand just for a second in response, "You see, Emily, I've been riddled with guilt because of the attention I received, especially from Aunt Popsy, who is held in great esteem among the family, and the jealousy that arose and the bitter feelings my sister held on not having had the same opportunities."

'"But, Dennis, the fact that she has realised that you are trying to help, well, I think it's a superb idea and very thoughtful," Emily said.

'"I'd better not overstay my welcome," I told her.

'"Dennis, my parents are away until late in the evening. Please stay," she asked.

'I didn't need asking twice and felt enormously excited that she obviously enjoyed my company. Not knowing whether it was my imagination, she looked at me several times and, may I say, in quite an admiring way.'

'You mean she fancied you, Uncle,' I said, lighting another cigarette and enjoying the tease. I knew what to expect; another quick cough, which was his usual expression of embarrassment, followed by another swift gulp of whisky.

'Emily mentioned her parents were willing her to take an interest in a student who was studying medicine.

'"My father has become a great friend of his," she said, "and is constantly inviting him for supper. Mother always makes a point of leaving me alone in his company while they all go out on the veranda for drinks."

'"Do you like him?" I asked.

'"I try to for my parents' sake but find it quite painful when all he talks about are his experiences as a medical student. Sometimes it's quite gory."

126

' "Is he handsome?"

' "Well, let's put it this way, he'd be more suited to someone else. There's talk about returning to England soon." I looked at her in surprise. "Not permanently, of course, but my mother is missing her parents terribly and my father is insisting that she leaves for the summer to be with them. I'm quite frantic with the thought of having to accompany her."

' "And will you?" I asked. She said that she most probably would, adding that she was a baby when she left England, but her passion was for India even though her parents were English. She thought England a foreign place to her.

' "Shall we walk?" she asked to my surprise. There was no hesitation and I stood up immediately to take her hand. She was slightly taller than me. The wisps of her long blonde hair glistened in the sunlight and blew slightly from her face in the breeze. She had the complexion of an English rose. We giggled over the most trivial of things, wandering in and out of tiny islands of shrubs that had established themselves firmly into the ground alongside the vast land that accompanied the beautiful home where she lived.

' "Do you remember how we met, Dennis?" she asked, reminding me of how I picked her up from the street as she cried out in pain, nursing, without any knowledge at that time, a broken ankle. She reminded me that I had carried her for miles until we reached her home, where I handed her safely over to her parents. "I wouldn't say that it was for miles, but it certainly felt like it," I told her, feeling quite proud that she hadn't forgotten.

' "I used to look forward to your visits, Dennis, although

127

brief, when I was strapped up in the awful plaster, unable to do much to occupy myself apart from read, and here we are today, still friends, enjoying a peaceful walk together," she continued.

'Strangely enough, we both knew in our hearts that true love would be an impossibility. Her dreams of a secure future in the years to come, providing the needs that she required, would come from a man with professional standing and our destinies lay elsewhere.

'Emily gave a huge yawn, for a lady. "I'll take you back," I told her.

' "No, well, not yet," she replied.

' "Shall we at least sit down?" I asked, feeling concerned. But without notice she grabbed my hand, clutching it tightly, and we ran together over the hilly grass. Suddenly stopping, we both knelt down together, hidden between a cluster of trees. I, with little pressure, pulled her head towards mine. I could feel her warm breath as I moved towards her lips. Our eyes met and we kissed. Her moist lips excited me and I slowly started undoing each button of her blouse. Her breasts, small and firm, tasted sweet. Engulfing my lips around her protruding nipples aroused me immensely. Our wails of delight came a little later.

'Oh my love, my dearest love,' Uncle said, turning to me. 'The first person I tell about that special day and it has to be you. I do feel somewhat bold, but realise that I shouldn't speak to you in such a personal manner. I'm sorry,' he said, looking quite embarrassed.

'There's no need for an apology, Uncle,' I replied. 'In fact, I find it rather romantic. I think I'll write it in my book. I'll make a special page dedicated to Uncle for daring to tell me intimate details of the passion he had with a beautiful lady,' I said, reassuring him with a smile and a raised glass.

He seemed a little more at ease. Uncle had become a great companion of mine over the days we had spent together. I was possibly more surprised than him regarding this as we both sat closely together in front of the slow burning fire, which glowed with warmth around us. But now and again chilling thoughts over the loss of Lily would hit me, and the learning process of controlling my feelings began sooner than I thought. I turned to Uncle, disguising the grief that I felt deep inside. 'What happened to Emily?' I asked as he sat there looking old and frail.

'I never saw her again,' he told me. 'Daring to cycle back a few weeks later, I called over to the gardener, his head bowed in concentration as I peered through the iron gates. "Will you tell Emily that I passed by?" I asked him, knowing that it would be too forward of me this time to call at the house without an invitation. He looked up towards me. "Won't be much chance of that, young man," I was told as he walked closer to the gate before resting his grubby hands on either side of the rails. "The Colonel's dead." I was shocked, and I asked if he meant Emily's father. He nodded and said the Colonel had had a heart attack a few weeks earlier. He seemed in shock himself and said that he'd worked with him all his life, but would stay on if the new owners wanted him. I asked who they might be but he didn't know their names. "They're British like me," he said. "But I doubt they'll have a girl as pretty as Emily."

'"Will you tell her that Dennis is here?" He looked

puzzled. "Emily," I said. "Please go and tell her I'm here. I insist." He told me that she had gone away. "Where to?" I demanded.

'"England," he replied. I asked him for an address, my voice by that time quite jittery. He simply said it was no good asking him as he was only the gardener. "There's not a soul left either," he added, looking up towards the house.

'I looked far ahead at the bench, the canopy raised and tied back, and imagined Emily and me sitting there together.

'"I wanted to tell Emily that the moment of passion we had shared ... well, it must never get in the way of our true friendship," I blurted.

'The elderly man lifted his cap and scratched his head, staring at me through the railings of the tall iron gates, his mouth wide open.

'"You'd best be off, boy. You'll be having the Colonel turning in his grave."

'I took heed of what he said and pedalled as fast as I could for home.

'The continuous sound of rotating blades humming from the fans in the drawing room on my return was too much for me. Mother looked up from the book she was reading and complained about the distraught look on my face. "I'm going to my room," I told her before any questions were asked.

'Closing my bedroom door firmly, I lay there on my bed staring up towards the ceiling until dusk settled in. I must admit I never bothered undressing, kicking off my boots as they landed in a heap on the floor. The night was humid, and I was quite restless. Fighting sleep no longer, I drifted off into a deep slumber.

' "Dennis," Grace called, knocking on my door. "Get out of that bed. You've been in it far too long." I grunted and looked at the clock. I staggered over to the door. The knock was repeated. "You look dreadful," Mother said, looking at me through the partly open door. "There's a day's work waiting for you. Clean yourself up. Aunt Popsy needs you to labour for her. She has guests arriving late afternoon."

'My concentration lapsed on my arrival down in the kitchen. I picked up a cup of tea that Grace had poured and drank it quickly. I coughed and spat it out immediately. The alcohol penetrated the back of my throat leaving a disgusting taste inside my mouth. Grace snapped at my stupidity, which had obviously embarrassed her. "Anyway," she said, "there's nothing like a strong drink to get you through the day. Off you go," she told me as I grabbed a glass of water on my way out.

'I took my time cycling to Aunt Popsy's, dreading the thought of her company for the day. The shutters were closed on my arrival and I climbed the steps up towards the veranda, where tables and chairs carved in wood sat all year through for Aunt Popsy's continuing array of guests. The door was swung open immediately and from the porch I was given a long-handled brush. I looked down at the worn out bristles before being squeezed tightly once again towards Aunt Popsy's bosom. "Now, Dennis, you know what a good job you have to do," she said, releasing me from her grasp. "Start from each side of the veranda so there isn't a speck in sight. Here, before you go," she said, passing a wicker basket over to me with her favourite lavender polish lying on top, "that's for the table. Don't forget to put some elbow grease into it, as Ernest would say," she added, patting me with a strong hand against my shoulder.

'My younger cousins spotted me and ran up and down the steps in playful laughter. Aunt Popsy took delight in watching through the window. "Go away," I told them when she disappeared from view. However, I had no choice but to tolerate their activities, brushing harder against the wooden floor in frustration. My throat felt irritated and I repeatedly coughed as the dust circulated in the air. The basket of rags and polish attracted them, each of them daring the other to spill its contents. After a knock on the window with instructions from Aunt Popsy, they gathered together and almost flew into the entrance of their home. "Little shit," I called after the boy, who rudely stuck his tongue out at me before disappearing inside. "Don't forget to dust the chairs," Aunt Popsy called after another knock to catch my attention.

'The job done, hopefully to her satisfaction, I stood on a pair of creaky ladders that were propped against the wall to check the tiny bulbs that lit up the outside of the house by night. The hanging row of wire looked quite untidy in the daylight, I thought, as I moved along screwing each bulb in tightly. I was disturbed by the same cheeky little brat who stretched his tongue out against the pane of the window as I stepped down off the ladder.

'By then the heat was getting to me. Aunt Popsy's

gramophone didn't help. She was playing her dreadful music at full blast, made worse by the crackling of the needle and then by Aunt Popsy joining in, singing along with the high pitch of her opera from years gone by. My head throbbed with her deep, husky voice bellowing out from inside the house. I had to get away.

'The outside loo looked inviting. I ran down the steps and locked myself inside the tiny wooden cabin. I had to sit on the toilet seat to get the full impact of my acting skills, knowing that sooner or later someone would pass and hear my groans.'

'Uncle, are you serious?'

'Yes, my love. Aunt Popsy was no fool and my plan of action had to be convincing. It wasn't one of the most desirable places to have closed myself in. Thank God the door wasn't level. Cracked by the heat, it allowed a little sunlight to creep through. I wasn't going to give up and began to groan much louder. Luck was eventually with me as I heard Aunt Popsy's voice. "Dennis, are you all right?" she called. "Dennis," she called again, staying silent for a few seconds before leaning the weight of her body against the door. I groaned again. "Have you got diarrhoea?" she asked. "Aunt Popsy," I groaned with a grin on my face. "Badly, Aunt Popsy," groaning once more. "I'll be back in a minute," she told me. "Have you finished?" she asked on her return. "Dennis, are you all right?" I crouched slightly before lifting up the latch and opening the door, clinging my arms around my stomach. She grabbed hold of me and forced a spoonful of medicine inside my mouth. It tasted revolting. "You'd better go home," she said, "otherwise we'll all be catching it."

'I refused the offer of a rest as Aunt Popsy pointed over to the hammock and I struggled over to my bicycle. "You go home then, Dennis," she said, giving me another hard slap on my shoulder before I pedalled off slowly, rapidly changing my speed once I was out of sight and giving myself a cheer by raising my hand in the air. 1 had no intention of going home. Well, at least not for quite a while. Emily had left for the damp, drizzly days of England and the place where she and I had made love lured me back. There was no fear this time returning to where she once lived, although I made sure that I disguised my bicycle by lying it flat on its side underneath the hedgerow. Although I did love Emily, it was a different kind of love to the one I held for Barbara. The passion Emily and I shared, although delightful at the time, left me riddled with guilt. To betray Barbara would have been the last thing on my mind when I visited Emily on that day, which now seems so long ago.

'I scrambled through the thorny bushes and ran over the hilly ground to where we had lain. The blades of grass had grown, leaving no sign of our encounter. Only the sound of the whispering breeze intruded into the silence that surrounded me and I ran as fast as I could, never to return there again. I cycled down from the country back through the busy streets of Calcutta towards home. It was late afternoon by then and I entered the drawing room feeling quite weary. Grace had taken to her bed I was told. Ernest asked me to keep as silent as possible. I immediately sat down, leaning heavily towards him. "She's got that terrible cough again," he whispered. "She doesn't seem to want my attention; I daren't go near her." I told him that perhaps it was because she wasn't well. "No, Dennis, no. I've asked her to stop going out when evening falls. It's chilly, Dennis, the night air. I know what goes on, Dennis. I'm no fool." He quietly wept, head bowed to hide the tears. I sat silently next to him.

'Eventually slipping away, I crept quietly up the stairs, stopped outside Grace's door and hesitated before gently knocking. There was no reply so I crept along the short landing to my room. The creak of the floorboards alerted your mother's attention. The door was quickly opened and she beckoned me into her room. I told her I was tired as she took the few steps over and pulled my arm. "They had a row," she whispered. "Who?" I asked, feeling irritated. "Mother and Ernest. That's why she's taken to her bed." I told her that our mother was not a well woman and reminded her that she had taken to her bed many times before. She just giggled, covering her mouth with her hand. "I'm going," I told her, frustrated with her immature manner, and I closed my bedroom door with a firm hand before kicking off my shoes and lying on the bed. There was endless turmoil going on in my mind, and I hoped that the gin that my father was drinking would send him, as usual, to sleep.

'Anyway, my love, I suppose I could go on for ever, and you would kindly let me,' Uncle said, squeezing my hand tightly. 'Mind if I use the bathroom?' he asked.

I immediately stood up as he passed the glass which contained the remains of his whisky to me and placed his hands slowly on either side of the chair in order to hoist himself up. My attempt at any help would have

135

caused him embarrassment. Ignoring his mild groans I left for the kitchen. 'Coffee?' I called as I saw him through the open door gripping on to the bannister as he tried to balance himself with each step that he took. 'Uncle!' I cried, rushing over to the door, 'why don't you use the bathroom downstairs? It would be so much easier.' He turned his head around. 'Down here, through into the porch,' I pointed, rushing forward to take the few steps towards him in order to help him down.

'Silly old fool I am,' he said out loud as we reached the bottom.

'Watch the step,' I called before he disappeared out of view.

The aroma of percolated coffee attracted him as he popped his head around the door on his return. My offer of a cup was accepted.

'I'll go and sit down, then,' he said, steadily making his way back.

I knew when I heard a welcoming sigh that he was sitting back safely in his chair. 'You seem pleased with that,' I said to him as I placed the hot mug of coffee on to the table next to him.

'Yes, it was a good buy,' he replied, scrambling through the pages of the old book on Churchill. 'This will teach the old bag that she is. Pop the scotch in, my love. Coffee doesn't taste the same without it,' he added, looking up towards the tall mantelpiece where the glass had been placed. 'We have this tempestuous relationship over the garden fence. Fine man,' he said, claiming victory when he actually found a picture of Churchill, yet looking frustrated as he peered below at the small print.

'These might help,' I said as I picked up his glasses that had slipped down the side of the cushion where he sat. 'You've got a mean look, Uncle,' I commented, watching him scrutinise every word.

'Mmm, let her test me on this if she dare.'

'Who on earth are you talking about, Uncle?' I asked, sitting down next to him as he scrambled through the pages once more.

'That interfering bitch that lives next door to me.'

'Good God, Uncle, is she that bad?'

'She catches me out every time. All I want is a peaceful read sitting in my own garden. "What's that you're reading?" she'll say, hanging her head over the fence.' I smiled as Uncle mimicked her voice. 'And lo and behold, wouldn't she have read it before me, finding a thrill in telling me what happens. She married this lecturer, university educated of course, as I would constantly be reminded. He's dead now, and with her rolling about all over him, I'm not surprised. But I'll catch her out this time, frustrated old hen.'

Uncle amused me with his catty remarks and how serious he was to win any confrontation on a book that he thought she would have no knowledge of. I was fighting sleep by then and no longer able to resist. I closed my eyes, leaving Uncle at peace digesting each page of his book.

# Chapter 4

I was there, at Rose Cottage. It was Christmas Eve. Looking up towards the paper chains my stomach churned with excitement as they hung, curving up and down from the ceiling. I was ordered to fill the hot water bottles and then tuck them under the pillows of each bed upstairs.

'Your voice is grinding,' Mummy told me as I stood on the tiny wooden stool that was riddled with woodworm, in order to reach the sink to fill each bottle, one by one, with running hot water. I decided to sing another song that might suit her better.

'You're out of key,' Teddy told me as he came in from the cold, closing the back door in haste. I switched immediately and sang 'Away in a Manger'. Teddy, my favourite brother, stuck his fingers inside his ears, making me sing out louder so he could hear.

A blow came to the back of my head and Teddy stopped my fall before standing between Mummy and myself in order to protect me. 'I've had to work my guts out to give you all a Christmas,' she screamed, 'while that little bitch is singing without a care in the world.'

I was carefully guided by Teddy back onto the stool again, standing as steady as I could. 'Oh dear,' he said. 'Now don't cry, come on.' I took a deep breath and tried to ignore the sting I was left with. 'There we go,' he said, screwing the tops back on to the bottles as I filled them. 'The tree is lit; have you noticed?' he asked.

I shook my head. The lump in my throat was awful and I swallowed hard.

'It's right outside our bedroom window. They've lit up the island that it sits on too. Listen,' he said, turning the tap off immediately. 'They must have heard you.' I was too choked up to question him as to what he was talking about before being picked up and lifted towards the tiny kitchen window. 'See, they must have heard you singing,' he said, watching a group of elderly women standing in the yard holding paper leaflets in their hands, flicking from one page to another as they sang Christmas carols. 'This is a nice one,' Teddy said, listening to the choir of voices singing to the words of 'Silent Night'. I turned my head around towards Teddy and immediately turned back to listen. He let go of me and I panicked. 'I'm only going to open the door so you can hear them much clearer.'

'It's Christmas, isn't it, Teddy?' I said, listening to their voices.

'Yes, it's Christmas,' he replied, placing his hands around me to guide me so that I could see them for real.

Our applause was noisy, Teddy urging me on to clap louder. 'Merry Christmas,' they said alternately, holding their leaflets down by their sides.

'And a Merry Christmas to you,' Teddy called, nudging me to say the same before they turned, leaving the echo of their steps to fade as they walked back into the entry.

'How about you getting straight back into bed when we've finished filling these,' he said, popping me back onto the stool, 'and I'll bring you up your stocking?'

'But I'm scared.'

'Of what?'

'Father Christmas.'

'What? Santa Claus is going to arrive to leave you presents and you're scared? Anyway, I'll come and read to you.'

'But there aren't any books.'

'Well then, I'll make something up in my head and I'll stay with you until you're fast asleep,' he said, urging me to take his advice as the last bottle was filled.

'No,' I told him, 'I'm waiting for Lily.'

'I'll write a note and when she comes home she'll read it and come straight upstairs to see you.'

'I've got a present, but shush, don't tell her. It's here inside my pocket.' Teddy wiped my hands dry before I attempted to lift it out.

'What is it?'

'It's a powder puff,' I whispered. 'It's made of felt and my teacher, Mrs Williams, helped me to cut it into the shape of a heart.'

'That's fine embroidery around it.'

'It's cross stitch,' I told him.

'No, I mean her name, Lily, that you've embroidered in the middle.'

I looked around to make sure that no one could hear. 'Mrs Williams did that for me, but Lily won't know, will she?'

'Don't suppose she will. Lily will love it.'

'Will she, Teddy?'

'Too right. Now come on, let's tuck you into bed,' he said, helping me carry the hot water bottles through into the living room.

I was distracted by the laughter I heard on the television and turned to look at it as we walked past but Teddy firmly moved me on up along the narrow stairs towards the dark landing.

'Watch out for the chamber,' he whispered, leading me around it before lifting up the latch to open the bedroom door, then pressing the switch down to give some light from the bare bulb hanging low from the ceiling.

'Get in,' he said as I waited while he pulled back the blanket. 'Get into bed. Feet up,' he told me, placing the bottle underneath them so I could feel the warmth. He returned quicker than I thought, holding out one of Daddy's socks and laying it next to my pillow.

'You're supposed to hang it up or he won't see it,' I told him, 'but I can't; there's no headboard,' I giggled.

'He'll see it all right,' he said, smiling at me.

I fought with excitement before finally drifting off with Teddy by my side.

'I knew you'd come,' I said, smelling Lily's fragrance as I rubbed my eyes to open them wide to greet her. 'Has he been, Lily?' I asked, sitting straight up. 'Do you think he'll bring you some of that nice perfume?'

'Oh, the Blue Grass I'm wearing. I hope so. He'll soon be here, but only if you close your eyes and go back to sleep.' She hugged me tightly before tiptoeing quietly out of the room.

The rustle of paper and the sweet smell of tangerine woke me. Teddy had already emptied almost all of his stocking.

'Here, pull,' he said.

The paper from the cracker tickled my nose as he

141

excitedly moved it towards me. I sat up. My hand was weak but I tried with force to pull as hard as I could. The cracker snapped with a spark and a crack. A tiny plastic package fell down onto the floor. Teddy swiftly reached down and picked it up, feeling excited once he saw the plastic soldiers that were sealed inside. It was ripped open immediately, the contents scattering onto the bed. His lips babbled with gunfire all around.

'He's been, you know.'

'Yes,' I said, watching him playing on top of the blanket.

'I can see you looking,' he said as I glanced once more towards my sock. 'Pick it up; it's yours,' he told me. 'No one is going to take it from you.'

I looked at him and smiled. I felt from the top to the bottom, pressing my fingers lightly around my presents on the outside of Daddy's long woolly sock. Almost frantic with excitement I pulled out the Christmas cracker that was leaning limply over the top. 'I'm going to pull this with Lily,' I announced, shaking it up and down with wonder as to what was inside. I saw the look of disappointment on his face and changed my mind almost immediately. Passing him one end while I clung on to the other, we pulled and I fell back sharply as Teddy won the prize. I giggled when the same pack of soldiers fell out. He laughed as he rolled down the rubber band to take out the paper hat before placing it on the top of my head.

'Merry Christmas,' Lily said, opening the bedroom door and rushing straight over to the window. Pushing it open, she lit a cigarette, shaking the match several times before the tiny flame died out. She turned and smiled while taking a drag, turning straight back to blow the smoke directly out of the window.

'Lily, look!' I gasped, picking out a plastic, beaded bracelet. I jumped off the bed and rushed over towards her. She smiled, wrapping her arms around my waist and she kissed me on my forehead.

This time machine-gun fire, with little spits mimicking every bullet that could possibly be fired, came out of Teddy's mouth. 'I wish he'd hurry up and kill them all,' Lily whispered in my ear, making me giggle. 'I'm not used to all this noise.'

She threw the stump of her cigarette out of the window where it lay on the frosty pathway below before taking me by the hand and leading me to the rest of my presents inside my stocking.

'I didn't hear him, you know.'

Lily looked puzzled as she lifted me onto the bed. 'Neither did I,' she said, realising then who I was talking about.

'A jigsaw,' I shouted, ripping open the clear plastic covering as the four wooden pieces fell out. Lily straightened my paper hat which by then had fallen over my eyes. Teddy read a joke from the tiny piece of paper that had fallen out of his Christmas cracker. No one laughed so, with a shrug of his shoulders, he screwed it up into a tiny ball and discarded it with the rest of the paper from presents he had hurriedly unwrapped.

I peeled my tangerine with ease and, ripping the segments open, gave half to Lily. The juice squirted into my face making my eyes water. I sneezed, Lily blessed me and Teddy carried on playing his war game.

'You can go down now,' Frieda said, opening the bedroom door and sniffing the air. I looked sharply at Lily.

'Oh, don't worry about her,' Lily said. 'Miss prim and proper has a lot to learn.'

Teddy picked up his plastic soldiers and stood them together on the bare wooden floorboards. 'Come on, Teddy,' I called as Lily picked me up and rested me on her hip. 'Teddy,' I called as she carried me along. He ran quickly onto the landing to join us.

I sniffed out. 'The chamber's full,' Lily said, holding her nose in fun as she walked past. 'Oh, Christmas tree, oh, Christmas tree, how full I see your branches,' Lily sang while I hung my arms around her neck as she stepped lower down on each stair. The door was left ajar at the bottom of the stairs. Lily took her last step before we entered the front room, and there stood the tree, lit up with millions of fairy lights. Lily walked around with me still in her arms, inspecting each bundle of presents that Santa had brought. 'Here we go,' she said, lowering me down gently.

'Merry Christmas,' I called over to Daddy who was struggling to light the paraffin heater. He acknowledged me with a nod and cursed before spitting onto his thumb as the stalk of the match he was holding burned quickly, giving him a nasty sting.

'Well, come on.' I looked up at her before she knelt down by my side. 'They're yours from Santa. Look, he's even wrapped them for you in special paper printed with branches of holly and clusters of bright red berries.' Lily leaned over, passing me a present no bigger than the palms of my hands.

144

'It's a box, isn't it, Lily?' I asked, feeling the square corners. Lily shrugged her shoulders. The wrapping paper rustled against the tips of my fingers as I tore ... and then I saw but couldn't quite believe. I took a deep breath before lifting the box closer to my eyes and peering through the plastic lid. 'A doll.' I whispered. I touched its face. It was what I had always dreamed of getting.

'Come on,' Lily said, 'pick her up.'

I shivered with excitement that at last my dream had come true. She wore a flanellete nightdress with a frill on the cuffs of her sleeves and her cotton socks were as white as snow.

'She hasn't got any hair, your doll,' Teddy spoke, stepping forward to take a peep.

'That's because she's just been born,' I whispered to him whilst rocking her in my arms.

'Aren't you going to open your other present?' said Lily. 'I'll hold her for you.'

I passed my doll to Lily and eagerly ripped the package open. 'It's a tea set,' I said, looking up towards Lily before starting to count the cups and saucers that were printed on the outside of the box. A paper plane zoomed past my head and I giggled as it landed near me. Filled with excitement, I rushed over, picked it up and threw it into the air, gliding it back towards Teddy's frantic calls that it was his. It was a magical moment – the ripping of paper, the smell of pine from the tree and everyone feeling the joy that Christmas brings.

Lily pulled the cardboard carton from inside the box and my tea set was opened. 'It's china,' I shouted to Lily, picking up the tiny teapot. 'I can make tea for Eric and

Mrs Crowswick now. I could smell the mince pies she was making through her kitchen window yesterday so I'll surprise them with a pot of tea and a special cup to drink it out of, and we can all sit down with mince pies to eat. Would you like to come? She has plenty of chairs around her kitchen table. She'll be pleased drinking tea from a new pot. There's a crack in the spout of hers.'

'You have to get dressed now that you've opened your presents,' Frieda told me, peering down at what Santa had brought me. 'There's a pan of potatoes to be peeled.'

'Why don't you peel them yourself?' Lily told her.

'The instruction from Mother is that she's to do them.'

'It doesn't matter, Lily, I don't mind, really.'

I dressed rather quickly that morning, rolling the waist up of the skirt I had been given that was no longer of use to Frieda, gripping it tightly with Teddy's snake belt to keep it up, and ran with joy back down the stairs. I felt quite surprised on how the atmosphere in the cold and dim living room was so different from the fun everyone was having in the front room. Mummy was standing in front of the fireplace, putting the rollers in her hair as she did every morning.

'Merry Christmas,' I said, looking at her through her reflection in the mirror. I tiptoed over to the hearth to see if Santa had eaten the piece of cake that Lily told me she had left for him. Mummy cursed when a hairgrip she was holding slipped through her fingers and dropped onto the floor. I quickly knelt down and searched in the dim light with my fingertips to try and find it. I was kicked quite sharply from behind.

'What the hell are you doing snooping around?' I stood

up feeling quite shaken. 'There's no presents if that's what you're looking for.'

'I was just looking to see if Santa—'

'See, I was right, you ungrateful little bitch.' A lump appeared inside my throat. 'Start to cry and you'll get a slap across your face.'

Frieda walked into the room with her new musical box, curving her hand around the ballerina while the music played so that I couldn't watch her dance. You're a horrible sister, I thought as I walked towards the kitchen door. Daddy was leaning down next to the cooker, prodding the turkey with a fork.

'It's Christmas Day,' he said, looking towards me as I dragged the sack of potatoes from one end of the kitchen along the floor towards the sink.

'I know,' I replied, sharing a few seconds of laughter with him.

'That's better.' He clicked his fingers. 'Pass me some tea towels; it's bloody hot over here.'

'Did you see him?' I asked, running over to help. 'Did you see him?' I asked again.

'Who?' he said, holding his hands steady on either side of the tray as he lifted the turkey out of the oven. 'Actually, I did,' he added with a sigh of relief as he placed the tray on top of the kitchen shelf.

'Daddy, you're not supposed to,' I said as I bent down to lift the stool to stand on, enabling me to reach over the top of the kitchen sink.

'He didn't know,' he answered, sucking the tips of his fingers from the crispness of the skin after touching the breast of the turkey.

147

'You're telling me fibs, aren't you, Daddy?'

'No, I'm not. I pretended to be fast asleep; that's why he left me an apple right at the end of my bed.'

'Didn't he leave you any handkerchiefs, the coloured ones that you like?' He didn't reply and I felt sorry for him. 'I'll make you a cup of tea,' I told him as I scraped the potatoes with a blunt knife, 'from the tea set that Santa has left for me.'

'What, he's left you a tea set?'

'Yes, Daddy, shall I show you?' I jumped when Mummy unexpectedly walked into the kitchen. She abruptly told Daddy that he should have been more careful.

'These tea towels are full of grease,' she moaned, grabbing them from him in a stern manner before leaving them lying on top of the drainer adjoining the sink. 'I want them peeling, not scraping,' I was told on her inspection.

Daddy said that he was going to have a shave as Mummy left. I pulled my face in disappointment that he was leaving. 'So can I be excused?' he asked, rubbing the tiny grey bristles on his chin with his hand. His departure was quick.

I changed the knife to a much sharper one and, this time, hummed the tune of 'Jingle Bells' quietly to myself.

Mummy returned to the kitchen. 'Don't peel them too thick,' I was told as she leaned over the sink to inspect.

'Did Santa leave you a present?' I asked Mummy.

'A load of debt, that's what he's left me.'

'I bet he wrapped it up in nice paper for you, isn't he kind?'

'God, what the hell did I give birth to?' she said, looking at me with horror before marching out of the kitchen.

'Shall I help you find it?' I asked. 'Sometimes I forget things too.'

'Mummy looked quite irritated,' Teddy said after he passed her on his way in to the kitchen.

'She doesn't know what she's given birth to so she's probably gone to find it.'

'Do you like my hair?' Teddy asked, standing there with every strand on top of his head plastered with Brylcreem, pulling the lid off the tin he carried.

'It smells strong,' I told him, sneezing as he came closer for me to look while trying to get a glimpse at himself through the tiny cracked mirror that hung by a nail against the wall over the kitchen sink. I sneezed once again before he left, with admiration only for himself.

The whistle of the kettle boiling caught my attention. Daddy had left it on a low light and must have forgotten about it. The whistle was getting stronger and the steam was hissing out in shoots through the tiny holes in the spout. As my hands were wet and dirty I called out Teddy's name, complaining to myself when there was no answer and so took one step from the stool in haste to switch it off. The stool tipped and I fell to the ground, crying out immediately. Come on, I said to myself, listening to the kettle's whistle grow weaker. My hands full of grit and stinging, I lifted myself up little by little. I was jolted by the neck of my cardigan.

'That kettle would have burned itself out and that would have been another expense,' Mummy said, pushing me to one side. The kettle hissed as she filled it with a small amount of cold running water from the tap before slamming it back onto the iron ring that sat on top of the cooker.

'Get back and finish those potatoes,' she shouted.

Frieda appeared, asking what all the commotion was about.

'Your bloody stupid father left the kettle on and she,' she said, looking towards me, 'hadn't the sense to switch it off in time.'

'I wouldn't put the blame on him, Mummy – after all she's always distracting him with one thing or another. She thinks she's a daddy's girl, but he must get so fed up with her. I've seen the expression on his face with my very own eyes. I'll bet she drives him mad. Anyway, there's a glass of sherry waiting for you in the living room,' Frieda said, coaxing her along.

Tears ran down my face as soon as they had left and I sobbed with each strip of peel I cut from around the potato. I'll ask Daddy if he doesn't like me, but what if he says he doesn't? I thought, sobbing even more.

There was a quiet knock from the outside of the kitchen window. I didn't look up, I just kept peeling. I didn't want my heart to break, not on Christmas morning, but the thought of Daddy disliking me made me feel scared. By then the tears were falling down my face fast and furious. The pattering continued and I panicked, lifting up my skirt to dry my eyes with the thought that old Mrs Crowswick, who lived next door, might call to wish me Merry Christmas. I practised how to smile, looking up towards the mirror before peering across and through the window. I took a huge gulp and stared. 'Father Christmas!' I said in a whisper, wiping my nose on my sleeve as he stood there, red cape and long white beard. 'It's Father Christmas,' I whispered to myself again, sniffing up hard.

'Thank you for my presents,' I called, feeling quite frightened of him.

I jumped as he swiftly moved from the window and I heard the sound of the latch lifting up on the kitchen door. I turned and stared. A large canvas bag was thrown in first. I looked towards the living room. There was no time left to run as he entered. I sniffed up at the strong smell of whisky. He gave me a wink and pulled down his beard. 'Grandfather!' I called. I was picked up from the stool almost immediately and flung high up into his arms. I felt as though my bones were being crushed and I didn't care, letting him hug me as tightly as he could.

'Santa sent me to wish you a Merry Christmas,' he said.

'Did you come on his sleigh?' I asked, holding my head back for an answer.

'I could have done, but he was too busy. I boarded the ship from Belfast and sailed over the dark sea through the night.'

'Were there pirates on board?'

'A few, but they were so drunk they never moved out of their seats.'

'Would you like a cup of tea from my teapot that Santa brought me? The cups are only tiny but I'll hold it for you. That's if your hands start to shake.'

'A drop of whisky stops that. It's like a medicine, just does the job,' he said, sitting me down on the stool before slipping his hand inside his coat pocket and lifting out a small bottle. The top was unscrewed and Grandfather drank whatever remained straight down. 'Now, what's a wee lass like you doing crying?'

I looked at him. 'Oh, I just felt so happy that it was Christmas Day that's all, Grandfather. I've been sent a doll, too.' He looked puzzled. 'Santa, Santa Claus left it for me,' I said, standing up carefully on the stool.

'You ain't peeling no spuds on Christmas morning. I'll have them done in a wink of an eye,' he said, lifting me up and standing me firmly on the ground.

'Grandfather,' I said as he rummaged through the drawer lifting out the potato peeler. Within seconds their skins were sliced and dropped down into the basin below. 'Is Nanna coming too?' I asked, stretching up towards the window in case she was sitting there in her wheelchair.

'She's looking after the canary. He needs to be fed every morning. Anyway, where is everyone?'

'Daddy's gone for a shave; he's got bristles on his chin and they were making him itch. Grandfather, does whisky taste nice?'

'When you haven't a drop left in the bottle it certainly does.'

I felt confused. 'Will you bring Nanna next time you visit Rose Cottage?'

'Most probably.'

'Grandfather, why can't Nanna walk?'

'There's a drop of whisky left in my case; unzip it and you'll find it tucked in somewhere.'

Lily suddenly appeared. 'I know,' I said to her as she looked towards me with shock.

'Oh my love, the love of my life, and grown up too.'

'Grandfather.' Lily rushed over and into his arms as he looked down over her shoulder at me with a smile.

'The lid's off from your tin,' I said, lifting up the small

amount of clothing that he had and shaking off the tiny leaves of tobacco that had fallen.

'Save what you can. Are my roll-ups there too?'

Lily offered a hand. 'Found it,' I said out loud. The bottle was lying underneath a sweaty polythene bag with sandwiches crumpled inside. The whisky swirled around the inside of the bottle as I lifted it out and passed it to Grandfather, who wiped his hands immediately before unscrewing the top.

'Heaven,' he said, taking a large gulp and passing me the bottle back. 'You can put it back in my bag,' he said. 'I'll have the rest for supper tonight.'

I waited until Lily had scraped up the loose tobacco with the tips of her fingers and put what remained back into Grandfather's tin, pressing the lid down until it clicked firmly into place. I picked out a rather baggy sweater of his, concerned that he might be cold due to the purple colour of his nose. Lily asked me to fix the hook and eye on the top of her dress. Kneeling down so that I could reach, I lifted the frill of her collar up. 'Don't move,' I said as I missed the hook. She waited patiently until it was finally fastened and, complaining of cramp, rubbed her hands against her leg as she stood up.

'Good God,' Daddy said. 'Pops, I don't believe it.' A hard slap from each other around their shoulders and a few tears, and the welcoming began. Mummy was called, and my brothers stood waiting one by one for a good old handshake from Grandfather. Lily was told to kick out the cat and the turkey was wrapped again in foil before we all left the kitchen. A Woodbine was offered by Daddy and was lit straightaway.

Grandfather placed half a crown on the table. 'That's for some sweets,' he said. We all thanked him and left the room.

Lily pinched a chocolate bell wrapped in silver paper from the tree. I giggled at her bravery. 'Don't tell,' she said, unwrapping it and eating it immediately.

'Wait for me,' I shouted, picking up my doll and running up the stairs behind her. She giggled with me and we ran into her bedroom, closing the door with excitement, knowing she had actually got away with it.

'What are you going to call her?' she asked, picking me up and sitting me down on top of her bunk bed. 'Your doll,' she explained, straightening my skirt over my knees.

'Lily.'

'Pardon?'

'Lily, that's going to be her name.'

'There are lots more names to choose from,' she told me as she went through as many girls' names as she could possibly think of before getting quite tired every time I shook my head to say no. 'Lily it is then,' she said. We both smiled and she kissed me gently on my forehead.

Frieda walked into the room asking Lily to hold the door open while she crouched down to pick up her presents from the landing outside before placing them on the wooden floorboards underneath the bottom bunk. Then she began counting out aloud how many she had.

'Show your ballerina to Lily. She dances around,' I told her.

'How do you know?' Frieda asked.

'Because of the music. It makes you want to turn around when you listen to it.'

'Yes, can we have a look?' Lily asked, pressing her hands gently on my knees so that I wouldn't move them up and down with excitement.

'I'm not turning the key again. You'll have to wait,' we were told, while she unwrapped a box of chocolates, taking pleasure in choosing one in front of us before closing the lid.

'Dance, ballerina, dance,' Lily sang, taking revenge on Frieda's selfish attitude and humming the rest of the tune while dancing around in front of me. I applauded her and Lily bowed with grace. Frieda tried to ignore the tease but deliberately picked up her musical box in front of us to check that it was locked.

'Where are you all?' Mummy screeched from the bottom of the stairs.

'Yes, well, there are jobs to be done,' Lily said, 'especially on Christmas Day, and I suggest all three of us muck in together.'

'I thought your high-class friends were teaching you to speak properly,' Frieda said to her.

This wasn't my war, for once, and I left the bitter attack between them, knowing that Lily would always win. 'Do you know why?' I whispered to Lily, my doll. 'Because Lily, my sister, is so much wiser.'

The room came to a sudden silence. Frieda had lost but I felt sorry for her. Sorry that she was so hard and cold. After all, I did love her; it wasn't her fault. Maybe she's sick in the mind. That's what Lily always told her. Maybe she is, I thought, as I watched her count each chocolate once again in the box she had opened.

'Well, come on,' Lily said, hoisting me up off the bed.

155

'Frieda, are you ready?' she called as she still sat there counting. Lily huffed but Frieda ignored her until the final count was done. The expression on her face didn't look good but Lily ignored that and stood there, determined that we all three go down the stairs together.

'That's from the Christmas tree,' Frieda said, spotting the empty silver paper screwed up in a ball where it lay on the bedroom floor as she was leaving the room.

Lily automatically knew what to do in the dining room. Grandfather wandered around leaving us to it as Lily pulled out the drop-leaf table from against the wall, extending it to its full capacity. A paper tablecloth was opened and shaken in Frieda's direction. I collected the box of Christmas crackers from the window ledge. The excitement was unbearable as I waited for them both to smooth the creases out and lay the cloth flat and even over the table. The job was nearly done with plenty of admiration from Grandfather. As the last cracker was laid, Lily frogmarched both Frieda and me through into the kitchen, tickling me around my waist on our way. Lily rolled the thin strips of bacon around the minia-ture sausages and I passed her the tiny wooden sticks to baton them down. 'We're a good team,' Lily said. I looked up at her and smiled. 'I'll put a ribbon in your hair before we sit down at the table for Christmas dinner,' she remarked, looking down towards me. 'Not yet,' she said as I excitedly passed another stick over to her, her fingers slipping with the fat from the bacon as she tried to roll it around. We laughed as the sausage kept slipping out.

Frieda gave me a little push. 'Make room,' she said,

sulking because she had been left with the sprouts to prepare.

Lily guided me around to her opposite side, protecting me from any sort of bullying. 'We're going for a walk,' Lily said, placing everything in order ready for the oven. She grabbed hold of the hairbrush from the window ledge and carefully brushed the knots out of my hair.

'The floor's to be mopped,' Frieda said, inspecting her long finger nails to make sure they hadn't been damaged as she put down the knife, her job done.

I watched with amusement as a money spider tried to make its way down the window on a tiny thread of web. Lily tugged the top of my arm and I followed her to the door, catching hold of my coat as she lifted it off the hook on the wall before we walked along the entry into the open air of the village.

'Merry Christmas,' Mrs Wright said as we walked along the front of her garden.

Lily nudged me as she helped me on with my coat. 'Merry Christmas,' I replied.

'Yes, Merry Christmas,' Lily called.

I shivered at the frosty morning biting my hands. 'Put them inside your pocket,' Lily said to me, waiting beside me until I tucked them inside.

Lily leant an ear to the sound of the church bells ringing. 'I'm going to ring those bells one day,' I told her, looking over the hill where the church tower stood. Lily looked down with question. 'When I'm bigger, of course. Don't look,' I said to Lily as the Grindle brothers stood outside their house aiming their catapults at us in a threatening manner.

The hill was getting steeper and my pace a lot slower. Lily suggested that we rest on a rather lumpy stone that was wedged in the ground on the edge of the farmer's field. She got flustered with embarrassment before we sat down because of the roaring whistle that Edward gave her from his bedroom window. Lily put her hand inside her coat pocket and wiped my nose with an embroidered hanky.

'Give us a drag,' Edward shouted as Lily struggled to light her cigarette, feeling the coldness in her fingers, before throwing the burnt match onto the ground.

'What would you like to be, besides a princess, when you grow up?' she asked.

I coughed as she puffed constantly, the tip of her cigarette glowing bright red in the cold air. 'If I'm not going to be a princess, which I might, I'd like to be kind, yes, kind when I grow up.'

Lily squeezed the tip of my nose. 'I'd like to get married.'

I looked at her curiously. 'Who to?' I asked.

'Well, I haven't met him yet. It certainly won't be Edward,' she said.

We both looked up immediately towards his window. He waved down at us to keep our attention. 'Can you marry anyone?' I asked.

'Yes, I suppose you can. That's if they want to marry you.'

'I was going to marry Eric. He's my best friend, Lily, apart from you, but he keeps picking his nose and he won't put it in his handkerchief.'

'Come on,' she said. 'I'm sure your bottom's cold,' she added, raising me underneath my arms. 'Don't look,' she said as we both stood up.

'Where?'

'Over at Edward.'

But I instinctively did. 'He's a bit of a creep,' I said as he blew another whistle between his fingers. 'He's got too many freckles, Lily. That's probably why you won't marry him.'

'Oh shit,' Lily said, 'Ethel's here. She'll be going to church.'

'How do you know?'

'Because she's got her Bible in her hand and I stink of cigarette smoke,' Lily muttered. 'Merry Christmas,' Lily said as Ethel came closer, stopping next to us as she fiddled with the ribbon in between the thin paper pages.

'I'm reading about the birth of Christ,' she told us, fixing the long thin strand of ribbon onto the exact page she was going to read from. 'Are you going to be in the congregation?' she asked Lily, closing the Bible gently. Her long grey woollen overcoat smelled strongly of mothballs and I sneezed twice, watching Lily as she hardly moved her lips, apologising to Ethel that she had to help prepare the Christmas dinner. I looked up at Lily, surprised, and was nudged again.

Ethel walked slowly with Lily a little further along the road. Lily linked her arm. 'Still feel as unhappy, my dear?' I heard Ethel say, her head bowed slightly. 'Why don't you come across and have a chat with the vicar some time soon? I'll come with you; it just might help. We've all heard the screams from inside Rose Cottage. It's got to end, Lily. You'll have to start trying to make a life for yourself. You're old enough now.' I kicked a few loose stones along the road to get Lily's attention, afraid of hearing any more of their conversation. 'Remember, I'm your Godmother,' Ethel said. 'Listen to my advice.'

Ethel kissed Lily's cheek and departed over the quaint bridge towards the church. My instincts on the short walk back to Rose Cottage left me with the dreadful thought that Lily would soon be leaving.

'Oh, that's a big sigh,' Lily said to me before we headed down into the short dark entry.

'A cup of tea?' I asked Lily when she lifted up the latch.

'Yes; no sugar though, I'm on a diet,' she said.

I smiled towards her and she took my hand, leaving the adults to chatter as she guided me into the front room. 'Oh, it's hot,' I said to Lily, leaning down and picking up the china teapot from the floor.

'It is,' Lily said, touching the spout.

'You're both going mad,' Teddy said, pointing his paper plane before directing it up into the air as Lily slipped away. 'If it tastes that good,' he said, 'I'll join you,' he added, winking at Lily as his plane descended quickly to the ground. I immediately tipped the spout of the teapot down towards an empty cup. 'It's not strong is it?' Teddy asked. I looked down inside the cup. 'It doesn't matter if it is,' he said, thanking me as I passed it over.

Grandfather had changed by then, looking quite smart in his brown checked jacket. He pulled a tiny bottle out from the inside of his pocket. 'Like a little rum in that cup?' he asked Lily, standing in front of the fireplace looking quite frail. His mop of hair was brilliant white. His cheeks sunk in slightly under his defined cheekbones as he swallowed from the bottle. 'Oh, the thirst after that long journey,' he said, pausing for a second before knocking the rest of it back quickly, just before Daddy walked in looking rather hot while straightening his tie.

Grandfather squeezed the empty bottle down the side of the tatty old armchair. Daddy didn't see and Lily breathed a sigh of relief. 'I'll bring you back a Babycham and we'll have a toast together for good health and happiness,' Grandfather whispered to Lily on his way out. The front door closed and Lily and I ran over to the window and clambered up.

'Isn't it nice,' Lily said, 'to watch Grandfather and his son walking together over the road to the village pub on Christmas Day?'

I was instantly pulled back by my hair with such force that I landed next to the Christmas tree. I was so close that I could feel the prickles from the branches against my chest.

'Where did you take it from?' Mummy screeched as she held out the silver paper that had been screwed up into a tight ball. She clamped her hand underneath my chin and raised my head up. 'Point to where you took it from, you simple child.'

'I can't,' I told Mummy, straining my voice. I was shaken furiously. My face stung so hard it burned with the force of Mummy's hand.

'I took the silver bell from the tree,' Lily screamed. 'Touch her once more...' Lily shouted, running towards me and shielding me with her body.

'And what?' Mummy asked.

'You're an evil, jealous mother and that makes me sad,' Lily said, moving me away from her. 'I'll be leaving Rose Cottage.'

'Go now,' Mummy shouted. Lily ignored her and lifted me up into her arms, holding me tightly, the tears streaming down her face.

'Sorry,' Uncle said, making me jump. 'But I had to wake you. Don't you think you'd be better off taking yourself to bed? You've been tossing and turning on that chair for far too long.' I looked at him, startled. 'Come on, I'll help you off that chair.'

'Don't, Uncle,' I replied, searching for a cigarette.

'I've drunk all the coffee you made.'

'Excellent.'

'I actually feel quite sober now.'

I picked a match up from out of the box and struck it straight away, taking one huge drag from my cigarette.

'You look quite flushed,' Uncle said. I didn't reply and took another deep drag. 'Drink?' he asked.

'Water, please.'

'You've been dreaming,' Uncle shouted while clattering around in the kitchen. 'There you go; ice cold too,' he said as I flicked the long length of ash from my cigarette into the glass ashtray before reaching out and thanking him. 'Good God, you were thirsty,' he remarked as I gave a sigh of relief on drinking the last drop. 'Don't worry about having to leave me,' he told me, 'if you want to retire for the night; only I'm wide awake now and I'm quite used to talking to myself.'

I pressed the stub of my cigarette down into the ashtray and lit another straight away. I sensed Uncle's glance.

'OK,' he said, 'looks like you want to hear the rest of

the story. Straight after your mother's departure, Ernest called me into the dining room and wandered around, carrying a heavy burden of emotion. I felt uncomfortable sitting there. He was drinking the gin fast, lifting up the bottle to see how much was left before pouring himself another. "Dennis," he said to me. "After considerable thought, and for me to do what I feel is in your best interests, I have decided to send you to St Vincent's in the Himalayas." I immediately straightened my back, my shoulders stiff. "We will take the overnight train tomorrow evening. You may only take a few personal possessions. The servants will be ordered to pack a bag for you with the necessary items of clothing that you require."

'I didn't feel the need to sit there and listen to any more. After all, what else could be said? I pushed my chair back in anger and stormed, without any thought, out of the dining room, slamming the door hard behind me. How could he just send me away? It wasn't long since I'd left my mother and my sister had just left the country. I felt discarded. The sunlight hit my eyes as I ran outside for air. Brushing the tears to one side, I ran and ran instinctively in the direction of where Barbara would be. I cried like a baby all the way. My body was weak and helpless, my heart full of fear and pain. I fell into a heap of grass, gripping the blades tightly, ripping them from their roots in frustration. The echo of my cries surrounded me and I listened to the sound of my sorrow.'

Uncle, by then, had gripped my attention.

'I felt bruised inside,' he continued, 'finally picking myself up and running the rest of the way into Barbara's arms. I couldn't speak as she rested my head against her chest to comfort me. She remained silent until I had the courage to hold my head up, searching down with one hand deep inside my trouser pocket for the stub of a cigarette I had saved. Barbara instinctively knew. "Here," she said, slipping out two cigarettes from the inside of her boots. She lit them both at the same time, striking a match on a nearby stone. We didn't speak as we knelt down, leaning our backs against the dry rotting wood of the barn door. Barbara leaned against me and we sat there within our little sanctuary, treasuring that quiet moment together.

'The dreaded thought of St Vincent's ran through my mind. I, uncertain about my future, immediately stood up. "Barbara," I said, looking down at her. She looked up, her eyes squinting before she protected them with her hand from the strong rays of the sun.

' "It's bad news, isn't it, Dennis?" she said as I gave her a helping hand to lift her up gently.

' "Shall we walk?" I asked, kicking randomly at pebbles that lay on the ground. She linked my arm and I looked down, my head bowed with sadness. I told her I was being sent away.

' "Where to?" she asked. "When?" Her link tightened around my arm and she stopped walking and looked me straight in the eyes. "When, Dennis? When for God's sake, tell me, when?" she cried openly.

' "Tomorrow evening," I said. She buried her head against my chest and gripped onto the lapels of my open shirt. I told her I was being sent to St Vincent's, where Ernest felt that I'd have a better education. I explained to her that it was run by priests and they'd be teaching me.

' "How far, how far are you going?" she cried. "Where the hell is it?" she screamed. When I told her it was high up in the Himalayas, her screams grew louder as she beat one hand and then the other against my chest. "No, Dennis, no," she wailed. I felt the dampness of her tears and the cold sensation of them trickling down my chest. I stroked her head to comfort her. Her long wavy hair felt like silk. God, I'm going to miss her, I thought, listening to her sob. She gasped and took a deep breath. I placed my hand underneath her chin and gently lifted her head. I pointed her face directly at mine and kissed her lips tenderly. "Make love to me, Dennis," she whispered.

'Maybe if we just stay here, lying as still as we are, I thought afterwards, the world will just go on turning and pass us by. My heart beat strongly and I sat up, bending my legs and stretching out my arms. I clasped both my hands over my knees. Barbara followed suit.

' "Look," I said, with a slight cough. "It's hell, I know, but I'll be back, Barbara. Yes, I'll be back," I whispered.

' "You won't, Dennis," she said, staring up at the clear sky.

' "Yes, I will, Barbara, and when I do there'll be lots to tell you."

' "Dennis," she said with a sigh.

' "We can go out riding together, can't we Barbara?" I asked. She thumped me against my shoulder causing me to fall sideways almost to the ground.

' "Come on, then, let's ride out now," she said.

' "What now?" I asked, surprised at her impulsiveness.

' "Yes, now."

'She lifted herself up and slipped into her boots. "Well?"

165

she said, offering me a hand as I dragged myself up. I stood and stared at her tying her blouse in a knot around her slim waist. She smiled with embarrassment.

'I felt an immense hatred for Ernest as Barbara and I walked arm in arm towards the stables. "I need another cigarette," I told her.

' "Over there on the ledge," she replied.

' "Where?" I asked as she pulled two saddles down while looking up into the darkness of the timber framework. She lifted her whip and pushed them. "Catch," she said as the packet nearly hit the ground.

' "So that's where you hide them."

' "Yes," she called, "they'd be pinched in seconds if I didn't."

'I stood once again leaning against the open door of the barn staring at her beauty as she tightened each girth. I wished it had been Ernest who had died instead of Grace. My loving mother would never have sent me away.

'Barbara looked sideways at me while pushing her fingers firmly inside her leather gloves. "Here, Dennis," she said, holding the straps up in a loop. I walked over and took the reins from her hand. My legs felt weak as I placed my foot inside the stirrup before hoisting myself over and up into the saddle. "You'll come back one day, remember that," Barbara called, already seated in the saddle. "Let's pretend we have for ever," she said, lashing her whip against the rear of the horse and galloping off. I was soon to follow. We laughed with the fun we were having. Barbara showing off her expertise left me slightly cold as I struggled to stay seated. "You're improving, Dennis," she said when we were eventually side by side.

166

'A slow trot was ordered and I followed suit. "I've taught you well, Dennis." I smiled, not revealing to her that I couldn't wait to get off the bloody thing. I was scared stiff. "I won't hear the echo, Dennis, the echo of your voice calling out my name," she said with sadness as the reins were tightened and we eventually came to a halt. We both stared down into the valley below.

' "Yes, you will," I replied, my stomach churning at the thought of losing her. "I'll call you from the highest mountain. I'll make sure you hear."

'She brushed her hand across her face. "Barbara, will you wait for me?" I asked.

' "What if I wait, wait forever and you never come running back into my arms?" she cried, gasping for breath in between her words. "I'm never going to let you go, wherever I might be," I told her. "You'll be right there, right there in the centre of my heart. I love you, Barbara," I said, tenderly.

' "Do you, Dennis?" she asked, turning towards me. I leaned over and wiped away her tears with my hands. "I'm going to be so lonely without you," she said.

' "I know, Barbara," I answered, reflecting on my own feelings, "I know."

'The clouds were gathering over the tips of the mountains, casting a shadow. Dusk was approaching and I dreaded the thought of the night, knowing that it would soon come and go before my journey began. We both gave a sigh and somehow managed to smile before slowly turning to make our way back. "You'll stay for supper won't you?" Barbara asked.

' "Of course."

'Dusk had finally set in and after Barbara had settled the horses a cold glass of beer was served on the open veranda. "I wonder how many stars there are up there tonight," she said, looking up towards the sky before pulling out the low cane-backed chair and sitting down. There was a silence and I somehow couldn't find any words.

' "I love India, Dennis," she said.

' "I know, so do I," I replied as we listened to the crickets croak in the undergrowth.

' "I wonder why you're being sent there, of all places. It seems so far way."

' "What, St Vincent's?" I asked.

' "Yes," she replied, "I should imagine that they'll be pretty strict."

' "Who?"

' "The priests, Dennis."

'I told her I was scared.

' "I know, Dennis, so am I," she replied.

'I asked her if she missed her parents being away so much.

' "My father, yes, my mother, no. She only married him for his money, you know. Anyway, father's got a mistress," she told me.

' "Really?" I said, surprised.

' "Yes, I hide the presents that he buys for her behind the bales of hay."

' "And you don't mind?" I asked.

' "No, Dennis, I don't. I asked him one morning if she was pretty. 'Very,' he replied."

' "And?" I asked her.

' "Well, that's all I know, Dennis." she said.

' "Barbara, is there anything you require?" Charlotte asked, making her way steadily towards us. "Hello, Dennis, nice to see you again," she said to me. Standing up immediately from my chair, I asked her if she'd like to sit down. She thanked me but said she was nearly ready to retire for the night.

' "Charlotte is the best housekeeper anyone could have, aren't you, Charlotte?" Barbara said, reaching out for her hand.

'Charlotte blushed. "Well, I'm not as fast on my feet as I used to be when you were a little girl, Barbara," she replied.

'Barbara told Charlotte that I was leaving the next day. She looked puzzled and Barbara explained that I was going to school, St Vincent's, up in the Himalayas. "Why ever there, so far away?" Charlotte asked. Barbara didn't answer but, with her voice breaking, told her she was going to miss me terribly. Charlotte covered her frail hands over Barbara's and squeezed them tightly. "Tell him he has to come back soon, Charlotte," Barbara told her, "I'll just die without him."

' "I'm sure he will if he's meant to," Charlotte replied. She wished me luck and I stood up and shook her hand.

' "Poor Charlotte," Barbara said as she watched her walk along the veranda, her back hunched with age. I ran towards her, linking her arm to escort her to the door.

' "Make sure you write to her, Dennis," she whispered, "when you're settled in, of course."

' "I will, Charlotte," I assured her.

' "Her heart's going to be broken," she added.

169

' "Mine's broken now," I told her. She stood and stared gently into my eyes.

' "I know, my son." It was a look of farewell from a wise old lady who I never forgot.

' "You're getting cold," I said to Barbara.

' "Only a little," she replied as she wrapped her arms across her shoulders and shivered as the outside temperature dropped. I insisted that she should get some sleep and that I would go home and do the same.

' "You'll be back, won't you?" she asked. "Tomorrow, before you go?" she added, turning her head to look up towards me as I stood there leaning over her shoulders. "We can go for a picnic if you like. Charlotte baked some cakes today. There's far too many. I can put some in a basket." I told her I would look forward to that and I jumped down the steps from the veranda before turning and blowing her a huge kiss and disappearing into the night.

'The dark, lonely lane matched my mood. On the walk back I feared nothing, not even the rustle of nature that surrounded me. I was surprised at how lit up the house was on my return, and cautiously pushed the unlocked door open. I felt my home was full of whispers and noticed my trunk laid flat on the floor against the entrance. The dining room door was ajar. I pushed it open but didn't step in. What I saw was certainly not welcoming.

' "You had better help him to his bed," I said to the servant crouched down in the corner of the room. He raised his head. "You'll be sitting there all night if you don't. Can't you see he's drunk? He's dead to the world." Poor bastard, I thought, not Ernest of course. "Come on, at least let's get him up from the bloody chair," I said, stepping in with frustration. "You can't sit there all bloody night," I shouted as the servant stayed crouched on the floor, clapping my hands to alert him to the situation.

' "You've been smoking that bloody stuff again," I said to him while lending a hand to enable him to stand. Ernest was a dead weight and we had made no progress after several attempts to lift him. I gave a sigh. "It's hopeless," I said, looking towards the servant who stood there with a bewildered look on his face. "Go to sleep," I told him, trying to explain to him that Ernest would eventually wake. He smiled, his gums protruding over his stained teeth, and retreated like a dog back into the corner of the room. Ernest's glass was deliberately left resting on the table next to him, leaving what little gin remained still lying in the bottom. Silly, I know, but I wanted no one accused of taking his last sip. I then left the room, leaving the door ajar.

'My legs ached with each step that I took up the short staircase to my room. It was almost an effort to unzip my trousers before lying on top of the bed in just my underwear.

'I awoke early the next morning, surprised that I had slept through the night. The hot sun crept through the gap in between the curtains. I turned and reached out for the tiny square clock on the bedside table, my eyes squinting while trying to focus on the time as I held it close up to my face. My body felt heavy as I slowly lifted myself up from the bed before standing and stretching out as far as I could. The bell rang loudly from below. I jumped with the noise, sensitive to the ring that tingled inside my ears. They would know downstairs that I had woken up because of the creaky floorboards under my feet. I pulled open the curtains and opened the window to take a deep breath of air, then wandered across the landing into the bathroom to take a shower under the slow trickling water.

' "Bloody well knock next time," I shouted, spitting out the froth of toothpaste from inside my mouth into the sink below as I stood there naked. The door was quickly closed and the servant was nowhere in sight on my return to my room. As I made my way downstairs I saw Ernest sitting in the dining room with his newspaper in his hand.

' "I'm going to see Barbara," I said, standing in the doorway, my feelings still of hatred as I looked towards him.

' "We'll be leaving at 4 p.m. sharp," Ernest said, looking at the large wooden clock ticking noticeably in the silence of the room. "So I will expect you home earlier than that. Dennis," he called as I turned to walk away. I quickly turned back. "I'm doing this for your own good. There's too much unrest here, especially in the neighbouring villages."

' "So I'll be better out of the way, is that what you're saying?" I asked.

' "Quite frankly, Dennis, yes," he replied.

'I walked quickly through the hall, kicking the trunk that had been packed for me with my foot on my way out, and jumped on my bicycle, pedalling as fast as I could in order to get away from the uncomfortable atmosphere I felt at home.

* * *

'It was as if I was almost frightened of seeing Barbara that day, although any attempt to stop myself from doing so would have been quite unthinkable. My thoughts, although foolish, I know, were to simply disappear. Just keep cycling, Dennis, a voice inside told me. Cycle so far away that no one will ever have the chance of finding you.

'I was about to circle the bend around which Barbara would be waiting. I felt sick inside with the thought that at the end of this day, I would have no idea when I would be able to call and see her again, my only true companion.

'I pressed hard against the brakes, stopping almost immediately, and left my bicycle slumped on the ground like a spoiled child before sitting myself down on the edge of the grass verge searching frantically inside the deep pockets of my loose-fitting trousers. I brought out two rather crumpled cigarettes and a bundle of tiny wooden matches. I leaned back and soon struck a match against the bark of a tree, lighting a rather limp-looking cigarette. I had taken pity on myself and took a rather large drag before blowing out the smoke, watching it disappear up into the morning air.

'My thoughts reflected back to Grace, my mother and, strangely enough at that moment, that very silent moment I had with myself, I forgave her for all the misjudgements she had made in the life she had chosen to live. "Oh, Mother," I wept, "why did you have to leave me, Grace?" I called. I felt wretched in my misery, filled with sudden grief. "If you are there in that other world, if you're really there, Grace, please guide me," I cried out aloud.

'Eventually, my tears stopped racing down my face,

173

leaving just a trickle running down. I lifted up my head towards the tall trees, their branches gently moving in the breeze. I almost felt afraid that I had invaded their peace, as I sat there in that lonely lane and threw my cigarette as far as I could before wiping my eyes. I stood up and bent down to pick up my bicycle from the ground. The trees looked quite eerie as I took one more glance up towards them and jumped back on my bicycle.

'I rang the weak old rusty bell in excitement, turning the corner of the bend. I pedalled faster and rang it again to alert Barbara that I was there. I gasped as she suddenly appeared. With pressure from both hands I pressed the brakes firmly and came to an immediate halt. I jumped off amid a spray of dust and stood still with my arms spread open like an eagle as she walked towards me.

' "Don't, Dennis," she said, as if she knew I was going to say how beautiful she looked. She was quite right, it was on the tip of my tongue to comment on how her pretty dress flattered her shapely figure, and I swallowed hard before holding her tightly in my arms. "The zip's not quite in position," she mumbled as I gently kissed her, moving my hands up and down her back, "only the needle broke on the sewing machine," she said, pausing in between our kiss. We both then started to laugh. Unromantic, I know, but it was probably needed to free the tension that we both felt.

' "Right," I said. "Now can I say how –" but I was distracted by seeing Charlotte approach, carrying a rather large picnic basket.

' "Dreams don't last, Dennis," she said, handing over

174

the picnic basket to me. "She looks beautiful, doesn't she?" Charlotte remarked, leaning down to straighten the lace at the bottom of Barbara's dress. "And she's been up all night long finishing sewing this dress so that she could wear it today, especially for you."

' "Charlotte," Barbara exclaimed in embarrassment, looking straight towards me.

' "You do look beautiful," I told her, "very beautiful," I added as I reached out for her hand.

' "I suppose I shan't see you again," Charlotte said, "until you return from school. You've a long journey ahead, Dennis, and I wish you a safe one."

' "But I'll see you—" I began, but Charlotte stopped me immediately.

' "You won't," she said. "This is your precious time together, yours and Barbara's, to share the memories of today. So when you bring her safely home I will be sitting in my old creaky rocking chair behind closed doors with my memories too, Dennis. Just allow me the pleasure, both of you, to stand here and watch until you disappear from view. After all, I was young myself once."

' "She'll go back and dream, Dennis," Barbara said.

' "About what?" I asked.

' "About how her life used to be."

' "You can't blame her for that," I told her.

' "I know," Barbara said, holding my hand much tighter.

'We climbed the grassy hill together and disappeared out of view.

' "We don't have to walk much further do we, Dennis?" Barbara asked.

' "I've just been thinking the same," I answered, and we

both nestled down together at the very spot where we stood, putting the basket down between us.

'I unstrapped the lid and Barbara lifted it open.

' "I'll be writing to you, long letters, of course, while I'm away," I told her, thanking her at the same time as she gently placed a tiny triangular sandwich onto my plate. Without any thought as to what was inside, on my attempt to eat it the mashed egg slipped through the thin pieces of bread and dropped back onto my plate.

' "Me too," she replied, looking down at the repulsive mess. "We'll have to tell Charlotte how wonderful these sandwiches are, Dennis," she said.

' "Yes," I answered, relieved at not having much of an appetite. We laughed a little before indulging in a slice of fruit cake that Charlotte had wrapped so neatly in a cloth. Lemon water was poured into tiny tin mugs and stirred with a spoon. We drank it slowly and listened in silence to the running water from the stream below. I, intimidated by the knowledge that I was to leave shortly, moved the picnic basket to one side and lay next to Barbara. We lay there for quite a while, quiet and still, on the soft blades of grass. If only time could have stood still, I thought, if only.

' "Let's fall asleep together and never wake up," she whispered, allowing me to gently caress her. Our kiss became more and more passionate and making love to each other that afternoon was wonderful.'

I gave a sigh. Uncle smiled and continued.

' "I'm going to hate riding out without you by my side," Barbara told me as we chose to walk back beside the cool flowing water of the stream. There was nothing I could say – I knew in my heart how she felt, but I tried not to show the misery, the misery of not being able to run towards her, and I pictured her brushing the stable yard, knowing the heartache she would feel alone there without me.

'Barbara stopped, bent down and took off her shoes. She rolled down her socks and slipped them off, giving a little shiver as she pointed her toes to test the water before stepping into the stream with a splash. We walked together hand in hand. The picnic basket was a little lighter on our return. We had left the birds to indulge on Charlotte's kindness.

' "You're miles away, Dennis," Barbara said, lifting her foot in the air before a trickle of water splashed lightly against me. I retaliated in fun, scooping up a handful of water. She ran off, laughing, missing the sprinkle of small drops of water that fell back into the stream.

' "Wait!" I shouted, cursing the basket that interfered with my run before I finally caught up.

'We sat on the bank, exhausted, yet full of laughter.

' "You tire me, Dennis, with all your energy," she gasped. I turned immediately and kissed her affectionately. "You do love me, don't you, Dennis?" she said.

' "Come on," I said, giving her a helping hand. She looked up towards me with a helpless expression. "Come on, Barbara," I said again, lifting her up and holding on to her until she found her balance.

' "Oh, Dennis," she said, as we slowly walked along.

' "Don't, Barbara, don't. It hurts me, too," I told her.

'She looked up at me and said, "Anyway, you'll hate it, hate it so much at St Vincent's that you'll run away straight

177

back into my arms. I'll look out for you every morning just in case. Just in case," she whispered. Aware of the view below us, she turned from my gaze and looked down at the old timber-framed roof of the barn.

'We helped each other down the hill. Barbara stopped, carrying her socks in one hand and, holding on to me with the other, she slipped on her shoes. The firm sound from her heels echoed along the empty courtyard towards the stables.

'I placed the basket down before following Barbara towards the horses.

' "I wonder if you'll ever ride him again," she said. "He's always been your favourite, hasn't he, Dennis?" she added, looking at me before hastily turning back. "Go, Dennis, go now," she told me. I looked startled but she continued, "Don't look back when you walk away. Please don't."

'I started to protest, but she stiffened her shoulder at my touch. "For God's sake, Dennis, just go," she begged. There was no look from her. Her back remained turned to me. "Go," she whispered, leaning her head against the horse's mane. Don't you know, Barbara, that this is the last thing I want to do, to leave, to leave you here alone without me, I wanted to scream.

'My biggest regret,' Uncle told me, leaning over and touching my hand, 'is that I kept those words deep inside before finally walking away.'

'Did you ever see her again?' I asked.

'You're racing me, my love. I need to go through those events in my mind. Without you listening to me they would be locked in for ever.'

I leaned over, struck a match against the hearth and

lit another cigarette. Uncle patted the cushion on my chair and beckoned me to lean back.

'We left by train later that day, Ernest, the servant and I, still and silent on the rugged journey through the mountains. I got bored looking through the murky glass at the views from the window. The loyal servant sat straight across from me. We glanced at each other from time to time, a stark reminder to us both that I would most probably be gone for quite some time. "You can use my bicycle until I return," I told him. The servant looked at me vacantly. I moved my hands, bending my arms stiffly as if I was holding onto the handlebars. Then, lifting my feet slightly off the ground, I moved them around like an idiot as if I was pedalling my bicycle. "You can ride it," I told him. He sat there, still with no excitement at my offer. "Don't pretend you don't know what I'm talking about, you old bugger. I caught you out last time. You'll probably be cycling around all over the bloody place as soon as you arrive back home.

' "Leave it, Dennis," Ernest said, "the man has little intelligence."

'I actually felt envious. Lucky bugger, I thought, sitting back against the seat wishing that I had none at all; then this trip would not have been necessary.

'Ernest must have read the newspaper a thousand times over, feeling secure with his nose looking down at every page, avoiding conversation. Even the odd cough I gave didn't distract him. I wonder how you're going to feel when you arrive back home and open that door, knowing that you will never hear the bell on my bicycle ring to let you know that I'm home, I thought, studying him as the train moved along into the darkness of the night. His feet inside tight-laced leather boots tapped against the dirty floor. I sat with pride and showed the courage of a man, knowing that the train struggling along through the mountains would eventually come to a halt.

'I obviously dozed off and was surprised that dawn had broken. A thick mist had gathered over the mountains. Ernest leaned over and peered through the window before checking the time on his watch. A flask of warm coffee was welcomed by him. The unsteady jerking of the train from side to side made the servant nervous as he poured it into the cup before passing it over. Ernest thanked him with an apparent choke in his voice; after all, he had barely spoken a word since our journey began.

'We came to a sudden halt. I, nervous of my destiny, stood up immediately. The small square basket fell over, leaving the contents rolling around the carriage.

'"Bloody railways," Ernest said. "We're not there yet, my man," Ernest told the servant, who by then was kneeling on the floor in a panic to put whatever had fallen from the basket back safely. A small grey pad remained unnoticed on the floor. I immediately bent down and picked it up. To my surprise, Ernest passed over to me from the inside pocket of his jacket, a tiny bronze pen as if he had read my thoughts. I immediately scribbled a message in large print and placed it on the reverse side, holding it up straight in front of my face.

'"Get on my bicycle on your return and deliver this to Barbara. Don't forget, you old bugger," I said to the servant. The servant smiled, ignorant once more of the words I had written.

' "Put the scribble away," Ernest said. "If you're going to write you haven't got long. I know who she is, Dennis. Her perfume still lingers." I didn't lift my head up to see the expression on his face, and pressed the nib of the pen against the paper.

*Dear Barbara,*
*My journey as I write continues. I feel no urgency to ask Ernest the time of my arrival, and I shudder with the thought of the train finally stopping at my destination, but at least I know in my heart…*

' "There is no time for sentiment, Dennis," Ernest told me as the train came to a stop, jolting me back into the seat. I stuffed the notepad deep down inside my trouser pocket and returned the pen, thanking Ernest before standing up.

'Steam from food cooking behind a tiny stall smelled delicious as we stepped down onto the platform. "A freshly baked chapatti and a bowl of soup," Ernest requested, insisting that it must be eaten quickly. I refused.

'The snow that capped the mountains held no fascination. The servant was allowed one minute to admire the view before joining us in the cart that was ready to take us to the school.

' "You'll be given an allowance, Dennis, at the end of each week. A small allowance, so don't be frivolous." On what, I thought. But for the cattle, the place was almost deserted as we moved higher up the mountain.

'"You'll make new friends, Dennis," Ernest said, "but I urge you to keep your mischievous side to yourself." At that specific time the servant broke wind. Ernest turned the opposite way. I wafted my hand up and down to embarrass him.

'"You've just farted," I told him.

'"Dennis, I won't have it," Ernest said. "It can happen to anyone. He's just as human as you and me." The servant, oblivious, smiled inanely.

'"I will reply almost immediately to any letters you write, Dennis." I looked at Ernest and nodded before he requested the driver to stop. I turned my head and looked up towards the huge monastery built upon the mountainside.

'"Is this St Vincent's?" I asked in a whisper, turning to look at Ernest.

'"It's not as bad as it looks, Dennis," he replied.

'I was ordered down from the carriage. "Keep those shoulders straight," Ernest told me as we walked the lengthy distance along the dusty pathway towards the main entrance of the building. We had finally arrived. As we walked through the barren doorway we were greeted by the Principal, who introduced himself as Father O'Connor. The thin layer of skin over his hands showed his age and his veins protruded as he shook first Ernest's hand and then mine. His Irish accent had clearly become weaker after years in India. He was a short, stubby man, bald at the top, his face fat and round, his eyes pale and blue, his complexion ghostly white, with barely a smile to welcome us. Draped in a black smock with just his toes peeping through his sandals, he suggested in a whisper

182

that Ernest leave immediately and remain silent to avoid any reaction from me.

'I sniffed up into the musty air before being introduced to a fellow pupil who was asked to show me along the ground floor to my room. Ernest had moved swiftly by then and my immediate response to turn and say goodbye was fruitless. I felt no confidence. The young man escorted me to my room in silence. I had forgotten his name on introduction and didn't ask to be reminded while he stood leaning with his back against the door that led into my room, and I hated the thought that this was going to be my only sanctuary.

'The grey painted room looked dismal. The bed was so low that it almost touched the stone floor. I sat on the thin mattress and jumped a little to test the springs. There were no pictures on the wall, just a wooden cross that hung at eye level on the narrow wall at the end of the bed, a reminder, I thought, each night before sleep, and each morning on awakening, of the presence of God.

' "I'll leave you to settle," the young man said. "Oh, by the way, I'm Sebastian, and you are?"

' "Dennis," I replied, shaking his long slender hand.

'After he had left, I ran along the corridor towards the main door just in case Ernest had had a change of heart and had returned to take me home. I was devastated and felt totally abandoned when I realised that he had already walked away from me.

'I turned, my legs weak with each step that I took, and walked back to my room in self pity. A heavy block of soap seemed to be my only luxury. I picked it up from a rather large steep bowl that lay in the corner of the room I now occupied. It had no scent. The narrow cracks of a split deep down inside gave me some indication of how long it had been lying there.

'A rumble of voices took my attention. I peeped out from the tall, narrow window at a gathering of boys before they eventually walked happily by, carrying cricket bats. I was soon left again in silence. I sat down on the edge of the bed with a feeling of unease, my head bowed in between my hands, and cried. "You can't hide me from the troubles of this world," I sobbed to myself, "to one day release me like a dove into a haven that doesn't exist. Ernest, why have you ... why have you sent me away?" I cried out, squeezing my hands together in frustration.

'There was a loud knocking on the pane of glass, which lasted several seconds.

' "Why are you not playing cricket? Everybody plays cricket here on Sundays," a croaky voice called. I lifted my head and immediately stood up, embarrassed, as a young man would be at having been caught taking pity on himself.

' "Open the window, lad," he called. I pushed as hard as I could but it still wouldn't budge. "Give it another push, lad," he urged. A gentle breath of air swept in, followed by numerous bugs. "Open it wider, lad," I was told. Chips of paint fell in fragments to the ground as I pushed the window with all my strength as wide as it would go. "This place will be rotting soon if it doesn't get the attention it needs," he said, inspecting the wooden framework. "And don't look at me with that expression of 'what does he want?', lad. I heard you wailing so I've come to see if it's you that wants something. Either you climb out through this window, or I'll climb in," he ordered. Slightly amused by his strong gesture, I took the offer and clasped my hand into his for support before scrambling through the open window.

' "Name's Edward Thompson, gardener. Come and lend me a hand. Grab hold of that spade," he told me. I quickly dusted myself down before he plunged it into my hand. "Ah, there's a nice little plot," he said to me, pushing a barrow filled with plants as I followed close by. "Come on, lad, get digging," he said as we came to a sudden halt. I started to dig where he pointed. "A bit deeper," he said, picking up a couple of plants and placing them carefully into the hole I had just dug. "I've been here for many years," he said, brushing his hands against the sides of his baggy overalls. "Not often I'll approach a lad, and many I've heard cry, but I've never heard a wail that sent out such a lonely message, and it tugged at my heart." It surprised me, I must say, to feel almost human again.

' "Don't feel sorry for me, Mr Thompson," I told him.

' "Life's too short to feel sorry for you, lad," he said as he walked away wheeling his barrow, expecting me to follow. To my surprise, I actually did. "Don't be scared of the place," Mr Thompson said, "it'll do you no harm."

'St Vincent's had a dark and gloomy presence, which sent a cold shiver down my spine. It was a long, quiet afternoon and I had no idea of where I was meant to be on that particular day. I stuck close by Mr Thompson. I dug and he did the planting along the narrow borders of the vast lawn. I wondered why he hadn't questioned me about my background, although if he had, would I have appreciated the intrusion?

185

' "Take those fags out of your pocket. He'll notice them straight way," Mr Thompson said. Confused, I immediately did as he asked and he grabbed them from my hand within a second.

' "Good afternoon, Father O'Connor," Mr Thompson said. The whispering breeze blew the cloak he was wearing, making it cling to his rather thin legs as he walked towards us.

' "I'm glad to see that you two have already met," said Father O'Connor. "Edward's been with us at St Vincent's since, well, ever since I can remember. Thanks to him we have the most beautiful gardens. Your trunk has been delivered to your room, Dennis, and a number of forms have been left on the desk with a pen at hand. You're given a choice of duties, three in all, either before or after lessons, which means that you check your timetable thoroughly before deciding."

' "Mr Thompson, may I be excused?" I asked.

' "There's no rush, Dennis," said Father O'Connor, "As long as they're on my desk first thing in the morning. Supper will be served at 6.30 p.m. in the dining hall each evening," he explained. I felt scared. Not with Father O'Connor's approach, or whether I should be helping Mr Thompson – I was just bloody well scared.

' "He's very proud of this place, isn't he, Mr Thompson?" I said, as Father O'Connor strolled slowly through the vast garden, leaving us behind.

' "So am I," he replied, kneeling down and burrowing his fingers deep inside the soil before bedding the last plant with pride.

' "I can't stand the place," I told him.

186

'Mr Thompson stood up sharply. "The air's much cooler now," he said, "so I'll be going yonder," he added, stretching out his arm to collect the spade. I loosened my grip from around the handle and passed it over. The squeak from his wheelbarrow grew fainter until he finally disappeared from view.

'I cursed myself on losing his friendship. "Damn," I said out loud as Mr Thompson left me standing there, making me realise how insensitive I had been in making such a bold comment. I wandered back alone in search of the open window that would lead me back to my room.

'The clouds had gathered low over the peaks of the snowy mountains, casting a grey shadow. I was desperate for a cigarette and, at that particular moment, would have accepted the risk of Father O'Connor finding them within my possession, had Mr Thompson not helped me avoid my first telling-off.

'I laughed out loud at myself for being such a coward as to allow Ernest to command, without any challenge from me, that here, here at St Vincent's, was where I should be. I also felt resentful towards Barbara for not advising me to put up a fight, and wondered if she really did love me. Why hadn't she run and begged me to stay, I thought, on that sunny afternoon when I quietly walked away. I felt frustrated at this war, this awful war that was going on in my mind. My chest felt tight and the grief for my mother had crept back into my thoughts. Grace, I silently cried, please guide me. I felt physically sick and knelt down on my hands and knees feeling an explosion from the back of my throat before vomiting. I threw up once more. Beads of sweat trickled down my forehead.

The sting from the back of my throat left me with quite an undesirable taste.

'Conscious of not wanting to attract any attention, I used all the strength left in my legs to stand up. Come on, Dennis, I told myself. Be strong; for God's sake, be strong. I felt weak with each step that I took along the dark, looming length of the building. Every window looked the same, tall and narrow. I listened to the squeak underneath my feet with each step that I took over the blades of moist grass before being distracted by an echo in the far distance of the constant clap of hands. I guessed that the game of cricket was finally over, which alerted me to move much faster in search of my room. It was easier than I thought as I discovered the remnants of the dried flaky paint that had dropped on Mr Thompson's request to open the window wider, still lying on the ground.

'I climbed back through the window and sat down once more on the edge of the bed. Drawn back to the window by the approaching hubbub, I peeped out and saw the same group of boys from earlier advancing like a shoal of fish, their bats swaying lightly from the movement of their steps as they walked happily by.

'I jumped from the sound of the internal bell ringing harshly in my ear. I looked down towards my wrist. The hands inside the tiny glass ring of my watch had stopped turning. The scurried footsteps along the corridor seemed to be heading in the same direction. Judging the time in my head, I realised that supper was probably ready. I felt reluctant to leave the safety of my room. My confidence was low and I wasn't going to make a spectacle of myself by wandering into the dining hall alone.

'I sighed at the thought of having to unpack. A short wooden rail screwed tightly against the wall held a few steel hangers. Not enough, I thought, pulling the trunk towards me before opening the curved lid. The packing was quite neat and I carefully picked up the top layer of shirts that had been perfectly pressed and folded. An envelope lay underneath and I recognised it from my own personal stationery. I ripped open the seal, pulling out the matching paper that was folded inside. Written in scribble, it read,

Mr Dennis,

This trunk of yours is half packed by now and I felt quite British allowing myself to write this letter to you – after all, the British are quite good at writing letters, aren't they, Mr Dennis?

'I immediately flicked my eyes down to the bottom of the paper to see who it possibly could have been from. Amazed, I carried on reading.

There isn't much to choose from in your wardrobe, so I'm packing the bloody lot, including a dirty pair of socks I found that you threw into the corner of your room. I'm going to miss the tricks you played on me, Mr Dennis, and the laughter I kept inside on seeing you jump every time Mr Ernest called for you. Your bicycle, if not used, will get rusty lying outside, so you don't mind if I ride it do you, Mr Dennis? I'll do a few spins and turns just like you did. Anyway, you old fart, as you always called me, enjoy your stay up in the mountains, and oh, by the way, just to let you know that in my school days I was top of the class in English, and I understood every bloody word you said, including the names you called me, so, as the British would say, Mr Dennis, up yours!

Your ever faithful servant, Bobo.

'The little bastard, I thought with amusement, conning me for all those years into believing that he never knew what the hell I was talking about. I shuddered at the thought of all those dreadful names I had called him. Addressing him as an old fart was a regular habit, and the cheek of his using my own lined paper to write to me. I laughed out loud. The little shit wasn't so stupid after all.

'A harsh knock at the door alerted me. I stood up immediately as the latch was lifted and Father O'Connor stood in the open doorway.

' "A whole plate of food has been wasted, Dennis, as you seem to have chosen not to dine. It won't happen again will it, Dennis?" Father O'Connor said with a frown. "And give yourself plenty of time to fill in the forms," he added before leaving.

'I was never allowed, while living at home, to call Bobo by his first name, but he had certainly amused me, especially when I found the socks which he had told me about in his letter at the bottom of my trunk. I laughed outwardly, hard and loud, imagining the little shit lying on top of my bed lighting one cigarette after another, courtesy of me, from the endless stubs I had left in the ashtray on my bedside table. I yearned to go back home and kick his arse.

'I sat down and began to fill in the forms with a biro.

I felt sure I would make some mistakes, but carried on regardless. My stomach frequently rumbled and by this time my eyes were starting to close. The adrenalin inside me had slowed down completely and I was ready to put my head down for the night so I signed my last signature ready to hand all the forms in the following morning. I folded back the blanket, ruffled my pillow, and soon fell asleep.

'I awoke feeling startled and sat up straight away. For a second I thought I was at home. Dawn had broken and reality hit me. I checked my watch. The fingers hadn't moved. Releasing it from my wrist, I shook it a couple of times and held it up against my ear to listen. Frustrated, I threw it along the bed and shot up. I felt the grit underneath my bare feet as I walked towards the door. I opened it slightly and peeped out, looking both ways along the empty corridor. I returned and grabbed my soap bag that lay among my clothing inside my trunk. I hadn't checked its contents, confident that what I needed would have been met. I crept out quietly into the long wide corridor in search of the washroom.'

# Chapter 5

Listening to Uncle was quite pleasing, and what did time matter? Poor Uncle Dennis, old and frail, had at last got a welcoming ear to reminisce to, but my thoughts, unknown to him, kept leading me back to the dark, gloomy days at Rose Cottage. As Uncle continued his story, telling me about the grim, cold washroom, walking in alone to the drip of water that fell into the dark, yellow-stained sink, I remembered Lily creeping through the open window of her bedroom with a bundle of clothes squashed underneath her arm, balancing herself along the flat roof. She held on to the drainpipe to guide herself down while carefully placing one foot after the other in the crevices between the bricks, giving me a final wave when her feet touched the ground. I continued to wave, hanging as far as I could out of the window, desperate for one more glance. Lily had escaped, leaving the haunted life of Rose Cottage behind her.

As I thought of her, I could smell the fragrance of Blue Grass and pictured Lily leaning against her battered old dressing table, dropping the scent onto her fingers, smiling at me in the mirror before dabbing gently behind her ears.

\* \* \*

'I slipped endlessly after stripping down and standing on the cracked stone base of the shower,' Uncle continued, 'trying desperately to work up a lather with the hard block of soap as I stood underneath the trickle of cold water. My wet feet flapped against the stone floor. Collecting the heap of clothing, I hurried along the corridor, shivering, and headed back towards my room. I sat hunched on the edge of my bed with only a towel wrapped around my waist and wept silently inside for my mother's loving touch. My hatred was purely for Ernest and my understanding of why Grace wandered in her married life didn't surprise me. Ernest was a cold, unemotional man.

'The bell rang again, this time slightly softer. I quickly dressed, slipping my feet through my sandals on the way out. I rushed along the corridor in the same direction as the patter of footsteps that had faded into the distance. Remembering Father O'Connor's abrupt manner the previous evening, I was anxious to be in the dining hall on time.

'I was completely embarrassed as a hall full of boys peered up towards me as I was turned away and ordered by the priest standing in the open doorway to go to the third floor, the top floor of the building, to be fitted with a uniform.

'I knocked once and waited. The door opened and I was invited in. It was a stuffy, poky room high up in the loft. I was measured by a gaunt-looking old man.

' "My hands aren't as steady as they used to be," he told me with a tremor in his voice. I immediately bent down and picked up the frayed measuring tape that he had suddenly dropped. I sneezed from the dust that filtered through the air as he lifted a light grey blazer from a hanger that was squeezed among others on a rack and shook it vigorously before opening it out. I turned on his instruction and slipped my arm into the sleeve.

' "That'll do," he told me, taking a step back. "Trousers," he said, slowly wrapping the measure around my waist. "There isn't much meat on you, son," he said as he checked my measurements through the half-moon glasses that rested on the end of his nose.

'We settled on the smallest size, which still left rather a large gap around my waist, so the old man threw me a pair of braces he had rooted out from an old set of drawers. "These will hold them up," he said, adjusting them so that the trousers stopped several inches above my ankles. "Start getting some food down you and you'll soon fit into them."

'I looked up towards the built-in rails as I clipped the braces around the band of my trousers. They were crammed with second-hand uniforms and I wondered, as I slipped on a well-worn shirt, if its previous owner had felt as I was feeling while standing there in that room, donning his uniform for the first time.

'My collar was lifted and a dark, thin, blue and white striped tie was placed round my neck. "You're done, lad," he said as I made a knot and pushed the tie up to cover the top button of my shirt before stretching the elastic of my braces until they fitted perfectly over my shoulders. I thanked him for his assistance as I lifted up the latch to the door.

' "Here," he said, "you're forgetting these." He handed

me the clothes I had been wearing. "Mr Hardman," he said, offering me his frail hand.

' "Dennis," I replied, shaking it with a gentle grip.'

A tear unexpectedly rolled down my cheek.

'Is it Lily?' Uncle asked, leaning over to touch my hand.

'Yes,' I replied, shrugging my shoulders in disbelief. 'Sorry,' I whispered.

Uncle squeezed my wrist gently. There was a barrier of silence with just the sound of the ticking clock. Uncle gave a slight cough and waited a second or two.

'Why don't you come back to London and finish your book? At least consider it. I won't ask you again, but I have an old desk and there are plenty of ashtrays, and there'll be a never-ending stream of coffee by your side.'

Again, there was a brief silence. I felt my writing was useless and the thought of putting pen to paper was a million miles away.

'Did Lily ever write to you?' I asked Uncle.

'Well, only occasionally,' he replied.

'Do you still have her letters, Uncle?'

'Somewhere. Most likely up in the attic.' I looked towards him, inquisitively. 'No, there wasn't much said in them. She would always race from one thing to another, as if someone at any time was going to snatch the pen from her hand.'

'She'd obviously written them from Rose Cottage,' I remarked, glancing towards the mantelpiece where her photo stood. Uncle looked up too, and sighed.

'Will you—'

Uncle stopped me. 'Yes, of course I'll let you read them. I'll search for them when I return and when I find them I'll post them to you immediately, unless, of course, you change your mind about coming back with me. But you must promise that they'll be returned because Lily was precious to me, too. In fact most of my memories, of one thing or another, are up in that dark little room.'

'Do you think you will ever fall in love again?' I asked. Uncle looked puzzled. 'Is it such a strange question for me to ask?' I said as his expression deepened.

'I am still in love,' he replied.

'With the past, Uncle.'

'Meaning what?' he asked.

'Barbara.'

Uncle laughed, but answered with an open heart. 'I would find it quite impossible not to be. She'll be old and grey now, but I'll tell you something, I would know her instinctively. There have been other women in my life, of course, but the difference is, I never fell out of love with Barbara. So deep rooted are my feelings that I can never let her go, hence the lonely old man sitting with you and enjoying your company on this lovely evening.

'Anyway, talking of Barbara, I was jolly glad she couldn't see me on that morning up in the loft at St Vincent's, with Mr Hardman, riddled with arthritis, dressing me in my uniform. I did end up looking rather ridiculous. With a stroke of luck, after thanking him once more for his help, I remembered I had to hand in my forms.'

I knelt down while Uncle carried on talking, lifted the poker and began to play with the tiny embers that were left inside the iron grate.

'Is it time for me to shut up?' he asked.

I turned and smiled. 'Of course not, Uncle,' I replied, sitting myself back down in the chair.

'I felt slightly frightened,' he continued, 'as I pulled at the uniform, trying to make it feel more comfortable before eventually finding the correct door with Father O'Connor's name imprinted on a brass plaque. I tugged on my tie. The knot was far too tight but I didn't dare undo it in case, at that precise moment, the door opened and I was confronted by Father O'Connor. The formality of knocking on his door and waiting scared me even more. I shuffled through the papers, before standing, shoulders straight, head held high, and knocked once more. I leaned my head close up to the door, having thought I heard a voice calling. I wasn't sure as I looked down towards the handle.

'"Come in," he bellowed. I quickly opened the door and entered his office.

'"Leave them there," he said, directing me with his eyes. I found myself tiptoeing over to his desk, where he sat scrutinising every word from a paper he was reading, and I placed them carefully down on the top corner. He coughed sharply on my way out. I turned. He sat in the same position, head bowed, reading intensely. Relieved that my attention wasn't needed, I tiptoed out, closing the door quietly behind me. I had thought of escaping, following any road out in the hope that it would eventually lead me back home, as I walked along the silent corridor. Would I be strong enough to challenge Ernest about my decision? If I did return home, only to be sent back like a little boy, I couldn't suffer the humiliation. Neither, I thought, could I suffer my stay as a student there, choked in the miserable atmosphere of St Vincent's.

'My footsteps echoed as I entered the almost deserted dining hall. My breakfast was noticeably waiting and I sat down to a plate of cold scrambled eggs. A young man was sitting with legs crossed next to the table opposite and tapping his fingers at an annoyingly fast rate on the top of the table cover. I scooped a rather large amount of eggs onto my fork, chewing on the undesirable taste, and swallowed while glaring at his discomforting presence. I took a sip of water and pulled my face at the tepid temperature, much to the amusement of the young man. He stood up and walked towards me, picked up the tiny glass salt cellar and sprinkled it over the remains of my breakfast.

' "Don't mind if I join you, do you?" he asked, pulling out a chair and sitting down. "After all, I have to escort you to class so you'd better hurry and eat that horrid stuff. I'm afraid it won't look good on your first day if you're too late. I'm Robin," he said in well-spoken English, looking horrified as I quickly devoured the lot.

' "I was bloody hungry," I told him, standing up.

' "British, obviously," he said before asking for my name.

' "Dennis," I told him as I wiped the corners of my mouth with my hand and began to follow him, a step behind. "Bloody well wait for me," I called, as he hastened his step.

'The classroom door was quickly opened.

' "Sit there," he told me, moving me along a narrow bench before sitting beside me. He picked out a long wooden pen, brushing his finger along the nib.

' "Brand new," he said, passing it to me. "The ink's there," he muttered, pointing to the tiny bowl that slotted into a hollow in the top right hand corner of the desk. A long length of plain white paper was passed along the desks. "That's Father Michael, an expert in Latin," he whispered to me, nodding towards the portly figure standing at the front of the class. Robin then folded the paper that had been handed to him, pressing his finger hard along the centre, causing a minor distraction from fellow pupils as he ripped it in half.

' "You don't understand, do you?" he asked, leaning slightly towards me.

' "What?" I whispered.

' "What he's written on the board. I didn't at first," he told me, "but just copy exactly what he's written onto the paper in front of you, and look straight over at him with interest when he talks; then he'll think you're knowledgeable on the subject, otherwise he'll make a scapegoat out of you for the rest of the bloody idiots sitting in front."

'The sheet of blotting paper had been well used with print stains covering either side.

' "Stop fussing," Robin whispered, as I struggled with my pen. "Clamp your hand tightly over it. If it comes out a bloody mess at the other end there's nothing you can do about it but pray."

' "Why do you keep looking at me?" he whispered as I glanced a couple of times towards him. "If you want to know how many spots I have on my face, I have three in all."

*Are you gay?* he scribbled while Father Michael gave a lesson of high-pitched drama by reading out the lines from a theatrical book.

*Is he right in the head?* I scribbled back, on Father Michael's finishing line, which was followed by the sound of clapping hands. *And no, I'm not, are you?* I wrote. He leaned over and smudged his finger over the wet ink where I had just written. Father Michael belched loudly before bowing once more over his enormous stomach for more applause.

' "Aahh, a new boy," Father Michael said, approaching us slowly.

' "Don't start making conversation with him," Robin whispered. "We've got to move fast for our next lesson and, anyway, he'll bore you to death. His nickname's Belching Bubbles. You'll see why in a minute," he told me.

'Father Michael stood close up. There was no formality of a handshake as he stood with both hands clasped behind his back. His breath smelled quite strongly of stale onion as he welcomed me into the house of St Vincent's before telling me its history. Robin nudged me as tiny frothy bubbles appeared around the corners of his mouth while he spoke of his love for the place with enthusiastic excitement.

' "I look like Charlie Chaplin in these damn trousers," I told Robin, leaving Father in his eccentric world with our apologies on the need to leave immediately.

' "Stand still," he said, stepping out into the corridor and moving a few steps along before stopping and turning towards me. His hysterical laughter echoed around me. I wasn't amused. He held his breath and apologised before leaning against the wall and roaring once more at their ridiculous length. "They don't even reach your ankles," he told me. His laughter, while coughing in between, became quite uncontrollable. "Where are you going?" he called as I swiftly walked away. "You're going in the wrong direction. It's this way," he shouted with the sound of laughter still in his voice.

'I wasn't going to have the piss taken out of me and had decided to go back up into the loft and complain quite harshly to Mr Hardman over his mistake on my measurements.

'"Where are you going?" Robin called again as I left him standing in the distance. I could hear his footsteps as he came running towards me. I was stopped by a fierce grip around my upper arm. "Our next lesson, which, might I say we are already late for, is in completely the opposite direction," he told me. I carried on walking with his grip still firm, pushing hard with every step I took while he clung on to me. "Look, I'm head boy and you'll do what I bloody well say."

'"Fuck off," I told him.

'"This is my very last day here," he said, "so don't be a bastard with me. I'm leaving tomorrow. I didn't want the job in the first place," he said.

'"What job?" I asked, rubbing the top of my arm on his release.

'"Of fucking about with you," he grumbled.

'"I'm sure this place has done you a power of good, Robin. After all, I wouldn't say that you're a prime example, and under the roof of God," I tutted, walking away.

'"Meaning?" he said, tripping over himself as he followed alongside me.

'"Well, your repeatedly filthy language for one," I told him.

' "You've no room to talk," he answered.

' "I'm not head boy," I told him, walking away.

' "You provoked me, you bastard," he called after me. Maybe he was right, I thought, deliberately tutting once more at his language.

' "Look," Robin said, catching me up and pulling once again on my arm, "we have a certain dislike for one another, just accept it, but if we miss this next lesson completely, well ... well, how do I explain to Father O'Connor?" he pleaded.

' "Tell him you went to fuck yourself," I told him, pulling my arm away.

' "You stubborn bastard," Robin called as I walked on, leaving quite a distance between us. "You don't know where the fuck you're going," he yelled.

' "Makes two of us," I called, turning my head in his direction.

'I had climbed the second staircase and reached the third corridor and was relieved that I hadn't passed any students, looking as ridiculous as I did. It would have been most embarrassing.

' "I want an apology," Robin called, running along the corridor before catching up with me. "You won't get rid of me that easily," he said as I jumped up the last two steps. I knocked hard on Mr Hardman's door. Robin, looking frustrated and rather breathless, stood by my side shoving his hands abruptly inside his trouser pockets.


The pain of Lily's cries came back to me. I tried to rid my mind of the haunting memories that swirled around inside my head while accepting Uncle's kind offer to make one last coffee for both of us. He complained of his aching bones as he slowly rose to his feet. 'I'll make it, Uncle,' I said, on seeing his discomfort.

'No, I need the exercise,' he told me, heading for the kitchen. 'I've spotted some cream,' he called above the rattle of the fridge door opening. 'We've still plenty of whisky left; how about an Irish coffee?'

'Sounds good to me,' I replied, resting my head back against the chair.

I fought hard not to remember, but the ghost of the past had crept back in, and the sound of Lily being beaten echoed around me. The strap of the belt was harsh. Burying my head beneath the pillow, I counted the seconds before the strap was once more whipped down against her helpless body and damned the thought that I, a helpless child, had no power to defend her. I could only bear the pain that Lily must have felt. She never spoke as later that evening I tiptoed along the dark landing, peeping through the partly open door of her bedroom. She knew I was there – Lily knew. Her silent tears rolled down her face. I tiptoed quickly back into the bedroom I shared with my brothers and knelt down, grasping hold of the round plastic bottle from underneath the bed I slept in. I knew I didn't have the wisdom of words that might have comforted her as I crept back to her room. I carefully lifted the top of the lid from the bottle, stirred the liquid with the small plastic stick, and began to blow tiny bubbles up into the air through its hollow ring. Lily looked at me with pain in her eyes but managed to give a little smile as a tinted bubble burst on the end of her nose. The liquid finally gone and all the bubbles blown, I stepped up two rungs of the ladder to the bunk where she lay and covered the ruffled blanket lightly over her petite body, blew her a kiss, and left, gently closing the door behind me.

A lump came into my throat as I remembered the next afternoon, when Lily climbed through the open window of her bedroom. I wept constantly that day as I knelt against the narrow window ledge. My dreams of her companionship were shattered as I watched her go. She had found her wings and the courage to fly to freedom.

Lily's absence only came to Mummy's notice a few days later. I was called down from my bedroom and I remember being looked upon with suspicion. I was told to stand straight and still on the tiny rug that lay against the hearth.

' "Where is she?" Mummy shouted, looking directly at me. "Don't pretend you don't know, you little bitch. When did she go?" I fell sideways with the sharp slap of her hand stinging the side of my face. "Tell me, when did she go, and where?" My tiny body burned like a furnace inside. I wanted to shout that I was glad that Lily had left Rose Cottage for good. "You can stand there for as long as it takes," Mummy said, "until I get an answer from you, you deceitful bitch."


'Goodness, what's that awful frown for?' Uncle asked as he came back into the room holding two rather large Irish coffees. 'It's me, isn't it, chunnering on?' he said, passing me a glass. 'At least the cream hasn't sunk,' he commented, feeling proud as he settled back into his chair next to me with his. 'Sorry, my love, I have gone on rather too much,' he said, taking a sip and complimenting himself on the taste, which consisted of more than the usual amount of whisky.

'No, Uncle, don't stop,' I answered. 'I'd like you to carry on. Did you and Robin, well, did you finally become friends? And Mr...'

'Mr Hardman,' Uncle reminded me.

'Yes. Did he offer to change those ghastly trousers you wore on your first day at St Vincent's?'

'What's bothering you?' Uncle asked, looking at me with concern. 'I can sense it in your voice. I just feel there's something more, something apart from Lily's death, and that worries me.'

I fought so very hard at that moment to hold back the tears, yet was unable to stop the few that trickled down my face. 'Please, Uncle, carry on with your story.' I was aware that my voice was faltering. 'Please, Uncle,' I asked again, turning my head to one side and wiping my hand gently across my face.

'Well, if you're sure,' Uncle said. 'This is bloody good,' he added, encouraging me to take another sip of my coffee. He was right, it was good. 'It'll warm you up if nothing else,' he added, 'and, yes, at last a decent pair of trousers was found for me.'

Uncle stopped and looked towards me. Satisfied that I was a little more relaxed, he carried on.

' "You startled me," Mr Hardman said as I lifted the latch and entered the room. He peered at me through a pair of half-moon glasses as I pointed towards my ankles. "They're far too short. I look ridiculous," ' I told him.

'Mr Hardman was sitting at a rather old single desk with a slanting lid. It was positioned under a tiny square window that gave just enough light for him to guide his pen, and was so tiny I wondered how on earth he managed to sit behind it. He got himself into a state and left the letter he was writing. "It's not often I make a mistake," he said, reaching for the pole and searching along a rack of tightly packed trousers. "Catch hold," he said, passing a pair down to me from his pole.

'I stripped down to my underwear and quickly slipped them on.

' "Here's another pair," he said as I quickly shook my head.

' "Try these."

'We were getting nowhere, I thought, looking at the floor that was strewn with trousers of different lengths. I sighed out loud.

' "Yes, I feel the same," he said, pausing.

' "Dennis," I said, "my name's Dennis."

' "Yes, yes, I don't need prompting; I hadn't forgotten. Try these on," he said, picking out one of the last pairs that remained on the rail. They nearly reached my toes, but they were the best pair yet.

' "We'll pin the bloody things," he muttered, leaning down against the floor and fumbling to place the pins through the material that he had doubled over. I was asked to strip down again and pass the trousers to him. I admired his expertise at what seemed to me, at that time, a pretty complicated piece of machinery as Mr Hardman sat at his sewing machine spinning the black cotton onto the spool and then, with the help of a magnifying glass, eventually threading the cotton through the eye of the needle. With a steady hand he turned the wheel.

' "Won't be long, Dennis," he said without a glance as I stood rubbing the chill that I felt around my bare legs.

' "Right, young man, step into these." I nearly stumbled in the rush to dress. "Steady," he said, holding his fragile looking arm out for support. I was surprised at him finding the patience to help after all that he had done. He clipped the braces around my waistband and I hoisted the elastic up towards my shoulders, squeezing one arm through and then the other. He gave a little smile at my generous thanks as I left his room once more.

'I jumped at the sight of Robin crouched against the floor outside, his head resting against the wall with a furious look on his face. "Want a hand up?" I asked in a jovial manner. My offer was refused as he got to his feet, brushed himself down and cursed underneath his breath.

' "Lessons are finished for the morning," he said, standing still and checking his watch, making sure that I noticed the thick band of gold that fitted tightly around his wrist. "After all that you'd better get changed. We all have our afternoon duties to do and you're on your own for these. I, of course, stay in uniform; the library isn't exactly what you'd call work, is it? And please don't forget," he said with sarcasm in his voice as we started to walk, "evening meal is at 6.30 prompt. I'll ignore you, of course; as if you don't exist. No one puts me through a day like you have. You've certainly earned no respect from me. Anyway," he added, stopping halfway along the wide corridor, "thanks for a lovely day in your pleasant company." He pulled one hand out of his blazer pocket before sweeping it through his head of thick blond hair, then strode away.

'I slowly made my way down the staircase towards the ground floor and wandered back in the direction of my room feeling almost hollow inside. I didn't much care whether or not I found it. There was no mistake as I opened the door with some caution. The lid of the trunk was still open and the scattering of clothes identified that these belongings were mine. I pushed the door closed. There was no eagerness as I undressed slowly with nothing to attract my attention as I stared around the blank, bare walls. There was little choice of suitable clothing for my duties ahead as I lightly kicked the scattered clothing around my feet before choosing a pair of fawn, linen trousers. I had worn these on my arrival, which I found it hard to acknowledge had only been yesterday. I felt as though I had been here for ever.

'The room was stuffy, so much so that I scrambled towards the window, half dressed and zipping up my flies, and pushed hard against it with the palm of my hand. My face became hot and flushed as I tried to open it. My adrenalin was low but with a little more effort the window finally opened. I sighed with relief, leaned out my head and breathed in the mild, damp air.

' "Knew it," a voice said. I leaned out, wondering where it was coming from. A few moments later a spade was leant against the outer wall. I took hold of Mr Thompson's offered hand and clambered through the open window. "Step into these," he said as he walked over to his barrow and held out a pair of clogs.

'Within seconds I felt the squelch of the grass beneath my feet as I walked the short distance. "You'll be glad of them," I was told as he noticed the expression on my face while I was trying them on. I looked at him in surprise. "Well, I knew you wouldn't come back to me, not of your own free will anyway, so I put a good word in to Father O'Connor's ear. You'd have only ended up in that hot kitchen scrubbing." he said.

' "Why?" I asked.

'Mr Thompson lifted his barrow and looked straight ahead. "I had to think of some way to give you those fags back. Get them out of my pocket, lad, and there's the matches too. Now go away over yonder while I prune this rosemary."

'I wandered off into the distance with a smile on my face. For some reason he actually liked me, even though my previous comments about St Vincent's were not received with his approval. I wondered as I sat down on the grass completely out of view, how on earth we would get on together working side by side, with me loathing the place which he dearly loved.

'I became a little dizzy after striking up and lighting a cigarette and taking one large drag. I blew the smoke high up into the air and thought of Barbara. The thought of being away from her seemed almost impossible. Me up here, surrounded by mountains and the almost claustrophobic atmosphere. God, I missed her.

'I caught sight of a beautiful lake below. Its waters were still and silent. I imagined fishermen casting their nets, chanting across to one another on their tiny boats, waiting patiently to haul in their catch. I cast my mind back to

Barbara, to our usual embrace before the sun would set, and then leaving on my bicycle, whistling with happiness along the winding lane for home.

'"Christ, you scared me," I shouted, standing up immediately as an old nanny goat appeared from beneath the bracken. I watched her wander up into the hills, a freedom that I longed to be mine. I hurled the stub of my cigarette down the steep embankment and sighed at the thought of returning under the huge shadow that St Vincent's held. Reluctantly slipping my hands inside my trouser pockets, I turned to make the short journey back.

'"Ah, you're back, lad," Mr Thompson called as he wiped his hand across his face. I noticed he had a quiver in his voice. "Bloody clippers," he said out loud. "The times these things are bloody oiled and cleaned. I'll have to request a new set. Well, stop staring at me, lad; there's work to be done." His voice was tense as he bent his thumb and finger through the ring of his clippers once more before sending a few more slender branches to the ground. It was obvious that he had been quite upset during my short absence.

'"Mr Thompson—" I began.

'"Don't ask, lad, just pick up the foliage and stick it in my barrow." I was filled with curiosity. My self pity had gone for that moment and I actually felt concerned. I took a deep breath and wondered what could reduce a man like this to tears. "Well, how did your day go?" he asked.

'"Not good," I answered.

'"Why's that?" he asked as he continued clipping. "Not made any friends?"

' "No, Mr Thompson," I replied.

' "Goodness, why? The place is full of young men," he said. I told him I'd spent the morning with the head boy, Robin.

' "You mean you were under the wing of Robin McIntosh? Say no more, lad," he said, knowingly. He inspected the leaves closely before handing me the clippers. "These all need a good spray," he said. "Still homesick?" he asked.

' "Yes, very," I told him.

' "Come on, lad," he said smiling, and we moved off to another part of the grounds.

'Mr Thompson explained that they grew all their own vegetables as I stared at the masses of them as we walked by an enormous plot. We got on quite well together, although not a lot of conversation was exchanged that afternoon. There seemed to be a comfortable silence as we worked side by side. I felt slightly scared as a group of priests in hooded gowns walked closely together with barely any sound from their footsteps. "They're only young men," Mr Thompson said as I stood and watched them walk by along the stony path and out of view. "But they've chosen to live their lives under God's roof. Anyway, come on, lad, you push it this time," he added.

'I held the two handles of the wheelbarrow and pushed until the wheel turned. "It's harder than I thought," I told him as I tried to manoeuvre it over the bumpy ground.

' "We're about finished," he said, looking up towards the thick, dusky clouds that were gathering. "Just as well. Glad to be able to soak my blistering feet inside a tub of hot water. What are your plans, lad?" he asked. I told him I was going to write to my father. He seemed surprised that I wasn't going to join in the usual activities. It was Tuesday, which Mr Thompson told me was crib night, but I told him I wouldn't be much company at such a gathering as I was rather tired.

'"Just a word of advice," he said as we made our way back. "Important too, lad," he added. "There's no other way I can say it so I'll get right to the point," he said as we continued walking. "Don't open your window during the night if you – Well, what I'm trying to say is," he said, clearing his throat, "if you're caught short, don't piss out of the window. Father O'Connor knows if anyone... well, you know... on the grass. It eventually starts to discolour it. Many a boy has been caught and held by the scruff of the neck. He'll do the same to you, so be warned."

'I was quietly amused at his foundering approach to the subject, his face flushed as he pushed that barrow hard against the uneven ground.

'"We'll empty most of that plot tomorrow so there'll be no feeling sorry for yourself lying awake in that bed all night. You'll need all the energy you can muster," he added, pointing over to the back entrance of the school. "Take those clogs off before you step in," he called as we parted company. I raised my hand up into the air to acknowledge what he had said.

'I could hear the faint sound of the bell ringing as soon as I entered the building, and I rushed through, clogs in hand, past hook after hook of cloaks and gowns. It was pretty dark in there, quite eerie. There was no air and a stale smell lingered. Glad of reaching the opposite side, I fiddled in the darkness for the touch of the latch. It was rather stiff and I had to use some force before it lifted. I flung open the door to a much stronger tone before the chimes of the bell slowly died. I ran towards a group of boys who were slowly moving forward and pushed my way through, leaving them jeering at me as I ran as fast as I could along the corridor until, finally, although slightly out of breath, I arrived outside the door of my room. I was aware there was no lock, which did disturb me, and as I rushed in I decided I would move my bed across the door to block any intrusion there might be after I had retired for the evening. I changed quickly into my uniform before walking calmly towards the dining hall.

'My bitter feelings towards Ernest remained uppermost in my mind, which took away some of the friction I felt at being ignored on my entrance through the open doors of the dining hall. Everyone had gathered around Robin. Spotting a table not too far away, I helped myself to a deep bowl of thick lentil soup, grabbed a roll of bread and sat down humbly on the long, narrow bench with only myself for company. Their chatter was of no importance to me. I searched my mind as to how to express in words my true feelings to Ernest. I cursed while trying to catch hold of the spoon, which slipped from my hand and crashed hard onto the stone surface of the floor. I didn't look up as the hall went silent, but continued to break the bread until it was moist enough to eat. All eyes must have been upon me as I swallowed, cringing at the bitter taste. I felt quite offended listening to the sudden burst of laughter, no doubt at Robin's sick sense of humour. "Hey, new boy, you've dropped something on the floor,"

Robin called with sarcasm as they all huddled in a group and moved forward. He stopped and suddenly kicked the spoon from underneath the table before picking it up and placing it harshly on top of the wooden surface. I tried not to flinch as he couldn't resist the temptation of spinning it around, to the amusement of his fans, while I ripped off another chunk of bread and dipped it very calmly into the bowl of soup without one glance towards him. I didn't admire myself for my composure, sitting there like a fool while he took the piss out of me in front of his selective audience before they wandered casually out through the open doors.

'I tried to swallow the churned up bread inside my mouth but I simply couldn't. I spat it out into the bottom of the bowl and made the long, solemn walk back to my room. Little did Bobo, our loyal servant, know that he had brought an unexpected smile to my face as I sat hunched on the edge of my bed and read through his letter once more, and thought how surprised he would feel if he knew just how much I missed him.

'There was no letter written to Ernest that night. Exhausted, I lay fully dressed on top of the bed and awoke to my surprise the following morning to the musical stroke of the bell. Alerted by its signal, I ran along to the washroom, dreading any inspection as I splashed my face with cold water, especially from Father O'Connor, who certainly wouldn't have appreciated the fact that I had slept through the night in my uniform.

'I took a huge breath and entered the dining hall, squinting as the morning sun beamed through the arched windows along the length of the inner wall.

' "You've been put on the list for a game of cricket."
Unable to see clearly in the distance, I recognised Robin's
voice. "It's my last game before I leave," he called. "The
boys have suggested it, haven't you?" he said, listening to
the hum of voices in agreement. "As long as you don't
drop the ball; that is, if you get a chance to throw it.
After all, we know what you're like with just a spoon in
your hand," he goaded.

'It was hard to ignore his sarcasm and I trembled as I
served myself a small portion of scrambled egg from a
huge steel drum, which happened to be the only food on
offer. I peeped down into a large steel jug and sniffed
the aroma of apples and, without haste, filled a glass
almost to the top, sipping a tiny amount as I made my
way to the first available table that I could find. Sitting
down with my back deliberately against the peering crowd,
this time it was I who sprinkled the salt freely on top of
the sloppy breakfast in front of me and cringed at the
taste before quickly swallowing as Robin and his entourage
walked past. Robin turned and walked back towards me,
allowing himself to believe that the pleasure of sprinkling
some pepper would bring amusement, as it certainly did.
I sneezed frantically while he tipped the pot and shook
it all around me and my food. I felt choked inside, listening
to their laughter disappearing into the background as they
left. I became almost desperate, desperate to get away
from the place, and ran back to my room in quite a
panic.

'I stripped off my uniform, crying bitterly at my misfortune
for ever being sent there. I hurled my belongings into
the trunk and slammed the lid down with fury. The patter

on the window distracted me. I turned my head towards it, my eyes a blur, before turning back and dragging my trunk halfway across the jagged surface of the floor.

' "Open the bloody window, Dennis," Mr Thompson called. Ignoring him, I pulled the door open and dragged my trunk a little further, wedging it open with just enough space to get me through.

' "Get out of my way," I shouted as Mr Thompson appeared, stretching his arm and resting his hand firmly against the open door. My emotions left me weak and I found myself walking backwards until I perched myself down on the side of the bed. He stood silently as I bowed my head and wept.

' "Hey, lad, come on. You've got goose pimples all over those skinny legs of yours," he said. I didn't look up. I didn't want to as I listened to the lid of my trunk being opened. "Before you run off anywhere," Mr Thompson said, throwing a pair of trousers over to me, "let's go and have a fag together."

'I tried not to look surprised although I was shocked at his remark. To share the pleasure of such a bad habit with the likes of Mr Thompson was quite unthinkable. "Don't, Mr Thompson, don't," I said, sitting with my head bowed.

' "Get those bloody trousers on or I'll dress you myself," I was told quite firmly. "Come on, lift that head up from below your knees. We're going for a long walk," he said.

'The window was opened and I listened to him breathing in the morning air while I dressed. He didn't turn, giving me time to compose myself. Grateful that no words were spoken, I lifted the lid of my trunk and picked out a white cotton T-shirt that Bobo had pressed and folded, slipped it over my head and leaned over, rooting further into the trunk until I found an old pair of webbed sandals lying at the bottom. The buckles rattled softly as I fastened the straps around my ankles.

'I coughed in order to give a signal to Mr Thompson that I was ready.

' "Right," he said, "let's go and get some real air into our lungs, although I don't suppose these will help," he added, taking out a packet of cigarettes from inside his pocket before climbing through the window with instructions for me to follow. "Lucky I've got the morning off ... I presume you have too," he said.

'I was strolling along a few paces behind him when he yelled for me to move a little faster. He waited until I had caught up before walking with long strides over the hill in the same rhythm. Once out of sight of the school, he sat down, enjoying the peace and beauty of the view below and the comfort of a cigarette. A grass snake moved swiftly, bending and turning through the thick blades of grass. I dropped my cigarette in fright. Mr Thompson was amused and leaned over to pick it up.

' "Let's get off, lad," Mr Thompson said, getting to his feet. "You're frustrated, I can tell. Take a deep breath," he told me as we walked together side by side. We both stopped as Mr Thompson allowed himself time to scrutinise one of the many tall monuments. I stood and stared.

'There was a mixed chorus of cheers, claps and boos whispering through the air. Mr Thompson noticed my distraction. "Play cricket?" he asked.

' "No, not really," I told him.

' "Well, that's no answer. Do you or don't you?" he demanded.

' "No, I dare say I don't," I replied, my attention once again diverted by the applause. We were standing by the dusty statue of a grim-faced man, his hands locked together. Mr Thompson looked towards me and asked if I could read the Latin inscription on the stone and I told him I couldn't.

' "No, neither can I," he said, sighing in disappointment as we wandered further along. "You know, Dennis, nothing is easy in this life; you just need to learn to adjust. Do you really want to wake up each day to live in misery?" he asked. I started to reply but he ignored any possibility of listening to my pleas, shielding his eyes with his hand from the sharp rays of the sun as he strolled along. I quickly followed.

' "What happened this morning, lad?" he asked as we walked side by side once more. I looked quite puzzled. "In that dining hall. Don't dare say nothing did because that's where you ran from. I caught a glimpse of you through those windows. I could sense the panic in you as you brushed past those tables in your hurry to get out. Well?" he said.

'I told him it was nothing, just a tease.

' "At what?" he asked. Then he told me to walk on as he had a few plants that needed checking over. I stood and looked at him. "I'll catch up, I promise," he told me.

'There was no other way to go but forward towards the cricket pitch. Thankfully, the game was well under way. All eyes, including mine, were on the ball as it spun around in the air before striking with force against the bat with a loud crack, followed by uproar as the catch was narrowly missed.

'My mind went back to my childhood games of street cricket in Calcutta. I laughed to myself at how we would group together. Whoever owned the ball would have the privilege of giving the orders and the bat was anything you could get hold of, as long as it was able to give a good strike. How I wished I was back there with them.

'I stopped short along the pitch, fearing the glances I received and feeling the tension of a very serious game.

' "Dennis," Robin called. "Try and catch." I flinched as he pretended to throw the ball.

'Mr Thompson leaned against the back of my shoulder. I turned slightly in surprise.

' "Well, lad," he said.

'I looked at him among the roar of the game.

' "Make a gesture," he said.

'I looked at him again.

' "For the ball," he added.

'I told him I only played cricket in the street.

' "I don't care where you played it, ask for the ball," he told me.

' "I'll ridicule myself if I do," I answered, but he was persistent and told me to give it a go. I took a deep breath and walked onto the pitch to the sound of clapping hands against the rhythm of my step.

' "Don't look back, lad. You keep on going, do you hear me?" he encouraged.

'Yes, I hear you, I said to myself, my knees trembling with each step.

' "I've come for the ball," I called to Robin, closing the gap between us.

' "You cheeky little bastard," Robin said as chants went up from the team for him to give me a shot at it. Robin hissed under his breath as we came face to face and reluctantly passed over the ball. It felt damp and weighed heavy as I curled my hand around it. "Stop wasting time and throw the bloody thing," Robin called.

'Calcutta was fixed in my mind once more and I thought of those friends, their only possessions being the clothes on their backs. They had nothing to hiss about in their minds. It didn't matter who won or lost, grateful for the chance of having a game even in the stench of the streets they lived in. I pictured their faces and made the run, quickening my step and using every muscle in my legs while running firm and solid along the ground. I twisted my arm with all my strength, releasing the ball from my hand with a fast and fierce throw. The stumps fell to the ground and the young man was out.

'Without hesitation, Robin called the game off. "I have to leave shortly," he called, checking his watch. Mr Thompson watched with pride as I walked back along the boundary pitch to join him.

' "You look more satisfied than I am," I remarked as he greeted me with an open smile. Maybe he was proud, proud that I had found the courage on his request to take the ball. There was an air of contentment as we walked back, Mr Thompson admiring the beauty of the gardens, and I satisfied that the challenge Robin had offered had left me able to hold up my head.

'We walked through the fine mist, down towards the sweeping driveway. Grains of dust crept in between my toes from the pebbles that crunched underneath our feet as we walked. Mr Thompson kept an interested eye on the flowered borders while I looked up towards the dismal entrance, my attention taken with the creak from the grey painted double doors as they slowly opened.

'A shiny black car drove steadily towards us, forming a cloud of dust from underneath the roll of its silver wheels as a man in a rather smart cap hooted the horn. The engine stopped and a slim figure jumped out and scurried around the vehicle. The driver opened the boot and ran to pick up a hefty pair of suitcases that had been placed on top of the concrete steps. Taking his time, he packed them neatly inside the boot of the car.

' "Wealthy, obviously," I said as we drew closer.

' "Yes, his father owns several tea plantations," Mr Thompson replied as the bold figure of Robin appeared, repeatedly tapping the scroll that he held in the palm of his hand, as he stepped down to an open door. He was tucked into his seat and the door firmly closed. I looked at Mr Thompson, his chin pressed low against his wrinkled neck scrutinising every move.

' "Good riddance," Mr Thompson muttered under his breath as Robin looked towards us through the glass window, nodding once with an air of arrogance.

'I tried to avoid trampling over Mr Thompson's flower beds as we were forced to step back out of the car's way as the driver turned it around. Robin's peering eyes searched me before he was slowly driven off. That morning Robin finally left, making the descending journey through the low cloud down the rugged mountain road back to civilisation. I kept my envy to myself. Sharing it with Mr Thompson would have been a bad idea as he whistled with contentment on the inspection of his hard labour.

' "Who lives up there?" I asked, looking up towards the stone pillars, examining the rows of tiny arched windows blackened out from the rays of the sun. "Only I sense someone's watching," I added.

' "Nothing to do with us, lad. It's a place for peace. For the monks' final days," he told me.

' "What, before they die?" I asked, trying to catch up with him.

' "Watch out!" he called, nearly trampling over a bunch of cacti that were hidden beneath the thick blades of grass as I caught up to him and we headed back over the hilly ground.

' "Have you ever been in love?" I asked. "Sorry, I shouldn't have asked," I quickly added, noticing his frown at my question. "Only I am. I'm deeply in love, with Barbara. She looks after the stables not far from where I live. She's very beautiful. I know that I should keep my personal thoughts to myself, but I can't bear to be away from her. It hurts to know that she feels the same. I'm going to leave my trunk behind and make a run for it. Well, those are my intentions at least, but I know that Ernest, my father, will swiftly bring me back. I'll look such a fool," I confessed to him.

' "You'd better hurry now and get into uniform," he told me as the chimes from the steeple bell rang out. "If you hurry, I'll wait and walk over to the chapel with you. Come on, get a little enthusiasm in those steps," he called, suddenly leaping ahead of me. "And don't look as though you want to scratch your head with mystery," he remarked, turning his head back towards me. "If you'd have checked the timetable pinned on the board in the main hall you would have realised that it's time for prayer," he reminded me.

'I stumbled over a clump of grass in frustration. "Well, talk about throwing me in at the deep end. Since the minute I arrived here, I've been left with little guidance, besides that bloody Robin. Some chaperone he was," I grumbled.

' "You've to fend for yourself here, lad. Now hurry," he replied.

'I didn't feel at all calm walking a step behind Mr Thompson along the narrow pathway. The last chime suddenly stopped, twanging with an echo out towards the cool air. I looked up towards the steeple. It seemed to reach high up to the heavens with a light cloud masking its peak. I felt quite dizzy as we made our final approach towards the chapel with its brickwork crumbling in parts.

'The old oak door creaked underneath the arch as we both crept in to a noticeable look from Father O'Connor as he continued to read from a worn, leather-bound Bible. Mr Thompson gently moved me on with a touch of his hand against my back. I was just about to squeeze myself along the first pew I came to when Father O'Connor closed his Bible and called me to the front. His voice echoed against the walls of the chapel, rising up and around the hollow of the arch in the roof. I moved immediately. The sound of my footsteps resounded along the barren floorboards. There wasn't even a whisper as

I stopped directly in front of him. His hands felt cold and stiff as he touched the tops of my shoulders to turn me around.

' "Dennis Joseph Ernest Dorrell," I cringed at my name being called out in full, "is welcomed here into this chapel and we pray that God will guide him to build upon his future here at St Vincent's," he announced. There was a rustle as the boys knelt down. I stood there feeling almost foolish but free to glance around at all the heads bowed in prayer in this beautiful little chapel. The candles flickered low against the outline of figures looking up towards God as they stood high upon the dark wooden ledges inside each arch of the stained glass windows. The font nearby standing on top of a pillar cast in white stone had stains of dried water imprinted inside the bowl. I imagined the cries of a newborn baby and wondered how many years had gone by since it was last used for baptism. The chapel seemed unprotected from the sneaky draughts coming through the uneven floorboards, making me shiver. I listened to the creak of benches as the small congregation proceeded to sit up straight.

'Father O'Connor alerted everyone with a request for Bible reading before making a gesture with his hand for me to return to my seat. This time the boys finally moved up a notch, allowing space for me to sit down.

'A scrap of a boy then stood up and, encouraged by the boys who remained seated alongside him, was welcomed by Father O'Connor. I had listened to endless prayers and readings from the Bible throughout my childhood, and to me this was just the same old ritual, except that this time the piss was taken out of the young boy good and

224

proper by the rest of the boys, because he had the misfortune of having a lisp. Father O'Connor listened, enchanted, to the words, completely failing to grasp the situation. I can't possibly take this seriously, I thought, as I sat there twiddling my fingers, feeling uncomfortable with the whispering and giggling. Not that I didn't believe, it was more comfortable to do so. I had cried many times for guidance from that great God above.

' "Thank you, Frederick," Father O'Connor said, coughing slightly to tune in his voice.

' "Well, that was a farce wasn't it?" I said, turning my head sideways to a freckle-faced young man sitting by me. He ignored what I said as he joined in with a soft and almost silent continuous hissing until Frederick had sat down.

'As we trooped out of the chapel I tried to catch up with the boy to simply give him praise on the reading that he had given, but he was herded in between the crowd and their departure was swift. There was a silence as I stood there, a lonely silence.

' "Oh, Mr Thompson," I said, looking startled as he seemed to appear from nowhere.

' "Not impressed are you, lad?" he said.

' "Would you be, sitting next to a bunch of hypocrites?" I complained, aware of the hollow echo in my step as I walked towards him. "It was just a piss-take," I told him, "and under God's roof."

' "Remember, lad, God doesn't need you to pray for Him. He reflects on prayer for each and everyone so that you can give yourself guidance. Maybe those lads didn't think they needed that at this particular time in their lives. There's one thing for certain, one day they will. Come on, lad," he said, holding the door open as he cautiously inspected a bunch of keys to find the right one.

'I shivered as the rattle of the keys turned in the lock. My head felt hot and I began to feel sick.

' "Is something wrong, lad?" Mr Thompson asked as I shoved my hands deep down inside my blazer pockets and huddled myself together. Before he had taken the key out of the lock, the door of the chapel started to spin around.

' "Hey, lad, what's up? Dennis?" he called. I felt my head sinking down towards the ground.

' "You bloody well scared me," he said. The sound of his voice seemed a million miles away. "Now here, sit up and take a sip," he told me. My head was too weak to lift off the pillow and my vision was blurred. "You're back in your room, lad, if you're wondering where the hell you are. Now come on," he said, lifting the back of my head and resting his arm underneath. "Come on, lad, take a sip," he coaxed.

'I wet my lips against the trickle of water. It quickly reached the back of my throat and I cringed as I swallowed.

' "That bad is it?" he asked. I felt relieved that my head was resting once again on the pillow by the careful guidance of Mr Thompson.

' "I'm not going to leave you, lad," he said as he peered at me closely. His face seemed to magnify over me. "I can see that despair in your eyes," he said. His voice seemed to echo from every corner of the room as I sank lower and lower. Sleep was inevitable and I closed my eyes without resistance.

' "Get them off me," I screamed, kicking my legs out in all directions. "They're crawling up towards me," I yelled in horror. I felt the force of Mr Thompson clutching my arms to hold me down.

' "There's nothing there, lad, you've been dreaming," he soothed.

' "There are snakes, millions of them," I screamed, "clinging around my legs. I can feel them. Get them off me," I begged, kicking out furiously to stave them off.

'My head seemed to split in two as I was lifted up from the pillow.

' "See, there's nothing," Mr Thompson said, wiping my brow with a tepid cloth. My vision was blurred. All I could hear was the haunting mumble of voices in the background as Mr Thompson requested a fresh bowl of ice-cold water while lowering my head back down onto the pillow. I sensed Mr Thompson crying, and I cried too. Then there was a blank.

'The humming and the cool air blowing down took my breath away. I caught the reflection of spinning fans as I slowly opened my eyes.

' "You've been drifting in and out of sleep for a while, but you're over the worst," Mr Thompson said, giving a huge sigh of relief. I fought hard to keep alert but I could feel myself sinking back. "Dennis," he called, "Dennis," as he shook me gently to arouse me from sleep. Conscious of his presence, I tried hard to force the lids of my eyes to open once more. "Good lad," he said as I responded to the touch of water as he placed the glass against the dryness of my lips.

'The raw smell of disinfectant seemed to flow inside my nostrils. A plain white sheet covered my naked body and my skin felt tight.

' "The rash you had doesn't seem to be as red," Mr Thompson said, peering towards my face. My eyes were hot and burning as if on fire. I felt scared and looked in vain into Mr Thompson's eyes. He must have sensed my anxiety. "I'm not going to leave you, lad," he said. "Scarlet fever, lad," he said. He walked over towards a large tinted bottle that stood on the desk, lifted it to eye level to inspect its contents and shook it vigorously. "But you've got through it, you've got through the worst," he called as he poured the thick white liquid generously until it filled the entire scoop of a long-handled spoon. He steadied himself with full concentration on delivering it unspilled. "Open your mouth," he told me as he pressed the tip of the spoon against my lips.

'I was praised for swallowing the distasteful stuff. Mr Thompson walked back proudly and placed the bottle back in its place, dispatching the spoon directly into a glass of clear liquid. A slice of mango appeared in front of my face on his enthusiastic return. I turned my head away.

' "You need to build up some strength, Dennis," I heard him say as I felt myself drifting back to sleep. I remembered my mouth being swabbed with touches of water. There was little response apart from the odd groan at being disturbed.

'I didn't know how long I slept or whether it was night or day. Mr Thompson snored gently from below. I lowered my head gently over the edge of the bed and peeped over at him as he lay there bundled up on a blanket. Mr Thompson's subconscious must have alerted him to my movement. His expression, although a little startled, was one of joy. "Hey, lad, there's a sign of improvement if nothing else. You've barely moved for days," he said.

'Mr Thompson, with a little struggle, lifted himself up from the floor.

' "How long have I been here?" I asked in a rather croaky voice.

' "A week already, but be prepared to stay in this room for quite a while," he said. I leaned slightly towards him as he pressed his hands firmly down onto the edge of the bed.

' "Hmmm," he said as he touched my forehead. I looked up towards him. "You've cooled down considerably but you're still contagious," he told me.

' "I stink, don't I?" I said as he sat me up, enabling my back to lean against the pillow.

' "It won't be long before you start to complain again about the cold showers you'll have to take each morning," he told me. I thanked him for reminding me. "Hey, lad, I'm just grateful that by the looks of it you're on the mend. Now pee into this," he said, bending down and lifting up a long narrow bottle.

' "No luck?" Mr Thompson asked as the minutes flew by, his back turned to save my embarrassment.

' "Would you have any, Sir, if your willy was pushed inside the neck of this awful contraption?"

' "Your wit amuses me, lad. Just pee into the bloody thing," he said.

'Anyway, the days went by, shortened by my need to

229

sleep. My only visitor was good old Mr Thompson, who regulated my medicine and kept a close eye on my well being. My daily bed bath was stopped and I needed no assistance to wash from a bowl of fresh cold water that he delivered every day, and I relished the fact that I could now walk to the corner of the room and do my bodily functions into a sanitary bowl with privacy.'

I gave a huge sigh. Uncle held my hand, this time not letting go. There seemed to be little sleep in me. Maybe I was frightened, frightened of the night, of sleeping in peace only to wake up and face another painful day without Lily in my life.

Uncle's silent tears rolled steadily down his face. I released my hand from his, picked up the handkerchief that lay next to me and gently wiped them away. I was confused. Was it Lily he was crying for, or his past that he spoke about with relentless passion? I glanced up once again towards Lily's framed photo, giving Uncle time to compose himself. Her stunning beauty smiled down on me. It was with a heavy heart that my dreams of Lily and me growing old together had been whipped away. These affectionate thoughts were quickly turned to Uncle. His fingers stumbling over the lid, I took his tiny cigar tin from his hands and opened it with ease.

'You've one left,' I told him, waiting for his nod of approval before picking it out and passing it over to him. I left him to strike the match. Mothering him would be quite an insult.

'You're leaving me, aren't you?' he said, halting the

strike of the match as I stood up. 'I suppose you've had enough of sitting next to this old goat reminiscing.'

'You're not an old goat, Uncle,' I called from the kitchen.

The aroma of Uncle's cooking still lingered and the brightness of the light beaming down made it once more feel like home. I grabbed hold of the narrow box of firelighters from the cupboard underneath the sink, sneezing with the fumes from the open packet. The rain lashed down against the outer window, shrouding any view. I reached over to collect Uncle's bottle of whisky, which stood next to a floral printed milk jug, elegantly moulded in fine china, and tiny enough to hold a handful of drooping buttercups that I had picked that terrible morning while roaming aimlessly around the garden before the dreaded clock told me it was time to slip on my long black coat and make my last journey to say my final farewell to Lily.

I gave a deep sigh, picked up the bottle and rushed back into the drawing room. Uncle looked surprised and stood immediately.

'It will be welcoming with the howling wind that has crept back, to hear the roar of the fire again,' he said, reaching out to take the box of firelighters from me. 'There's a glass up there,' he said, looking towards the mantelpiece. 'You're tense, my love.'

'Not really, Uncle,' I replied, reaching up. The base stuck slightly on top of the shiny wooden surface as I reached for the thick-rimmed crystal tumbler.

'Don't bother washing it,' Uncle said, leaning down and striking a match as he watched me peer down and look at the remnants stuck in the bottom before resting it on top of the circular wine table that stood next to Uncle's chair. The cap felt quite tight as I twisted my hand around to unscrew it from the bottle. The strong smell of whisky drifted up towards me. Uncle could hear the rumble as a generous amount flowed from the bottle down into his glass, which gave him the encouragement to stack the fire generously so as not to interrupt the evening by having to tend to it again once he had sat down.

The fire took hold quickly, with wild flames of orange stretching up between the crackling wood. The stump of his cigar was lit before he snuggled himself back into his chair.

'Cheers,' Uncle said, raising his glass as the room flickered with shadows cast by the light of the roaring fire. 'Not sharing a glass with me?' he asked. I shuddered at the thought. Uncle smiled, leaning over and ruffling my cushion before I sat back next to him and curled up my feet once again.

'I was pretty lousy at writing letters, my love. I should imagine, looking back, that young boys always are. Each time Aunt Popsy visited us, I was expected, on Grace's instructions, to write her a letter of thanks. No doubt it was because a substantial amount of money changed hands at each visit, to Grace's advantage of course. I was thought of by Aunt Popsy as the educated one, and my mother's need to impress on that matter meant her looking over my shoulder while I sat on Ernest's creaky chair, my back hunched over three crisp pieces of notepaper that were dropped in front of me.

'"You must fill it in with exciting news," I was told before a pen was pushed into my hand and I waited for her usual groan of frustration as it was swapped from my right into my left before I began to write. "Keep dropping it in the ink," she would say. I satisfied the request, with the constant stretch of my arm, by frequently dipping the sharp nib of the pen into the pot that was fitted into a slot at the far end of Ernest's desk. "Tell her how beautiful she still is," I was told as I lapsed into thought. I remember looking up towards her and pulling a face. "Dennis," she would say, giving a little push on my shoulder, "learn how to be charming." I'll never forget that sultry manner Grace had, and her obvious beauty, which she took full advantage of.

'What's that sullen look for?' Uncle asked, turning his head towards me. 'I know,' he said, in a hollow tone, reaching over and gently squeezing my hand. Maybe he had just remembered at that moment how familiar it all was to me. Uncle took a sip of whisky, pondered a little and drank some more.

'You can continue, Uncle, I really don't mind.'

'Are you sure, my love? Only I'm rather self-conscious of digging in too deep.'

I gave him a warm smile and, without any hesitation, he continued his story. 'I don't know why I went back in my mind to those letters I had to write regularly to Aunt Popsy,' he said, re-lighting his cigar and blowing a ring of smoke up into the air. 'Maybe because Mr Thompson had left notepaper and pen by my side during the long hours I spent confined to my room at St Vincent's. The fever had certainly taken its toll. "I look wretched, don't I?" I said to Mr Thompson on one of his regular visits. "I don't need a mirror, I can tell by the way you look at me."

' "You are rather gaunt," he told me in his usual deep voice.

' "And extremely weak," I replied as he helped me by propping my back up against my pillow.

' "You must start eating again, Dennis. A little more each day, and it's my job to see that you do just that. And stop pulling that gruesome face at me; the food here isn't that bad."

'He passed me a glass of tepid water. I was grateful, not for that, but of having the strength to hold it myself and sip it with ease. Anyway, my love, it was Mr Thompson's idea that I should get my brain active again and writing, he thought, would be the way to start.

'Mr Thompson asked permission to root through my trunk, picking out a pair of rather over-washed pyjama pants and a short-sleeved cotton top.

' "Socks," he said, mumbling to himself as he rooted deeper. "My God, may I?" he asked, picking out an oval frame, the silver discoloured around the edge. "She's beautiful," he whispered, lifting it up to eye level.

'I beckoned him over, using all my strength to sit up straight and leant forward slightly with my hand outstretched, waiting impatiently. His eyes stayed fixed on the picture as he slowly stepped towards me. "It's Grace," I told him as he placed it into my hand.

' "Grace?" he asked.

' "Yes, my mother. Bobo must have sneakily placed it inside my trunk."

' "Bobo?"

' "Yes, the servant. His astuteness surprises me. He can't have had time to polish the silver," I said, gently brushing my fingers over the tarnished framework. "He would have known that Ernest, my father, would have seized it immediately as he wanted it kept solely in his possession. She died, you know, just over a year ago."

'Mr Thompson leaned over to have another look. "She is rather beautiful. An Indian princess, I would say."

' "She was, Mr Thompson, to me anyway." My eyes glazed over with emotion at the memory of my dear mother. I clasped hold of her picture tightly and placed it against my heart.

'Mr Thompson breathed deeply as he sat down by my side. There was a silence for a while before he loosened my clammy fingers from the grasp of Grace's picture.

' "I saw her, you know. She was here with Ernest. She stood exactly there," I said, pointing my finger, "just behind you."

' "Place this on your desk," he whispered, standing with the picture in his hand.

' "You don't believe me, do you, Mr Thompson?" I asked him as he slowly walked over. "But I did," I called, coughing with frustration on raising my voice. I expected an answer from him but there was none. Throwing the sheet I was lying under to one side, I crawled out of the bed, standing with a slight stagger.

' "Hey, lad, what's up?" he asked.

' "I'm going to write to Ernest," I replied in a rather grumpy manner as I held onto the edge of the bed for support. Mr Thompson came to my aid immediately and reached over the bed for my pyjama pants.

' "Lean your hands on my shoulders," he told me as I shivered, standing there in just my underwear. Because of my weakness, I had no other choice but to obey his instructions. I stepped into each open leg one at a time as he helped me dress. "Why don't you leave that until another day? You know, writing to your father," he said, taking in another deep breath while reaching over for my top.

'I didn't have the strength to answer and explain that a letter written by my own hand was of utmost importance to me, while I tried as hard as I could to stretch my arms through the sleeves. As soon as the jacket touched the top of my shoulders, refusing further assistance, I slowly walked over to my desk. The room span around in my head several times but I kept my eye on my bearings and, with a conscious effort, sat myself down on the low stool, enabling me to rest both arms on the sealed lid that slanted down towards me. The latch of the door was opened and Mr Thompson, without any acknowledgement, left the room.

'I sat there for a moment staring at Grace's picture, which sent me fleeing into a merry-go-round of the past where the sounds of voices clashed. Ernest would arrive in the kitchen most mornings, more often than not disgruntled, and would always poke his nose into domestic matters. He never learned how contemptuous Grace was at that early hour as she, as always, would scorn his intrusion. This was such a common occurrence that I would merrily let it go over my head and, in the middle of it, enjoy a good hearty breakfast. Oh, how I missed the rumpus that went on throughout my childhood years.'

Uncle sighed, took another sip of whisky, and continued.

'The long-fingered pen weighed heavy, because of my weakness. Feeling anxious about how to address my letter to Ernest, I moved the sheets of writing paper along so that they lay in front of me. The ink-pot seemed far from my reach as I leaned over with a steady hand and dipped the nib into the thick black liquid. Blotting paper at hand, I bowed my head and started to write.

*Dear Sir,*

*My stay, although short I know, hasn't been a successful one. I know that you will be disgruntled after reading these few lines, but I beg you to bring me home. The few lessons that I have had up to now have been of little interest to me. This place holds no gentle atmosphere and I feel quite uncomfortable. I am no longer a boy, but a young man, and I urge you to respect my feelings, even though I have little confidence on gaining a swift reply.*

*I can't recall much during these last few weeks, Sir, while lying in my bed with a high fever, but I heard from mumbling voices in the background that you were sitting by my bedside with Grace, my dear Mother, standing close by. I know what you're thinking, delirious, but, nevertheless, Mother's voice echoed in my mind. I tried in vain to reach out to her while she soothed my raging temperature with a wet cloth. I spotted the sheen from her long black hair as she moved around the room. She was there, Ernest, with you and me. She actually raised her voice to you. Her full red painted lips opened and closed repeatedly as she spewed out words of anger on your lack of compassion towards me, then requested in a much calmer manner for you to go and fetch fresh water.*

237

'I remember, my love,' Uncle stopped to say, 'holding my pen still and looking towards the picture frame into Grace's deep dark eyes. My tears dropped heavily onto the paper, wetting the dried ink and blurring the words that I had written. I reached for the blotting paper, which trembled in my hand, and I jumped at the sound of the door opening as Mr Thompson returned to my room. Straining to the thunderous noise splitting inside my ears, he stepped inside and closed the door. I felt sensitive to every sound, even to his footsteps.

' "Hey, lad, come on," he said, walking over to me and taking the pen from my shaking hand before helping me up.

' "My mind feels like a battlefield," I told him, trying to straighten myself up and walk as steadily as I could with the help of his arm.

' "My fault, lad," he said, pulling back the sheet from the bed. "Making you run before you can walk. Get your head back on that pillow."

'My eyes felt on fire. "Bloodshot, aren't they?" I whispered as Mr Thompson looked into them. I tried to focus on him but he had wandered away.

' "Your days of reckoning are a long way off, lad," he called, alerting me to the sound of liquid being shaken as he came back into view. "Open your mouth, lad," he said, unscrewing the top of a tinted bottle.

'The tiny spoon felt like an intrusion inside my mouth. I shivered from the taste that lingered on my tongue long after swallowing. Mr Thompson shook his head and then smiled at the painful expression I showed on my face. My body raged with a temperature. I tried in a whisper to give the full address. Mr Thompson leaned his ear closely. "You'll send it won't you ... the letter to Ernest?" I asked, aware that I was drifting back into a deep sleep. I pictured Barbara's smiling face and didn't fight any more. I would take the image of her with me into my dreams. I could hear her sweet voice echoing my name before she left me. The dream deepened, leaving me to face the black murky waters of the wide open sea. "Dennis, Dennis take me home. Dennis, come take Lily. Calcutta is where we belong," Jenny's voice wailed over the strong current as she called for me. There was no fear sailing in the narrow boat. Frantic, I pushed the blades of the oars down into the rising current. I could hear Lily's faint cries and I was desperate in my search. Grace appeared from beneath, her ghostly silhouette dancing on the water. "I'm not truly gone yet, Dennis," she said, her face unscathed. Her laughter echoed through the mist. "They're mine," she was saying, laughing in my face through her dark sunken eyes while gripping the pearl necklace with the bare bones of her hands around the neck of her skeletal frame. The waves began to swell. Grace rose with them, and then sank, only to rise again. "You're taking me home, Dennis, only me," she laughed.

'I suddenly shot up from my bed and scrambled to the edge. Beads of sweat rolled down my forehead. It took several seconds before I realised and thanked God it was only a dream.

'I don't know how many days or nights I lay crunched up on the edge of the mattress. There was no sense of time for me any more. What little appetite I had had seemed to have diminished altogether. I sensed the friction in each of Mr Thompson's visits when, suddenly, it all came to a head.

' "You haven't shown the slightest intention of getting better have you, Dennis?"

'I shook my head, which was bowed between my hands. It was certainly not in agreement, but with the frustration of how bloody ill I still felt.

' "And your refusal to eat – come on, lad, admit it, there's been hardly any attempt on your part."

'I sat still in the same position, feeling sick in my stomach.

' "And you think staying silent on this matter will help. Well, I don't see how," Mr Thompson blurted.

' "I've got bloody indigestion, haven't I?" I told him, raising my head slightly before bowing it once more.

' "Anyway," he said, "it's time you got some fresh air."

' "It's not my fault I've been stuck in this room."

' "Yes, for far too bloody long," Mr Thompson replied. "Give a good belch, lad," he told me, "that will get rid of it."

'So I did, several times. My head remained bowed, with the view below of Mr Thompson's hobnailed boots. There was no need for him to step closer only to listen to me belch once more.

' "There's nothing lining your stomach," he complained, "otherwise you'd be out and about."

'My head started to spin. "Hold on," he said as I heaved. A smelly rubber bowl was pushed under my chin. I felt nauseous and I wanted to vomit. My stomach retched.

' "That's right, lad, bring everything up," Mr Thompson

said, holding the bowl as steadily as he could. There was a rush as Mr Thompson covered the bowl with a paper towel and left the room, returning almost immediately with a tiny mug. "Here, gargle and spit it back out," I was told as he passed me the mug half filled with water, as if he knew of the bitter taste left in my mouth. I sensed he was tired of my continued ill health. So was I. The strain of my being heavily dependent on him was showing on his already weathered face. I took a mouthful of the tepid water.

' "Now swill it around," I was told, which I did, before spitting it out with force. "Now we're going places," Mr Thompson said, taking the mug from me and tipping the remains out of the open window.

'The blanket that I had sweated on during the last weeks of my high fever was draped around my shoulders. It weighed heavy on my attempt to stand, proving my weakness. Mr Thompson offered his help and moved his arms forward. I gripped hold, feeling the strength of his firm muscles, and I gradually lifted myself up off the edge of the bed.

' "Keep your balance," he said, letting go. "We're going to walk, lad, you and I, out of this room and along the corridor. It's time we got some of those muscles working in those skinny legs of yours. I want to see you pushing that barrow soon over yonder hills, and there'll be a fag at the end to reward you. Miss you, somehow, not being out there alongside me."

'I was quite surprised at his touching confession. I think he was, also. I managed to smile, just a faint one, towards him.

' "Are you ready?" he asked, standing shoulders straight and head held high. I made an attempt to salute him. Mr Thompson smiled at the gesture. "Come on, lad, let's make a move."

'The door was opened and we both stepped out into the musty air. "There's no rush, lad," he said, reassuring me with the offer to link his arm. "Your eyes look deep and sad," he told me, glancing towards me as we slowly walked along arm in arm. "Still not settled are you? But you must take into consideration that your health won't have helped."

' "I'm frightened," I blurted out, "that I'll never see my home again. But there's more than that. It's Barbara." Mr Thompson must have picked up on my sensitive cough.

' "I gather she's your sweetheart," he said.

'We walked on a little longer. "Yes, Mr Thompson, I'm deeply in love and so is she."

' "Pretty?" he asked.

' "Yes, very," I replied.

' "But you're only young, lad, and—"

'I stopped him. "No, Mr Thompson. I want to spend the rest of my life with her. I shouldn't have left her all alone that day. She must have felt ... well, I can't explain, but I know. I can see her now, sweeping the lonely stable yard as she must have done so many times since I left, looking out for me to appear through the film of dust in the air. I know that she would have cried out for me many times, but I never appeared, Mr Thompson, to hold her tightly in my arms."

' "You're torturing yourself, Dennis," he told me.

' "Yes, maybe, but I truly know, Mr Thompson, that her

heart will be broken. I've got to get back to her. Will you take me?"

'Mr Thompson sighed. "There are rules that have to be adhered to here at St Vincent's," he said.

' "Oh, bugger the bloody rules," was my reply.

' "This walk is doing you good, Dennis. I see you're getting your spirit back," he told me. Beads of sweat started forming on my forehead. "Well, I think that's enough exercise for one day. Let's go back. Look," he said, "there is such a thing as compassionate leave here which could be, I suppose, if it was put in writing, that your health is deteriorating."

' "At a fast rate," I told him. "You mean I don't have to stick a scroll in my hand to get through those bloody doors?"

' "That's more like you, Dennis. You're getting some fire back into you. But it isn't as easy as that, Dennis. You would be required to have a full medical check before any consideration could be given. If you ask me, there's nowt much wrong with you now the fever's passed."

' "But there is," I cried out, turning immediately towards him.

' "You haven't let me finish, Dennis. If it involves the likes of your sweetheart back home, well, that's emotional isn't it? So you wouldn't stand a chance of leaving on those grounds. It's no good you lying back on that bed, Dennis," he told me as I flung myself back down as soon as we entered my room.

' "Granted you've been ill, but it's time you stopped feeling sorry for yourself. You're left with a bout of feeling homesick if you ask me. Well, there's no cure for that but to get up off your bloody arse and get on with it," he told me.

'Mr Thompson walked over to the window and gave a long, deep sigh. "There'll be a low mist tonight. Can see it gathering over the tops of yonder mountains so I'll shut this window. If you want to share a bowl of soup you'll catch me in the dining hall, 6.30 p.m. sharp."

' "You mean you're not—"

' "No, I've done all I need to do; the rest is up to you. Remember, lad, you'll get tired of taking pity on yourself, and when you do you know where I am," he replied.

'The door closed behind him and I was left in a daze, angry with Mr Thompson. How dare he just leave, and why the sudden change of attitude?

'I tossed and turned that afternoon, determined to stay in my room. After all, to expect me to join him after I had been so terribly ill was a joke. The afternoon was the longest I had spent. Used to sleeping through, I was now aware that I had got through the worst. My brain was beginning to respond to the world around me, including Mr Thompson's comments.

'Restless, I clambered from my bed, steadying myself before making my way towards the tall, narrow window. Mr Thompson was right, I thought. The mist was thick by now, hiding the peaks of the mountains from view. It looked quite eerie, sweeping down in a shroud towards the valley below. I already missed Mr Thompson, probably knowing that I wouldn't have the privilege of his company that I was so used to sharing during the weeks confined to my room, and I felt utterly miserable. The view from the window wasn't helping and, turning away, I spotted

Mr Thompson's reading spectacles lying on the tilted desk in the corner of the room. I dragged my feet along the floor as if I was some old geriatric, and stared at them with sadness before reaching over and picking them up.

'The sudden sound of the bell rang in my ears as I stumbled back towards the bed, still gently holding on to the beaten frame of Mr Thompson's spectacles. I leaned over and checked my watch. Both hands pointed down towards the six. Mr Thompson's dusty old spectacles pulled at my heart strings. Poor sod, I thought, as I perched them on the edge of my nose. The glass lenses, scratched with the use of time, meant that I could barely see through them. Mr Thompson must have struggled reading to me through the restless nights I spent in and out of sleep – and I could barely remember a word. I questioned myself, standing alone in my room. Could there be a possibility that Mr Thompson, deep down, felt as lonely as me? After all, there was no mention from him of a mother, father, or brothers and sisters. There was no great aunt or uncle he talked about. A fool's guess, maybe, but that didn't stop me feeling a sudden need to return that pair of spectacles to him by hand.

'Well, my love, I didn't linger on any more thought. I searched through my trunk for something suitable to wear. Sweat filled my brow once again, but I managed to smile remembering Bobo's letter as I lifted it out, leaving it for another time to read again and to take in the little bastard's brazen words.

'I pulled out a short-sleeved khaki shirt, the sight of which instantly took me back to a late morning at home in Calcutta, when Grace burst into the kitchen dropping a load of shopping bags onto the floor. I was standing there, looking idle, I suppose. A look of disapproval was given and she beckoned me over.

' "Keep still, you're wriggling like a worm," she told me as the same khaki shirt that I had just pulled out from my trunk was taken from a bag and held against the back of my shoulders. "Stand up straight," Grace said, measuring it with her eyes. "This is just you, Dennis," I remember her saying. "Quick, quick, try it on." She was more excited than me. Anyway, my love, little did I know at that particular time that it would be the last item of clothing that she would ever buy for me before she died.

'I sat there, stupid me, in my room at St Vincent's and sniffed the material, thinking that I might, just might, still smell her scent. That familiar floral cologne that she wore that day when hugs were exchanged and thanks were given. I, feeling like some kind of sissy as she held me tightly in her arms.' I gave a sigh. Uncle gave a much deeper one. 'I wonder if she knew that her life was going to be cut so short. It was just the way she embraced me that morning, as if she never wanted to let me go.'

Uncle shrugged his narrow shoulders and, for a second or two, bore the signs of sadness on his face. The clock on the mantelpiece noticeably ticked in the silence of the room. Uncle, all of a sudden, realised. 'I'm sorry,' he said, leaning over to gently squeeze my hand. 'I was just, just for a little while, missing the love, that precious love that Grace always gave me. Silly old fool that I am.

'Anyway, my plan was for me to dress and show Mr Thompson that I wasn't as weak as he thought, but the most important thing was for me to return his spectacles.

At least I could show my gratitude for the endless hours he had sat and read to me, although I must point out that I wouldn't otherwise have considered the thought of walking back into that dining hall, not since that day I was insulted by Robin and his team of cronies. But if I had to walk back in for the sake of Mr Thompson, so be it.'

'Did you wear the shirt?' I asked. Uncle looked puzzled. 'The one that your mother bought for you.'

'Certainly not,' he said in quite a loud manner, making me jump by his immediate reply. 'There was too much sentiment going around in my head so, on spotting my uniform hanging wearily from the wooden rail on a steel hanger, the shirt went straight back inside the trunk. I pulled the lid down sharply as if feeling all that love that had once surrounded me was safe inside.'

Uncle laughed, telling me about the struggle he had stretching up and reaching for his uniform.

'I disliked it immensely and had a change of mind several times with the difficulty I had trying to fasten the collar of my shirt and fixing the tie; never mind the dusty old blazer that had to be shaken several times before I finally slipped it on.

'That's a hearty smile,' Uncle said, patting my knee. I had imagined Uncle, who was short in height and slender in build, making such an effort to reach up and collect his uniform, despite the misery of wearing it.

'The corridor was long, cold and empty,' Uncle continued. 'No pictures hung on the walls on either side of the dim, grey-washed stone walls. The wooden floor bore no shine and the musty smell still lingered, but what was I to expect? After all, this was St Vincent's.

247

'I battled with each step I took, determined to have no fear to walk once again into the arena of that ghastly dining hall. After all, I reminded myself, I was only going in there to return Mr Thompson's spectacles, which weighed next to nothing in my hand.

'I stopped and took in a deep breath, composing myself before nearing the door at the end of the long corridor I had walked down. I could hear the buzz of conversation and the clatter of cutlery as they all ate. I had no fear, not this time, on my entrance – or so I told myself. I gave a faint cough, not one, may I say, of a gentleman who was about to make a grand entrance. With no more time to think, step by step I finally walked through the open door. Mr Thompson was in direct view. He glanced up towards me and stopped for a second, the spoon still raised in his hand. He made no effort to greet me and continued to eat his supper. The clatter of knives and forks ceased, to be replaced by the scraping of chairs being pulled away from each table. Mr Thompson sat, head slightly bowed, and ripped apart a roll of bread, making no conscious effort to acknowledge my presence. There was no way I could turn back. To be thought of as a coward was unthinkable. I held out his spectacles and walked the short distance over the bare stone floor towards him. Most of the boys were now standing, and there was a sharp noise that sounded like clapping. I tried to ignore them as I approached Mr Thompson.

' "The applause is for you, lad," he called over the hail of noise before looking sideways at a group of boys who had bunched together. "Looks like you've taken Robin's place, well, at least in their eyes."

'My face burned brightly with embarrassment. "You'd better give a nod of appreciation," I was told as the clapping died down and everyone scrambled back to their seats.

' "Well, come on, lad, sit yourself down. That bowl's for you. I took the liberty of pouring you some soup. It'll be cold by now. Here, dip that in," Mr Thompson said, passing me a crust of bread.

' "What the hell was all that about?" I asked, leaning over the table to wait for Mr Thompson's reply.

' "Should imagine it's when you took the ball off Robin and bowled the batsman out. Remember, lad, that game of cricket? I've never gloated as much in my life. If you ask me, those lads sitting over yonder felt the same way about him as you and I did. Cowards the lot of them; that's when they were in his company. Well, that's changed now he's gone. Only reason he was head boy in the first place was because of his father's generous handouts, which of course we here at St Vincent's were extremely grateful for. Anyway, that's history. I'll be off now. Presume these are mine?" he said, standing with the spectacles in his hand. "And don't look at me like that. Your friends are over there, lad," he added.

'I didn't feel happy that Mr Thompson was leaving me alone in the dining hall. "You stay where you are, lad," I was told on my attempt to stand, leaving me quite bewildered when my table overflowed with hands of friendship as soon as he began to walk away. I realised that that was what he intended doing, leaving me to the sudden scurry of newly made friends. I knew that I would never forget my first unpleasant experience of this dining hall, neither the taste nor the atmosphere, and I wasn't going to allow myself to cave in to the friendship that was offered from the hands of snobs. I was baffled by the sudden intrusion, and felt quite suffocated by it all. My heart was not here at St Vincent's, but where it used to be, with the boys in the tiny streets of Calcutta. After all, what better practice could I have had than the simple game of cricket that we used to play?

' "We heard that you nearly died, Dennis," one boy called over the head of another. The invasion was from a slightly built, dark-skinned boy who had found the courage to push through and pull out a chair next to me. His worn-out blazer hung down over his narrow shoulders. The tattered badge embroidered on his pocket was barely recognisable as that of St Vincent's. His bony knees stuck out without intention through the thin material of his narrow fitted trousers as he sat down next to me. He pulled the wooden chair as close as he could until the worn-out boots that he wore, with laces loosely fastened, were tucked underneath the square frame of the table. He leaned forward, clasping his thin, bony hands against the table top, making no conscious effort to disguise the dirt underneath the short tips of his jagged fingernails. The boy turned to me and, through a row of brilliant white teeth, smiled. The mutual liking for each other was spontaneous. His dark, chocolate eyes seemed full of mischief.

'One of the boys, a tall spiky-looking character, leant across the table. "I see you've still not had your bloody hair cut," he sneered at him, with cheering from the rest.

' "Get those scissors out," they chanted. The small boy ducked and leaned slightly on his chair towards me, but not in time. The tall, lean boy grabbed on to the crown

250

of his head with his enormous hands and ruffled his hair quite vigorously.

' "There'll be no taunting tonight," came the call from a pale, lanky young man with shimmering red hair and a spray of golden freckles across his nose and cheeks.

'I felt a slight panic and searched up at peering eyes that looked towards me before the crowd quickly dispersed, leaving almost silently in tiny groups.

' "What's your name?" I asked the boy who remained sitting in his seat next to me.

' "He doesn't speak nor hear. He's deaf and dumb. I'm Stephen," the freckle-faced boy introduced himself, offering his hand.

' "Dennis," I replied before he sat down opposite me.

' "His name's Eddie, but don't be fooled by his boyish smile. He's sat outside your door every night for hours on end in that draughty corridor since you were taken ill. Don't look so surprised, Dennis. He's kept an eye on you since the first day you arrived. He lives up in the loft and knows every nook and cranny in this old building. There's no doubt he would have been watching you from a great height, especially when you were helping out in the garden before your illness struck. This is his permanent home from what we gather. He's got the freedom of the place. Well, that's what the other boys and I think; the way he'll walk into a lesson and walk out again, and nothing's said. Mystery if you ask me," Stephen said. "He's never matured," he continued, "and most likely never will, but I'll tell you this, he's as cunning, if not more so, than the rest of us. Come on," Stephen told the boy, "don't hold back. He's one of us," referring to me.

251

'It was then that I realised he could lip read. Eddie glanced quickly towards me before pushing his hand deep down into the torn seam of his blazer pocket. A pack of loose tobacco and roll-ups were lifted out and placed on the table. Eddie then held his hand out, grinning widely. He obviously enjoyed the tease for some reason. Stephen wasn't amused and clicked his fingers twice. The atmosphere around the table became very tense.

Eddie continued to search in the deep pocket of his blazer. The strain showed on Stephen's face, turning almost to a look of anger. A minute piece of hardened mud was eventually pulled out. I recognised immediately what it was and looked straight over to Stephen.

' "Ever smoked pot before?" he asked, giving a hefty sigh of relief while weighing the stuff in his hand.

'A handful of rupees was thrown to the boy and he was told, by a nod from Stephen's head, to scarper, leaving me to face Stephen alone across the table. A joint was offered as Stephen kept his eyes fixed on me. I politely refused, complaining of a splitting headache, while standing up and wiping my sweaty brow on the sleeve of my blazer before excusing myself almost immediately.

' "Well, how about a game of cricket in a day or so?" Stephen called as I made my way out. "We need to choose a captain so it'll be between you and me."

'I felt agitated by his comment. I didn't turn, but raised one arm up into the air and flapped my hand loosely up and down, giving him a sign of having no interest in their petty game, before I finally disappeared from view to walk back along the narrow, musty corridor. I left no shadow as I walked along. There was no bright sun beaming down through the skylights above. The sun had lost its fire and dusk was apparent. I was conscious of someone behind me – or was it just my imagination? The sound of heavy steps continued. I stopped as if to take a breath. The corridor fell silent, and once again I thought that it must have been my imagination. Nonsense, I thought, as the patter of footsteps continued.

'I was determined not to turn around and face who it was. "You can piss off," I called, "ghost or no ghost," feeling a touch braver as I reached the door to my room. With one fierce kick of my foot the door flew open. I swiftly turned. The heavy sound of feet rushed past me. Recognising the dark silhouette of Eddie, I gave chase, but my energy was soon used up. Sweat dripped, it seemed, from every pore in my body and I damned myself for using what little strength I had on such a fruitless chase. Nevertheless, I was curious about the boy and, by the nature of his actions, he clearly was about me. Eager to find out more, I decided that the following morning I was going to make a point of finding him. My door was left ajar in case my silent visitor was interested in returning.

'My sleep had been deeper than I thought. Wrestling with the fierce sound of whistling from outside, half dazed, I shot up from my bed and faced the window, only to see Mr Thompson standing there in the early misty dawn of the morning.

' "Stop scratching your head, lad, and get out here with me. It's so bloody peaceful out here, a walk will do us both good."

253

'I started to dress, but was concerned that I wouldn't be able to keep up with him.

' "Come on, lad," he called as I squeezed my head through the neck of my jumper. With one arm by then inside my sleeve, I was conscious of his waiting and pushed open the window with a firm hand.

' "Could have given me more time," I complained, pushing my other arm down into the opposite sleeve as I climbed out to join him.

' "Dawn moves quick here, lad. Don't want to lose the momentum, do we? Your laces – fasten them," I was told, stopping me in my stride over the dewy grass. I did wonder about the reason for such an early call with the urgency for me to accompany him. I begrudgingly followed. Birds flew above us, swooping down on their prey. "The more bugs they eat the better for me," Mr Thompson said, saluting them with his walking stick as we walked along briskly.

'The sudden dip down into the valley was unexpected. "Steady, lad," Mr Thompson called, grabbing me by the arm. The early morning mist lay heavily on our descent. I looked up, dizzy of course, to the shady peaks of the mountains. "Aye, lad," he said, still guiding me by the grip of his hand, "one doesn't venture into those mountains lightly. They rattle with death." I looked towards him. "The mountains, lad, that they dared climb. Most of them clever lads, cleverer than you and I will ever be. Of all the mountains in the Himalayas they had to climb, they chose the tallest and most treacherous one of all. Somewhere over there if I recall," he said, pointing sharply with his stick.

'The mass of snow-capped peaks were masked by the light mist that hung down, moving slowly over them like the spirit of a ghost. Mr Thompson had been right. The tallest rose above the clouds making it impossible to see.

' "You're brave enough to sit in the cold and listen?"

' "Yes?" I replied.

' "Well, you can hear the rattle of empty tin cans rolling around. I presume they're what they took their food up in, and were left behind after each and every one of them fell to their deaths. Anyway, that's history. Happened a long time ago. Still, I suppose there'll be many more who'll chance it," he said with a sympathetic tone in his voice.

'We battled over humps of rocks to the valley below. Where on earth was he taking me? After all, it was the crack of dawn. I complained bitterly, but only to myself, as I grabbed hold of anything that grew along the wayside to support me on the slippery descent.

'Our stop was almost immediate. After I had scrambled my way further through the loose chippings of stone, I was cautioned by Mr Thompson's grip around my arm. We stood side by side, not moving a step further.

' "She's here."

' "Who?" I asked falteringly, aware of the grim expression on his face.

' "Mrs Edward Thompson," he called in a faltering voice. I looked towards him. He stood, his eyes fixed firmly down on a hand-made wooden cross standing solidly in the ground. Mr Thompson stepped over, gliding his fingers softly over the name of Kitty that was carved in the wood. Suddenly realising what he had just said, I took a huge

255

gulp. "There's nothing you can say, lad. Don't want you to either. She was a peasant. Still, no fancy flowers in my hand to lay down." I looked down towards him. "Still don't want you to say owt. I was an orphan. Father O'Connor had chosen me out of a dozen or so from the refuge centre on the outskirts of Calcutta, run by the Sisters of Charity.

' "Sister Evelyn called me over one morning when he was visiting. 'Father,' she said, 'this young man has been with us for a long time. We don't know where he's originally from or the whereabouts of a mother or father. He was left on our doorstep; such a tiny baby he was. We named him Edward and ever since then he's been in our care, a shining example. He now tends the gardens in the many convents we have sprawled out around here, and if anyone's fingers are green, Edward's are.'

' " 'May I borrow him, just for a while?' Father O'Connor asked. 'Only the gardens up at the monastery ... well, they're not as tidy as I would like.'

' " 'I'll miss him,' Sister Evelyn remarked, pushing her round spectacles closer to her eyes so she could see me more clearly. 'Well, Edward, you're free to go,' she said, choking back a cough.

' "I didn't have anything to pack so it was no inconvenience to simply scrub up to leave almost immediately with Father O'Connor. Old Sister Evelyn must have had a premonition that I would never come back and would stay at the monastery for the rest of my life, which encouraged her to clasp her hands around my back and shed a tear or two.

' "I worked hard in those days up yonder at St Vincent's

256

and took to wandering on time off. Never talked like this before, my lad. Don't expect I will again, not on matters as personal as this, but now I've got this far I might as well let you in on the rest.

'"I hadn't experience, lad, then. Never really thought about it until my wandering took me a little further than it should. I lost the battle of a young man who was innocent of all thought when I saw her. This petite young figure of a woman; her dusky complexion and her hair black as coal and as shiny as the sun, which hung down, stopping at her waist, attracted me immensely. The heavy basket of washing she was carrying made a hump in her back, and her shoulders drooped. When she saw me she suddenly dropped it and ran inside the weather-beaten farmhouse, which looked as if it offered little protection from the cold, bitter howling wind. Did she think I was some kind of an intruder? It certainly hadn't been my intention of stepping onto anyone's property. In fact, I was taken by surprise. I didn't turn and run in panic, but walked over and picked up the basket that she had dropped and continued up the stone pathway, to be greeted almost immediately by a well-worn, dumpy, elderly man who was dressed to suit his surroundings.

'"He immediately invited me to step over the threshold. Goats roamed close by. The old man raised his stick and shooed them away. 'Mama's sick, Kitty's getting frailer each day and I'm of no use with this,' he said on his introduction, leaning on his stick and pulling up the leg of the trousers he wore. 'Been without this leg for fifteen years,' he tried to explain in broken English, before beckoning me in.

'"I sat for a while on a wooden seat supported by two

thick stones. In fact it was the only seating in the bare, cold room with just a ray of sunlight casting its way through the poky little window, apart from Mama's old chair with hardly a scrap of material left on the arms, showing the bare stuffing inside. Mama sat there huddling a shawl around her covered bosom. Her mouth opened in a smile, revealing teeth the colour of a dark blend of coffee, which showed her age. Kitty didn't smile, but turned her head away in shyness.

' " 'This place started to crumble years ago,' the old man said. 'We have nowhere else to go.'

' " 'Papa,' the beautiful woman said, standing immediately from the ground where she knelt, embarrassed by his complaining, especially to a stranger.

' " 'Kitty's our only help,' he explained, as she ran out through the door.

' "After explaining that I had come down from the monastery high up in the hills, I was given an open invitation to visit whenever I liked. So my trips back down to that poverty-stricken household became a regular habit. So did pinching from the kitchens at St Vincent's. I learned to walk briskly, cutting the time of my journey by half. The haversack I carried on my back was always crammed. Occasionally, the odd roll of bread would drop out on my steep journey down, which I would eat quite heartily, knowing there was still plenty of food left to share. Walls were rebuilt; goats were milked and wood was chopped; and Kitty and I fell madly in love," Mr Thompson told me, and with a huge sigh knelt down and combed through the soil that lay on top of her grave with the tips of his fingers.

' "She fell pregnant," he said, with grief in his voice,

"and my journeys back to see her became much more frequent. I still tended the gardens at St Vincent's, rising much earlier; my continual absences when my work was through went unnoticed. I felt anxious for Kitty's well-being, very anxious. Mama was waiting to die and hardly moved off her chair. Papa, well he was always smoking something to numb the physical and mental pain he endured. Panic began to set in. From a young boy, I had been protected by the priests. I had no wealth and few personal belongings; the Bible my main one. Who was I to turn to? Would I be cast out of the monastery for my straying ways? My need to marry Kitty before our baby was born was crucial. My burden felt heavy as I trod over the sandy soil one evening when I stopped, stopped still and turned. I'd never done that before, and there, on the ridge of the hilly mountainside stood Father O'Connor. His black gown brushed against his feet in the gentle breeze of the early morning. He didn't beckon me and we stared from a distance. He gave me the freedom to carry on and I continued my descent down the rugged hillside. I turned back once more, but only the thick blades of grass swaying to and fro remained to be seen.

' "The two double doors stood open on my return, calling me to step inside the monastery. 'She's pregnant,' I blurted to Father O'Connor, when I spotted him tidying books on the top shelf in the library. He showed no interest in me. 'I love her, Father, very much,' I told him with slight panic in my voice as I stood at the open door. He stepped down from the ladder and welcomed me in, patting the dust from each hand before rubbing the palms of them together. He pulled out a spindly wooden chair, and then another from beneath the lower shelf. 'I knew you would have to pass by here. Sit down, boy,' I was told. 'I would have been disappointed if you had just walked past and made your way to your room,' Father O'Connor told me, sitting down next to me. 'I've watched each morning from my window as you wander over those grounds, my boy. Then you simply disappear out of view. It didn't take me long before I realised where you were heading.' Questions were asked on why I had got so familiar with them, so familiar that I had stooped to the sin of stealing. 'Falling in love with the girl was the risk you took,' he told me, 'and now there's a baby on the way. Heavens above, boy, what on earth is going to happen now?' My heart felt weak and I had no answer. 'This building might be magnificent, and so it is,' Father continued, 'but we depend mostly on donations and what we do receive has to be handled very carefully, and, as Catholics, you have brought a great burden, not only on yourself, but also on the Church. We, as priests, are here to guide and I have decided to use my own discretion on this matter, so it will be kept, for the time being, between you and me, and God, of course.

' "Father O'Connor then prayed in Latin. I, of course, barely understanding a word, kept my head bowed. He immediately stood up and my legs felt weak as I joined him in a mark of respect. Father, with a slight nod, bid me a good night's rest before making his way out of the library. 'Close the doors, boy, before you leave,' he called to me on his departure with a light tone in his voice. I must admit, as the doors were shut and the thick iron bolt squeaked on locking, I had never felt so alone with the sheer turbulence that was going on in my mind. It was to be a restless night.

' "I didn't have the stomach for my gardening duties the next morning, which ain't like me, lad, but I wandered aimlessly along the lawns and borders. My main thought was that I loved Kitty and that there would be no other choice but to pack my few personal belongings and leave St Vincent's for ever. Mind you, I was scared, lad; so scared of leaving the only life I had ever known to wander over that hill never to return. Aye, you might sigh, lad," I was told as I stood watching Mr Thompson, with his weathered hands, turning over every grain of soil on the mound that covered Kitty's grave.

' "Well, I left that very same morning. There was no food, just an old weathered Bible I carried in my hand. What use was I to Kitty, I thought, with just a Bible full of words to offer? Choked with emotion, I descended the sloping hill. There was no looking back. My choice had been made. I pictured the carcases of goats I would have to kill to feed my new family, or would I have to creep out in the night and steal like a beggar?

' "I thought I heard the sound of my name whistling through the air. Was God telling me not to think like a fool? I looked up. His place was way above, under the blanket of thick grey clouds that covered the sky. God was too far away to guide me. The beat of my heart began to race. The sound of my name echoed into the deep valley. My eyes glared in between the slender trunks of the tall pine trees and below, through stalks of leafy bushes, as I made my way down. 'Who's there?' I called, frightened of my own voice as it echoed around me. 'Edward, Edward.' This time the sound of my name became almost clear. I swiftly turned around. 'Father O'Connor!' I exclaimed.

' "His long black cloak was tucked closely against his short legs as he slid down the hill. 'Edward,' he said, gasping for breath, 'I need to lose some of this weight. I'm certainly not as fit as I used to be.' He finally caught up with me and said, 'Listen, the main thing is that we get you wed.' I stood with my mouth wide open. Shocked to realise that Father O'Connor was a true companion. 'I've little time,' he told me, clinging to his Bible, 'so let's get on with it.'

' "The squelch of Father's footsteps over the clumps of grass was the only sound to be heard as he followed behind me on the pathway that led us along to Papa's goat farm.

' " 'I'm asking permission to marry your daughter,' " I blurted out to Papa on our arrival at the farm. Papa was sitting with his stick by his side on his creaky rocking chair on the open veranda. He pointed his stick towards the open door and Father O'Connor, with a nod towards Papa, followed me in.

' "Kitty was huddled on the stone floor, leaning her head against the sides of Mama's swollen legs as she sat there in her chair. 'Will you marry me?' I asked. She smiled up towards me with slanted sparkling eyes. I hoisted her up gently and held her in my arms, looking over Kitty's narrow shoulders down to Mama. Mama looked up and smiled. Papa, taking his time, limped in and the room went silent as Father O'Connor read out the wedding vows. Papa banged his stick up and down on the floor when Kitty and I were pronounced man and wife, and Mama cried.

'Mr Thompson knelt down and wept, covering his face with his hands. I must admit,' Uncle told me, 'I cried too.'

' "I was given the offer of staying on and tending the gardens at St Vincent's," Mr Thompson told me moments later, his voice faltering on his words. "I would be paid a small wage and Father O'Connor suggested I be given a vegetable plot, and whatever was grown I would be free to take.

' "I worked all the hours God could send. My home at Papa's house was a mattress on the floor in a tiny room where the sunlight would beam down from the narrow window above, and where Kitty and I shared our most tender moments of love.

' "She gave birth on a cold early morning, 5.00 a.m. to be precise, on the 14th of November 1935, to a son. The child gave no cry as I laid him against the warmth of Kitty's bosom. Kitty began to lose a lot of blood. Too much. I realised that she was haemorrhaging. I panicked. 'Mama,' I screeched, turning directly into the room where she sat. Mama didn't move; she couldn't, but stared towards me with fear in her eyes. 'Papa, Papa.' His eyes rolled. I tried to pick him up but he was a dead weight so I left him still crouched in the corner of the room where I had found him. 'I'll be back with help,' I cried to Kitty. Her eyes had dark rims around them as she lay there holding on to our son.

' "I ran out like a raging bull, cursing at the slippery

grass as I struggled to climb as fast as I could up the hilly mountainside. Sighting St Vincent's, my voice bellowed across the long stretch of lawn. 'Help!' I shouted, 'help!' falling over my own feet as I ran along with urgency, trying to alert someone's attention. 'Will someone help?' I shouted through the cupped fingers of my sweaty hands. 'For Christ's sake, help!'

'"Bare light bulbs flickered on here and there. 'Help!' I screamed. Windows were lifted and heads peered out. 'Help!' I screamed once more. Father O'Connor appeared in the distance dressed in a long striped nightshirt. He slipped on his sandals and ran towards me, covering himself as he slipped his arms through the sleeves of his black gown. 'Kitty's losing blood, lots of it,' I told him, trying to catch my breath.

'"'Call the house doctor,' he called to Father Michael, who was rushing out of the building towards us. 'Tell him to go to the farm down in the valley,' he shouted.

'"Father O'Connor slid most of the way down the hill. I followed directly behind. The thorny bushes grazed our skin as we tumbled our way down to the farm where Kitty and our newly born son lay.

'"We barged through the open doorway and immediately ran into Kitty's room. 'There's a doctor on the way,' I whispered, kneeling down by her side as she lay on the bed, eyes wide open, with her slender arms wrapped around the child as if she never wanted to let him go.

'"Father O'Connor leaned over from the opposite side, felt Kitty's pulse and then sighed. 'What,' I asked him, 'what?' 'She's passed away, Edward,' he told me before closing Kitty's eyes. 'The baby?' I asked. 'He's alive, Edward.

264

See his little heart pumping.' I shielded myself over Kitty and my son as the doctor, a tall, pale, wispy man, rushed in with a rather breathless Father Michael. He knew Kitty was dead. They both sighed and moved to take the baby who was wrapped in Kitty's arms. 'I'm not going to lift that child from his mother,' I told them. 'Give my son a little more time to lie against her, in her arms, while they are still soft and warm.'

' "Father O'Connor bowed his head and waited. 'Come on now, Edward, let the doctor do his job. Edward, pick up the child. Edward, are you listening? You've held them both long enough. It's no more healthy for your newborn son than it is for you.'

' "I was advised to stand outside. 'Some fresh air, that's what you need, Edward,' Father O'Connor told me. Do you know, Dennis," Mr Thompson turned to say, "I didn't have the guts to pull my baby son away from his mother and walked out of the room. I crouched down on the creaky platform of the open veranda and cried. 'Some fat use you are, Lord,' I cried out in anger, looking up at the sky before burying my head in my hands and sobbing. A hand gently touched my shoulder. 'You'd better step in, Edward,' Father O'Connor said in a quiet, calm manner. I brushed my tears aside, stood, and took in a deep breath before Father O'Connor led me inside. Father Michael stood with his head down holding the baby, who was wrapped in goat's skin, a piece that Kitty had saved from Papa's first skinning of one.

' "The doctor introduced himself as Nicholas Henderson. He was a well-spoken young man, bald on top with a rather pale complexion on a face that was thin and drawn.

I shoved my hands deep inside my trouser pockets and waited for what he had to say.

' " 'There's a possibility that the child is mute,' he told me, looking towards me with his pale blue eyes.

' " 'What possibility?' I asked sharply.

' " 'Every possibility, Mr Thompson,' Dr Henderson quickly replied.

' " 'The child has made no sound, Edward,' Father O'Connor told me.

' " 'And should he so soon?' I asked. Nicholas Henderson nodded his head.

' " 'We'll have to give him all the care that is needed, Edward,' Father O'Connor said. 'I suggest the Sisters of Charity take over the responsibility, at least for the time being. It's the proper thing to do, Edward. What other choice do we have?'

' "My arms felt weak as I stretched out to take my child from Father Michael, yet they were incredibly strong when I picked him up and held him tightly. I sighed, looking down at my beautiful son locked in my arms, and I shed a tear or two at that very moment.

' "Whispering went on around the room and Father Michael immediately dashed out. 'We've not long have we, Father, the child and me, before he's taken?' my voice quivering on every word. Father O'Connor nodded.

' "I left the room where Kitty lay, with my son tightly in my grasp, and wandered towards where Mama sat. I saw the pain on Mama's face, that terrible look of grief. 'Mama, Kitty's dead, I know, but look,' I said, kneeling down next to her, 'you have a grandson.' Mama's dark brown eyes filled up with tears. Laying him on her lap,

266

she managed to reach out her hands, which were riddled with arthritis, and touch him as gently as she could, brushing lightly against his forehead with the tips of her short stubby fingers.

' "I waited a while, just a short while, before picking him up and snuggling him once again in my arms. 'Papa, your grandson,' I said, walking over to the corner of the room where he was crouched. I leant down to show him. Papa's eyes rolled. I managed to pat him on his shoulder and hoped he would get a glimpse, just one glimpse, but opium had filled his brain and I felt hopelessly sad.

' "My dream of sharing a life with Kitty had suddenly come to an end, yet I still shared part of it, that dream, with the baby son she had left me, who lay fast asleep in my arms.

' "I was hopeless at choosing a name when all of a sudden he was to be taken, so I blessed him with mine before handing him over to the arms of a nun."

'And Mama, Papa and your son, what happened to them? I asked Mr Thompson, with urgency in my voice.

' "Mama died in her chair, as expected, within weeks of Kitty passing away. Papa, well, he made sure that whatever he took the night Mama died was enough to follow her to his grave. At least they're both together. They're buried further down the valley at the farm, the only home they ever knew. Mind you, it doesn't exist any more. Eventually, over the years it crumbled to the ground bit by bit, but it's a place where newborn goats wander freely and Papa will know by the treading of their feet that his wish was granted to be finally laid to rest on his beloved farm."

'I could hear the faint sound of bells chiming around the valley where I stood. My heart skipped a beat and I took a step back. Was Kitty going to rise from the dead? The sound became much clearer. Mr Thompson looked up. I turned. Were Mama and Papa going to be there right behind me, Mama sitting in her chair and Papa leading two goats in the hazy mist?

' "Right, lad," Mr Thompson called. I jumped at the sound of his voice and turned back immediately. Mr Thompson smelled the sweet soil he held in his hand before sprinkling it through his fingertips. He complained out loud about his aching limbs while getting to his feet. The bells rang much louder.

' "St Vincent's?" I asked.

' "Sounds like it's a matter of urgency," Mr Thompson said, making his way towards the hilly mountainside. I made sure that I followed close by. "Those bells never sound out at this early hour unless it is..." he called, sounding quite breathless as he climbed up the hill.

'We scrambled our way up, both grabbing hold of the tufts of grass bedded deep into the sandy soil to help us on our climb.

' "I've met your son," I called as I followed swiftly behind.

' "Wouldn't have much to say for himself, would he, lad?" Mr Thompson called back.

' "Enough," I shouted.

'Mr Thompson turned, reached out his hand and hoisted me up to the top before we ran together across the lawn. "You see, lad," he shouted to make himself heard over the loud ringing of the bells as we continued running, "I owe my own and my son's life to St Vincent's. Eddie was eight years old when the Sisters of Charity brought him back to me. They'd taught him a lot, a lot more than I ever could have. This is our sanctuary, Dennis," he called, looking straight ahead as we ran side by side. "And when I die they'll only have to take me the short journey down the mountainside so that I can be buried right by Kitty's side."

'The bells' tone became lower and only a slight echo remained before they eventually stopped, leaving our panting breath more noticeable. Father O'Connor came into sight as we ran the remainder of the distance. He looked like some ghostly figure. His long, floating gown hung down over him without movement in the stillness of the morning. He stood, hands clasped, waiting on the edge of the stony footpath in the damp rising mist. A tall figure appeared behind him. I squinted with the salty sweat that rolled down my forehead leaving a harsh sting in my eyes. Was it Ernest? I thought in a moment of madness, rubbing my eyes fiercely to rid my blurred vision. I practically stumbled over the wide border filled with shrubs, feeling shock.

' "Your belongings are being packed at this very moment," Ernest told me as Father O'Connor stepped to one side. "We will have to leave the country in the next forty-eight hours. All British personnel will have to go. We no longer have any part in the ruling of India."

'Ernest looked pale, grey in the face in fact, standing there with trembling fingers which he locked on noticing my look. It was obvious to me, knowing Ernest as I did, that a skinful of gin down him would have stopped the shakes.

269

' "Mr Thompson, may I introduce you to my father, Ernest Dorrell," I said. Ernest grunted, impatient with any formality, then took Father O'Connor aside in private conversation.

' "Fancy coming home with me, Mr Thompson?" I asked.

' "Fancy staying here instead?" Mr Thompson replied with a serious tone in his voice.

' "Want a bet on it?" I said, trying to be jovial.

' "No, because I'll win, won't I, lad?"

' "I'm not at all sure about that, Mr Thompson."

' "No, lad, probably not for the time being. Today, lad, you've got what you wanted, but you'll never forget your stay here, and one day, just one day in your life, lad, you'll stroll up that driveway and come back to see us with better memories than you're leaving with today." I shrugged off his comments while accepting a pat on the shoulder. "Good luck, lad."

' "Well, I'll be off," Mr Thompson called over to Father O'Connor. "Jobs to do." Father O'Connor gave his usual nod; then, with one final pat on my shoulder, Mr Thompson walked away.

' "Dennis," Ernest called, beckoning me over. I tripped over myself looking back as Mr Thompson strode off over the grass. "Dennis!" Ernest said with a snap in his voice. I held up my hand. Ernest knew to keep silent.

'I stood and stared that misty morning until the land finally took Mr Thompson from my view. I felt a huge lump inside my throat and my eyes suddenly filled with emotion.

' "Dennis, you'd better go and check that your room is left clean and tidy." Ernest's voice seemed far away. In

270

fact it was as if, just at that moment, I felt Ernest's presence to be void as I wiped away the tears I had shed. Ernest coughed in a deliberate attempt to get my attention. "Bobo isn't as young as he used to be," he went on to say. "The burden of packing all of our belongings back home has taken its toll on him, so I suggest you go immediately to your room and help the poor man out."

'The thought of Bobo being so near to my belongings made me suddenly feel as if I was turning into some green-eyed monster. I ran with great force along the stony path. Although breathless, I stood as silently as I could outside my window, wiping the dew that coated the glass with the sleeve of my sweater, and peeped in. There he was, the short-arsed little shit, with his back turned, sitting at my desk, pen in hand, pretending to be some scholar. The cuffs from his sleeves still hung low, covering his hands, leaving only his long, thin fingers in view. His greasy black hair touched the tip of the frayed collar of the nylon anorak he wore. Grace had given it to him a long time ago when she was certain, from my abhorrent reaction, that lilac was a colour I would definitely not wear. It was much too large in the sleeves for Bobo, but his excitement was too much to bear when it was offered to him. Grace complimented him on how good he looked in it. I scoffed at the thought. Feminine, it's too feminine a colour, I tried to explain to him, but Bobo was having none of it, and he was warned by me at that time never to wear it in my company. Remember, Bobo, I'll not be seen dead next to you wearing that, I had told him, as he looked down admiring himself. His urgency to show off to his friends was obvious as he fled from the kitchen.

271

' "Dennis, you're too hard on him," Grace said. "Leave the poor man be." Her advice at the time was sound; after all it wasn't as if Bobo and I would ever be out together at a social gathering.

'My patience, standing there on that damp morning, surprised me, holding back the urge to jump through the bloody window to get my hands around his neck. Bobo then stood, after scribbling on paper after paper. He bowed his head, moving it up and down towards the grey painted wall as if the wall had come to life and there was a crowd of people applauding him on his work. I remained silent, peering in with my face squashed against the pane of glass.

'Grace, had she been alive, would have whispered over my shoulder, "Let Bobo enjoy the few minutes of his dream, his dream of always wanting to be a scholar. Let him imagine what it might feel like in his short visit to St Vincent's, and even if his dream only lasts a few seconds, let him have that privilege."

'I felt then, at that very instant, that I had a heart, and Bobo was right there, right there inside. I sighed quite heavily. The vapour from my breath blocked my view. I rubbed vigorously with the sleeve of my woolly sweater, which squeaked against the glass, alerting Bobo to my presence. He jumped and squinted a couple of times before realising that I was standing there.

' "Open the bloody window," I called. Bobo rushed immediately to it, using all his strength.

' "Don't look so bloody surprised," I told him, climbing through. "We had to meet again some time," I said as I brushed myself down. "Bet you didn't think it would be as soon as this."

272

'Bobo mumbled some sort of apology, bowing down to me while retreating backwards to the far corner of the room. I felt quite sick. We were no longer in the kitchen back home, where Ernest and Grace would fight almost daily, and Bobo would have to constantly duck and weave in between the odd pieces of china being thrown, but we were both here, in this grey, oblong room. I kept the moment tense, just for another tease, which was quite naughty considering that I really did feel for Bobo. After all, the only life he knew, I suppose, was scrubbing floors and running around like a headless chicken for a society he thought was better than his.

'He had aged since I had last seen him. He looked towards me with his dull, solemn eyes. I lifted a cigarette, one of three left, from deep down inside my trouser pocket, and passed it over. His thick lips opened, wetting the tip as he immediately placed it in his mouth. A loose match was struck in between the cracks of the stone that covered the floor, but failed to light with the dampness. Bobo waited until I struck lucky, inhaling deeply before blowing smoke out through his mouth and down his hairy nostrils as if he were some dragon.

'I could hear the sound of voices approaching. Father O'Connor's strong Irish accent softer than the bold upper-class manner of Ernest. I ripped the cigarette immediately from Bobo's mouth and threw it through the open window. Ernest sniffed the air as he entered.

' "We'll be leaving by carriage the same way as we came on your journey to St Vincent's, Dennis, and then by train," Ernest said.

'I noticed the shiny wooden handle of a pistol he was

carrying, weighing down the inside pocket of his tweed jacket as he leaned over to check that the trunk had been fastened securely.

'"You won't be teaching him any more bad habits on our journey down, will you, Dennis?" he said, referring to Bobo as he looked out of the corner of his eye towards me. "Only the whole of the journey will be treacherous as it is, without any tomfoolery."

'I sensed the tension Ernest felt, clicking his fingers for Bobo's attention. The few words Ernest said were in Punjabi, harsh I should imagine, as Bobo struggled with the weight of the trunk. Ernest seemed to find some compassion as he grabbed hold of one of the iron handles, leaving Bobo with a tight grip on the other, and helped him carry it out of the room. Ernest's voice melted away in the distance along the corridor as I continued to lean against the open door. Bobo had kept silent to Ernest's banter, no doubt complaining of the utter inconvenience I had caused. It pleased me being right. After all, it was Ernest's gallant idea to send me here in the first place.

'I didn't expect to kneel on the hard surface of the floor near to where the wooden cross hung down and pray for guidance for those people I had met here in the monastery. Even Robin, the old head boy, got a silent mention. I asked the Lord for extra special guidance for Mr Edward Thompson and his son.

'I could hear the familiar sound of Father O'Connor's sweeping cloak and the creak from the strap of leather that crossed the sandals that he wore. I didn't turn, but kept my head bowed in the hope that my silent prayers would be answered. Father O'Connor coughed lightly, a hint I

274

presumed. Struggling to my feet, I walked over to the door to make my exit, turning for one last glance at the cross that bore little importance to me when I had first arrived here. Now I felt I was carrying away with me some comfort and guidance from it before I started my journey along the musty corridor that would eventually lead me out through the main doors to leave St Vincent's for ever.

'Drawing close to the dining room, I could hear the clatter of pans and the clinking of cutlery. I glanced quickly through the wide open doors into the vacant hall, not stopping to reminisce about how desperately lonely and left out I had felt that first morning, sitting over a plate of mushy scrambled egg which I had forced myself to eat while being made a spectacle of by fellow pupils.

'Father O'Connor tried to make light of the shudder I gave on my way past and stopped for a second to look through into the hall that would soon be full of starving young men.

' "Will you be here until you die?" I asked when he eventually caught up and we walked in a respectable slow fashion side by side. "I don't mean to shock you, sir, with my question," as Father O'Connor frowned, "but will you? Well, what I'm trying to say, if you don't mind me asking, sir, is that ... well, you've got to have had a life somewhere, before you grew up and decided to become a priest.

' "You have filled me with frustration at your negative attitude since the day you arrived here," Father O'Connor told me, leaning against the deep ledge of a tall stained glass window. "Your question is frank, and the bravery of asking such a personal question as that, before you take your final few steps back into your world, a world far away from St Vincent's, amuses me. Now is not the time to go into my past. All you need know is that St Vincent's is heaven compared to the Belfast I grew up in, and I will be happy to end my days here."

'Father O'Connor gave a nervous cough, giving me no time to apologise. "We lived rough on the outskirts of Belfast," he began to say. "My mother lived for the Church. God was the only one she believed would guide her. The Bible would be snatched from her tiny hands many a time when my father came home with a skinful of whisky inside him. I would creep down and watch her vacant chair rock many a time before lifting the Bible that lay sprawled across the bare floorboards, after my father had dragged her up the dark wooden staircase and raped her. He had to prove that he was more important than God himself to my poor mother. The Bible, that old worn out Bible she read, was soon to be stripped of its pages and ripped into shreds with the strength of my father's thick, strong hands.

'"My mother, in church on a bleak, wintry morning after we had finished praying to God, pushed me in front, making me her shield as we stepped from the pew but was caught red-handed slipping the Bible she held that belonged to the church, underneath the drape of her woolly shawl that hung down from her shoulders."

'I leaned down with my knees crunched, resting my back against the rough wall opposite Father O'Connor. His eyes showed the emotion he felt on choosing to answer my question. "She was branded a thief and disowned by the Catholic Church where she worshipped. The only friends she had were nosy neighbouring women who would congregate in my mother's kitchen. There wasn't much

276

room. The stone cooker, a weathered-looking kitchenette and a folding down kitchen table that wobbled at the legs, took up most of the space. Three neighbouring friends in all, who still managed with their over-sized bodies, each with folded arms and clasped hands underneath their droopy bosoms, to stand there inside displaying scenes of distress for her. Totally false, of course," Father O'Connor stressed in a much sterner voice.

'"My mother was a pretty wee thing, long curly auburn hair, always neatly tied up in a bun, and emerald eyes that, no matter what, smiled. She was so finely boned you could almost imagine that with one crush she would break into pieces. I ran through the streets many a time, peering through smoky glass windows, spotting my father once or twice drooling over a thick pint of Guinness as he sat leaning over a round wooden beer barrel. I would run home fast, sweat rolling down my thin chest, trying to get my mother to sleep in my bed. It worked a few times. I, lying on the bare floorboards underneath my bed where she slept, scared stiff of his footsteps as my father staggered up the creaking stairs late at night.

'"One morning my mother let me dress in my short grey pants and long grey socks. She looked drawn, and her face troubled. She scolded me a few times for not checking that all my schoolbooks were in my satchel, while listening with one ear up that dark staircase in case my father had sobered up. He would be lying there in his bed while the normal pattern that went on each school day carried on. She had over-packed a bag made from string and with a shaking hand unlocked the key in the wee front door, and we stepped out on to the pavement

277

of our sloping street. My mother's eyes searched all around her before she whisked me by my elbow down the steep slope until we passed every street and reached the station. Her wee hands trembled against the click of her worn purse as it was opened, and she dropped the pennies into a tiny slot. The ticket master took hold of them one by one, then stared admiringly towards her through the dirty thick square glass window he sat behind. My mother looked around, all around, as the podgy-faced man rolled out two tickets that curled down from a black metal ring he held with his grubby fingers. My mother shoved the tickets inside her purse and clicked it shut before I was led again by my elbow onto the narrow wooden platform of the litter strewn station.

' "The train moved in slowly, hissing with puffs of smoke that rose up into the cloudy sky. My mother gripped me even tighter and took another look around before lifting me onto the step. We both sat down on a cracked leather seat, my mother shoving me up to the grubby window. I somehow knew that we were leaving for good. The train moved away from the station and my mother sat back for the journey that would take us far away."

'I felt not only intrigued, but honoured that Father O'Connor felt comfortable enough to give me an insight into his past, trying to ignore the strong urge I had for the puff of a cigarette in anticipation of what he might tell me next. I remained silent and very still.

' "A downpour of rain suddenly appeared, lashing against the train as it sped along the track," he continued, "barring any vision out through the steamy window. Mother sensed my look towards her as she stared straight ahead and squeezed my hand tightly, leaving me feeling safe about whatever decision she had taken.

'"The train stopped several times here and there for a few minutes. I, waiting in anticipation, wondered when it would be our time to leave as people stepped out and on to the platform, and others stepped in before our journey began again. I opened my satchel, which had remained strapped over my shoulder since leaving home that morning, purely out of boredom. After all, the marks and comments from my teacher were nothing to be proud of. Needless to say, my lunch for school, which Mother had made me, was pulled out first. Mother opened the lid of the box that had been pressed down tightly, and we enjoyed some rather curled up brown bread with salmon paste inside. A hard green apple, rather bitter in taste, was bitten in turn. My drink of bottled milk would be waiting at the school I attended back home, curdling by now.

'"As the train stopped once more my mother stretched across me and we peered through the tiny window together into the quaint timber-framed station where the sun's rays beamed directly through, and an old man sat on a green painted bench smoking his pipe with a rolled up newspaper underneath his arm. That was when my mother decided, urging me up from my seat, that this was where a new life for us would begin.

'"We wandered through the tiny cobbled streets; me tightly holding my mother's hand as we passed the faces of strangers. We soon entered the village square, quite by surprise, and found a row of fancy shops with hats and pretty dresses and brightly coloured shoes, which my mother stood and stared at through windows as shiny as a sixpenny piece. She scoured the shop windows and spotted a cottage advertised for rent on a plain white postcard written in clear black ink. She left me standing outside and came out smiling. 'It's not far,' I was told, 'and I've enough money too,' she said, fixing her eyes on another card advertising a job as housekeeper with lodgings.

' "It's up there. It's a long walk for you, wee laddie,' a flush-faced, plump old man said as he held onto the open door of his grocery shop, checking that his advertisements were neat and straight. My mother stared up towards the big, old sandstone vicarage built on top of a hill, looking down over the valley of trees and bright green fields.

' "Where are you from?" he asked while holding onto the braces of his baggy grey trousers, obviously wondering why two strangers had suddenly appeared from nowhere. My mother grabbed hold of my hand and led me away.

' " 'You've got to come from somewhere,' he called.

' " 'Don't be answering,' I was told as my mother sharpened her step until we disappeared from his view. I did pull back, just for a second, peeping through a cast iron railing down to a couple of stone steps, then through a poky little window that displayed many a boat carved in wood, with brightly painted flags to hoist. 'I'll be sailing on one of those one day,' I told my mother.

' " 'I'll buy you one for Christmas; you can sail it in your bath.' I felt the tension in her as she pulled me away. The journey didn't take us much further, just down a narrow dirt track to the run-down cottage that my mother hoped to rent.

' "A young man with arms as long as flagpoles headed

over the fields towards us, jumped off his roaring tractor and negotiated with my mother on the cost. 'Well, it's my father's cottage. As long as he knows,' the young farmer's son told her, stuffing the money into the pocket of his heavily soiled overalls, before returning to his tractor and driving it over the vast fields until we saw him no more.

' "My mother and I found a smile for one another as we struggled together with the rusty iron key to open the lock. A rusty old oil-lamp was soon lit. My mother sat there on a tiny wooden bench just inside the door, turning to look through the miniature glass window, its frame rotted with woodworm, that looked out onto the rich green fields before giving a lengthy sigh. I slipped her flat sandals from her tiny slender feet before cuddling up beside her. 'It'll have to do, wee William, until I can find work,' she told me. 'We'll get a fire going first thing; that'll get rid of the dampness,' she said, sniffing the air.

' "Dusk was closing in. Exhausted, my mother and I held onto each other's hands and made our way up the tiny flight of stone steps. The wooden door creaked with the eeriness of the night, and we shivered underneath the blanket as we lay our heads down onto the thin sprung mattress on top of the cast iron bed. I heard my mother whimpering during the night. I wiped her tears with my bare hands. 'He won't be coming up those stairs, not any more,' she cried as I held my arms as tightly as I could around her.

' "I woke to the sound of a cockerel, but after a restless night, twisted myself around underneath the blanket and fell back to sleep.

' " 'I'll be going to find work. There's a speckled egg

boiled in the pan for you, son,' I was told as I found my way into the kitchen. 'Lucky, if you ask me, that those hens wandered so close,' my mother said, slapping a piece of rag up towards the low beamed ceiling at the ghostly looking cobwebs, swaying with the force of air at each attempted strike.

'" 'It's the vicarage, isn't it, Mother, where you're going?'

'" 'Well, I wasn't going to tell you just in case.'

'" 'You'll get it, Mother.'

'" 'I don't know, son.'

'" 'Course you will,' I told her.

'" 'There's lodgings too, which means we won't have to stay here in this cottage another day. It's filthy and damp.' My mother looked towards me with an anxious expression. 'The Lord might not be with me, son. Not after stealing a Bible from his church. I'll be going to confession at the first opportunity to try and rid myself of this guilt I feel. I did a bad thing, William, stealing from God's house. How on earth will he find forgiveness? And, if news travels fast, there's no hope of getting the job.'

'" 'God forgives all who sin; that's what you've taught me to believe.'

'" 'You're getting taller, young William, and wiser. There'll be no more short trousers for you to wear soon. To think that you're eleven coming the end of the month.'

'" She threw her mac over her shoulders and grabbed her purse from the dusty kitchen table. 'Find a brush from somewhere and sweep this floor for me. I'll be bringing a loaf back and something we might both fancy to eat. Find what pots you can and set the table.'

'" The door was slammed shut and I watched my mother

from the wee kitchen window slip her arms into the sleeves of her mac before running down the dirt track. I was faster on my feet than her and plucked a cluster of clover from the wild garden outside.

' " 'Mother, Mother!' I called, running towards her, passing her my bouquet as she stopped and turned.

' " 'William, you bring a smile to my face like no one else can. I'll carry these lovely flowers in my hand all the way for luck, son.'

' " 'Good luck, my beautiful mother,' I whispered before she finally disappeared from view. She won't be long, I thought, fearful of this lonely old place.

' "I checked that nothing had been left before hanging my mother's string bag on the open latch of the kitchen door, ready to wait for her return, when I would run into the garden and she would tell me her good news before whisking me off to live high upon the hill.

' "With no watch or sense of time, I followed the sun's direction. It had moved slowly, peeping in and out of scattered clouds and I realised the morning had turned into afternoon, leaving a dark shadow over the cottage. I stood and watched as far as the eye could see along the narrow dirt track, hoping that at any time I would catch a glimpse of my smiling mother. My hunger had passed as I anxiously waited. The tweet of the birds flying overhead had faded, and the sun was dying down, making me shiver with goose pimples at the sudden breeze. The green grass swayed in the desolate fields around me, and I ran and ran as fast as I could down the track in search of my mother. The village seemed almost deserted. The market had folded away, leaving litter scattered on the ground in the barren square. Shutters and blinds were pulled down before my very eyes. The stout butcher nodded to me underneath his linen cap while lifting a steel tray with racks of lamb decorated in fine white paper socks, and the old man who assisted him turned the key in the lock. I peered through the thick glass window of the red telephone box.

' " 'Have you seen my mother?' I asked a total stranger as she walked by leading a curly white poodle by her side. 'She's not very tall and has long wavy auburn hair and sparkling green eyes. She'll be holding a purse in her hand if you did. Her name's Frances O'Connor,' I called as the lady snootily passed me by.

' "Suddenly, I noticed the sandstone vicarage that looked down over the village. I kicked myself for not thinking as I headed up the long sloping hill. She'd probably got the job as housekeeper and no doubt would have had to start work immediately. I gave a sigh of relief and wondered how my mother had managed to walk so far. The muscles in my legs were already aching.

' "The narrow windy road had been partially cordoned off as I reached the top. I made my way carefully around the perimeter of bollards. A sign made from tin was standing on the side of the road, facing opposite my direction. I presumed it was a warning to prevent any oncoming traffic from driving through. I was urged by the priest as I walked along the narrow verge below to take the broad stone steps up to where he stood.

' " 'I gather you were coming here?' he asked. I was surprised at how young he looked for a priest, as he stood in a long flowing black gown in the peaceful grounds of the wide open graveyard, among the smell of the colourful sweetpeas that were shared out, equally bunched, on the tombstones of each grave. 'The church doors are always open for any visitors, no matter what age,' he said, obviously also surprised at how young I was to take an interest in God's house.

' " 'What time will my mother finish her work?' I asked as I approached him, 'if you don't mind me asking, sir. She came for the job of housekeeper early this morning.'

' " 'Ah, yes, a delightful young lady.'

' " 'You won't be disappointed in her, sir. She polishes and shines everything until it's as shiny as a new sixpenny piece. Would you kindly let her know that I'm here, sir?'

' " 'I'm Father McKenzie,' he introduced himself.

' " 'William,' I told him on the shake of a hand. 'I won't be idle while I wait. I can do some weeding if you like, sir.'

' " 'Where have you come from, my son?' he asked.

' " 'From the cottage down in the valley,' I replied.

' " 'Only you have a strong Belfast accent.'

' " 'That's because my father was raised there, but he died a long time ago,' and God forgive me for lying, I thought. It's just that I didn't want Father McKenzie to track down any link there could be on my mother's background. If they found out that she stole the Bible from the church she would most probably be sacked on the spot.

' " 'Ah, your mother is here now. Rosemary, bring some tea out and a glass of water for the boy,' he called over, 'while we chat. You'll find the necessary items somewhere in the kitchen. Just have a look around. Probably in one

285

of the many dusty cupboards,' he called out as she vanished behind shut doors. 'I'm afraid I've had to leave her to her own devices with the tragedy of what went on in the narrow lane below. A sudden death right outside the church. Poor woman. From what I'm led to believe she dropped her purse in the middle of the road. Right there,' Father McKenzie pointed. 'An onlooker was saying that she was in so much of a rush to cross over that her purse slipped from her hand and spilled open. Before she had chance to gather the coins together she was mown down by a tractor turning the bend in the road far too fast.'

' " 'Sir, if you don't mind me saying, I think you've got a little mixed up. My mother's name is Frances, Frances O'Connor.'

' " 'So Rosemary is not your mother?'

' " 'No. Frances. Frances O'Connor is my mother. She's got long wavy hair and eyes of emerald green.

' "Father McKenzie wavered on his feet and I saw sorrow in his eyes.

' " 'Did she get the job; tell me she did, Father, please, please tell me.'

' " 'I'm sorry, William, but with your description and the time that your mother should have arrived—'

' " 'She's dead, isn't she? She's dead,' I screamed and screamed, banging my fists against his chest before collapsing in his arms.

' "I was soon to identify her body. I was next of kin, so Father McKenzie thought. The last thing I wanted was for my drunken father to be notified, to slaver with false words of love over the slab she lay on.

' "I passed my eleventh birthday stricken with grief. It was now me alone without my dear mother by my side. It was me who lived in the vicarage high upon the hill, as the kind Father McKenzie took me in.

' "My education was to continue with Father McKenzie as my tutor in the old reading room, a quiet dark place inside the vicarage walls, which had books of every description stacked from the floor to the high ornate ceiling above. My dear mother was buried within the church grounds, Father McKenzie's influence saw to that, which enabled me to look down through the arched window of my room over the plot where she had been laid to rest.

' "There was always a strong feeling that my mother was by my side and listening to me from beyond the grave. As I approached the age of fifteen I knelt at her grave one day and told her that my mind had been made up and I had chosen to give the remainder of my life to work with God's charities. Father McKenzie left me to stew for a period of time, asking no questions for he knew in his heart that I had truly chosen my journey in life.

' "The fragrant smell of sweet peas had blossomed again. Father McKenzie stood in silence with luggage in both hands as I filled a vase with fresh water and a colourful array of flowers and left them with my mother, sheltered in front of her marble headstone with her name, Frances O'Connor, printed in gold. I turned just once for that one last glance. The bee was already at work, sucking out the nectar as my mother's flowers swayed in the light breeze, and I walked away in silence with Father McKenzie by my side down the wide stone steps before our long journey began to our final destination here at St Vincent's."

'I swallowed very hard as Father O'Connor said no more. Ernest was waiting. He ranted and raved like a wild dog. "Don't you realise how humid it is out there? It will be mid-afternoon before we catch that train, and that in itself is draining enough. Any more loitering by you and we'll miss the damn thing. Dennis, the trunk is waiting to be lifted. Bobo hasn't got the strength he used to have, so I suggest you give this matter your immediate attention," he told me in a much calmer manner.

' "Move your arse," I told Bobo as I jumped down the steps, immediately picking up the handle on the side of the trunk. "Playing for sympathy, are you, just because your bones are getting old and brittle?" Bobo had the cheek to wink at me, lifting the other end before hunching his back as we carried it towards the carriage. "You cunning little bastard, but you always have been, haven't you, Bobo, to gain sympathy that you know you'll get from Ernest? Get lifting high before I kick your arse," I told him as we placed the trunk on the wooden bench next to a middle-aged Indian, who looked as if he didn't hold too many scruples, but was chosen to guide the cart with two weary-eyed oxen down the sloping pathways through the mountains.

' "Tell me," I asked Bobo as we both struggled to tie the thick twisted rope to secure the trunk for our journey, "or I'll soon show Ernest that you still have muscles on those wiry arms of yours that you think your long baggy sleeves will hide, did you make contact with Barbara?" Bobo looked at me in confusion. "Barbara, the stable girl. Horses," I said, neighing in mimic towards him, forgetting at that point that he understood English.

288

'Ernest swiftly walked down the steps and ordered Bobo to be seated immediately. I dusted my hands and looked towards Father O'Connor, who was standing on the steps in front of the wide open doors at the entrance to St Vincent's.

' "Your watch, Dennis," Ernest said. "It was lying on the floor in your room. Put it on your wrist." I placed the round face of the watch up against my ear and listened to the tick before leaping the short distance to where Father O'Connor stood.

' "Would you please, sir, give this to Mr Edward Thompson with this message? Tell him that every time a second ticks by, and minutes are made, these will be times when I think of him wherever I may be in this world. I'm not going to say farewell," I told him, kissing the palms of his limp hands, "because you'll always be with me."

'Embarrassed, my eyes filled with tears. I ran swiftly and sat facing him from afar as the wheels of the carriage began to turn. I looked up towards the blacked-out windows built up high in the roof of the monastery and wondered if Eddie was sitting there looking out.

'A film of dust from the carriage wheels was left floating in the air. I could still hear Lily's cries ringing in my ears, me waiting in the long dismal corridor of St Helier's to be invited into the room where Lily was born, and now I was going to England to cradle her in my arms once more. My vision of St Vincent's was blurred as I sought to capture it once more before the mountains suddenly took us steeply down and away from its haunting view.'

\*　\*　\*

Uncle appeared spent and quickly announced that he would retire. He stumbled towards the staircase, then held tightly onto the shiny wooden bannister as he slowly climbed the stairs. I was flattered that he had shared with me his tender memories that could never be left behind. I could hear his unsteady footsteps along the creaky wooden floor above. The guest room welcomed a most interesting character and I was sure that my dearest Uncle would be in for a very peaceful night.

The soft springs of my mattress gave me no comfort after a restless night of haunting memories as I lay staring up at the white spirals on the ceiling. The ruffled sheets were cast aside. My body overcome with sadness, I sat with my feet dangling over the edge of the bed. The twittering of birds encouraged me to wrap myself inside my dressing gown, securing the belt around my waist. I slipped my feet into my fluffy slippers before making my way across the room. The cord to the long velvet curtains was pulled, and I released the stiff latch of the Georgian window. The rise of early morning mist left ghostly shadows among the twists of branches in the woodland beyond. I leant out through the open window, looking towards the garden below. Dewdrops trickled down towards the roots of thin blades of grass and I sniffed in the scent of dawn.

The house martins were at peace here for their annual stay in the grounds of Rutherford House and, with hard labour, had built secure homes for their loved ones underneath the eaves above my bedroom window. I caught sight of tips of tiny pointed beaks peeping out above the edge of half-cupped nests of mud, the birds chirruping along to the mixed chorus of early morning song. My grief left me for a fleeting moment, and I smiled to myself that soon the chicks would find the strength and courage to spread their tiny wings, and fly out into their own world to freedom.

The en suite to the master bedroom was as old as the house itself. The mosaic floor, cold to the feet, swirled in colour. It wasn't my favourite place but I needed a cool shower. Maybe it would relieve the burning anxiety I felt inside. Still tense afterwards, I slipped into a loose cotton dress and the comfort of a well worn pair of sandals. My hair gripped securely in a French pleat, I almost felt ready to face the day ahead. But I screamed inside, wanting the pain of grief to go away.

As I stepped into the kitchen, Uncle was dropping his luggage with a slap against the stone floor. He gently put his arms around my shoulders.

'Hope the skyline brightens up, my love. It's going to be ghastly enough leaving you here. It's such a beautiful place, but lonely for a young lady alone.'

Uncle's paisley cravat matched the gold buttons on the double-breasted blazer he wore. With his perfectly pressed cream slacks and smooth, tanned leather sandals, Uncle knew he fitted the bill.

'You look rather smart,' I told him.

'And you look rather pretty, my love, in your floral dress.'

I smiled. Uncle smiled back.

'Boiled, fried or scrambled?' I asked, lifting a carton of eggs from the fridge.

'I'm not hungry, my love.'

'Then scrambled it will be,' I told him, cracking open

the shells against the rim of a wobbly old saucepan and allowing the yokes to slip down into it. 'Tea or coffee?' I called against the whistle of the kettle. There was no reply. 'Then coffee it is.' The rattling of the teaspoon against delicate bone china alerted Uncle to my approach. He stood and briskly walked over, taking hold of the shaky cup and saucer from my unsteady hand.

'I know there's not much time before I leave, but I've lit the fire. Could we have breakfast by the glow of a burning log?'

Uncle and I made a good team. Toast jumped up from the toaster; the kettle whistled once more; the radio was tuned into Radio 4 and the kitchen came alive. Uncle dressed the bareness of two copper trays with crisp white linen cloths.

'Scissors?'

'Over there in the drawer,' I told him.

Uncle whistled his way along the kitchen and, with the lift of the latch, left through the back door. I peeped out through the window and watched before his search along the garden path took him from view. Rashers of bacon sizzled and a tomato popped under the heat of the grill.

'Don't look,' Uncle said, hands behind his back, on his return.

Plates were warmed and breakfast was ready to be served. Uncle slipped off his blazer and folded his cravat, then instructed me to go and be seated on a chair by the fire. Uncle's walk was steady as he placed the tray across my lap. A rose of pink petals with shoots of fresh green leaves, moisture glistening on its stem, had been carefully placed on a slant next to a flute of pink champagne.

292

I looked up towards Uncle.

'It's my way of saying thank you,' he called on his way back into the kitchen. 'You'll write to me?' he asked, settling himself into the comfort of his chair before tucking the corner of his serviette under the loose collar of his shirt.

'Of course,' I replied. 'Uncle?'

'Yes, my love?'

'The plumber had to be called to Rutherford House a few weeks ago now. The pipes in the cellar rattle whenever they please and it became quite haunting. I hate walking down those stone steps into the echo among hanging cobwebs that blanket bottles of corked wine, and a grandfather clock that never ticks. Down there I found a diary, a large one, too. It was peeping out between the rusty iron legs of an old tin bath. It was rather dusty; the dates had faded and its pages were empty and damp. I carried it back into the house and left it to dry on a ledge where the rays of the morning sun slowly pass by. I'm going to use it to write to Lily about my journey in life.'

'Your sister loved you so much,' Uncle said while scraping the butter along a thin slice of toast. 'It did come to my notice when you were a little girl, her deep concern for your well-being. Dare say at that specific time there was very little she could do, my love.'

'The diary will have a title printed in gold, *Letters to Lily*.'

Uncle rested his knife and reached over to gently squeeze my hand. 'You'll mention me now and again, won't you?'

'Of course, Uncle; you'll be the first. I'll write, *Lily, our dear Uncle Dennis has been such a gentleman on his stay here at Rutherford House, guiding me gently with words of comfort, his company interesting to say the least.'*

Uncle looked proud, patting each corner of his mouth with his serviette before reaching out and lifting his glass. 'Cheers, my love,' he whispered as I continued.

*'Lily, Uncle left this morning for London, and if I may say, I was jolly glad to see the back of him.'*

Uncle spat out the sip of champagne with laughter. I giggled.

Uncle insisted on helping. The washing up was shared, and the remaining champagne poured into his glass. He thanked me while slipping on his blazer, with cravat tucked neatly in place.

'There will be no goodbyes, my love. I've said too many in my lifetime and I will leave on foot. Although, unlike Dick Whittington, my journey will start as soon as I can flag down a bus to take me to the station.'

'How ridiculous, the road goes on for miles before you reach civilisation.'

'The longer, the better. It will give me time to gather my thoughts. You see, my love, I miss Lily too,' Uncle said in a gush of tears. 'Born in Calcutta and buried in England, that's one hell of a journey,' his voice quivered.

How foolish of me to wallow in my own self-pity when Uncle felt her loss just as keenly. An old man now, yet as a young boy that precious moment Uncle shared with Lily, a baby in his arms before her journey across the Indian Ocean, had left an everlasting bond.

Only the creak of the tall iron gates told me Uncle had left that morning. As he had promised, there were no goodbyes. I ran fast, then faster between the bare trunks of trees, past clumps of daisies, around bold stems of thistle until I reached the far end of the garden to where the wishing well stood. I touched the crumbling bricks and, leaning my head against the stone, I cried, cried so hard as if a little girl again, feeling pain, such horrible pain through my tears.

In my sombre mood, I hadn't noticed that eventually I had made my way back through this vast garden. I opened the door and Rutherford House seemed such a lonely place. I wandered into the drawing room, sat against the hearth and stared towards the white ashes in the grate that, not so long ago, had crackled with burning wood. My temptation to find Uncle and insist I drive him to the station would be foolish. After all, he was a very determined man.

'Churchill,' I whispered as I noticed Uncle's book laying against the armrest of his chair. I picked up the heavy, bound book; a bookmark peeped out, waiting for Uncle to carry on with his most interesting read, and my heart ached with sadness for this lonely man, my dear Uncle Dennis.

Trees with wild hanging branches cast a shadow along the stretch of the long, narrow lane. With my fingers gripped around the steering wheel, I pressed my foot down against the accelerator once more. With his book by my side, I was determined in my search. As I was nearing the end of the lane, I spotted a weary man. His slow walk told me that his feet had taken the burden. His frail physique made me wonder how he had managed to get this far. I turned the key and left the car. Pebbles crunched underneath the soles of my sandals on my brisk walk towards him. I placed my hand on his shoulder. Uncle slowly turned, tears dripping down his face.

'Why don't you come back to Rutherford House for a while? A shot of whisky would do you good.'

'I'm going home,' he whispered.

'Look at the sadness in your eyes,' I told him. 'Give me that suitcase.' I gently took it from his cold hand. 'Anyway, you're not in any fit state to travel alone. I'm coming home with you, Uncle,' I said, passing him the keys. 'Besides, it isn't often you get the chance to drive a Jag.'

With a gentle touch, my fingertips wiped away his tears. Uncle smiled. I smiled too.